THE HIDDEN TRIBE

Borgo Press Books by S. Fowler Wright

Arresting Delia: An Inspector Cleveland Classic Crime Novel
The Attic Murder: An Inspector Combridge & Mr. Jellipot Classic Crime Novel
The Bell Street Murders: An Inspector Combridge & Mr. Jellipot Classic Crime Novel
Beyond the Rim: A Lost Race Fantasy
Black Widow: A Classic Crime Novel
The Capone Caper: Mr. Jellipot vs. the King of Crime: A Classic Crime Novel
Crime & Co.: An Inspector Cleveland Classic Crime Novel
Dawn: A Novel of Global Warming
Dead by Saturday: An Inspector Cleveland Classic Crime Novel
Dream; or, The Simian Maid: A Fantasy of Prehistory (Marguerite Cranleigh #1)
Elfwin: An Historical Novel
The End of the Mildew Gang: An Inspector Cauldron Classic Crime Novel (Mildew Gang #3)
Four Callers in Razor Street: An Inspector Combridge & Mr. Jellipot Classic Crime Novel
The Hanging of Constance Hillier: An Inspector Cleveland Classic Crime Novel
The Hidden Tribe: A Lost Race Fantasy
The Jordans Murder: An Inspector Combridge & Mr. Jellipot Classic Crime Novel
The King Against Anne Bickerton: A Classic Crime Novel
The Mildew Gang: An Inspector Cauldron Classic Crime Novel (Mildew Gang #1)
Murder in Bethnal Square: An Inspector Combridge & Mr. Jellipot Classic Crime Novel
The Police and the Public
Post-Mortem Evidence: An Inspector Combridge & Mr. Jellipot Classic Crime Novel
The Return of the Mildew Gang: An Inspector Cauldron Classic Crime Novel (Mildew Gang #2)
The Rissole Mystery: An Inspector Combridge & Mr. Jellipot Classic Crime Novel
The Screaming Lake: A Lost Race Novel
The Secret of the Screen: An Inspector Combridge & Mr. Jellipot Classic Crime Novel
Spiders' War: A Novel of the Far Future (Marguerite Cranleigh #3)
Three Witnesses: A Classic Crime Novel
Too Much for Mr. Jellipot: An Inspector Combridge & Mr. Jellipot Classic Crime Novel
The Vengeance of Gwa: A Fantasy of Prehistory (Marguerite Cranleigh #2)
Was Murder Done? A Classic Crime Novel
Who Murdered Reynard? A Classic Crime Novel
The Wills of Jane Kanwhistle: An Inspector Combridge & Mr. Jellipot Classic Crime Novel
With Cause Enough?: An Inspector Combridge & Mr. Jellipot Classic Crime Novel

THE HIDDEN TRIBE

A Lost Race Fantasy

by

S. Fowler Wright

THE BORGO PRESS

An Imprint of Wildside Press LLC

MMIX

CONTENTS

CHAPTER I.

"IT was good of you to come," Leonard said gratefully. "I was afraid that you would. But I hoped that you might not hear."

"Grimblett brought some chatter from Cairo. It was so absurd that I should not have listened at all if it had partly confirmed from another source. Of course, I knew it was false, but I thought I'd like to find out what the truth is, and stand by if you were in any jam. So I got a week's leave."

"Well, it's over now. I resigned yesterday."

"You *what*?"

"I said I resigned. It seemed the best thing to do."

"You don't mean that you couldn't—"

"No. I don't mean that I'm under any suspicion now. If I had been, I don't suppose I should have taken that course. There's been an inquiry held, at which they were unanimous that Blinkley lied to get out of paying a bet; and after that the Major apologized to me for the mess."

"Then why—?"

"Because I felt like it. It was all right for them to back down, but there wasn't much excuse for having talked before in the way they did, and I was fed up. You know I've never got on well with Atkins, or one or two of the others, and it seemed the right moment to throw my hand in."

The two men who spoke sat at a cracked marble-topped table in the veranda of the Paris Hotel (a good name is as cheap as one of lowlier sound) which overlooked a straggle of sand-blown palms, and the flat mud-bank and spreading surface of the Nile that shone bluely beneath a reflection of cloudless sky.

They were so closely alike in build, in features, in voice, and the mannerisms by which individuality is most clearly revealed, that even those who had known them longest would have relied less upon these characteristics for identification than the uniforms that they wore. The naval uniform indicated Second-Lieutenant Denis

Kinnear, R.N., of *H.M.S. Relief*, now stationed at Alexandria, while that of Lieut. Leonard Kinnear (the younger brother by fifty-three minutes) was the military one of a British regiment which had its headquarters at el-Orda.

Denis considered the information he had received in a silence of understanding sympathy. Affinity of feeling between the twins economized words, as it often would. He asked: "What shall you do now?"

"I've got an idea of trying a little exploration."

"Exploring? Where? I didn't think there was much left to be done. Not on this continent, anyway."

"Oh, but there is! Do you know that you might walk for five hundred miles northwest from this spot where we're sitting now and, after the first ten or fifteen, yours might be the first human eyes to survey the scene since the world began?"

"Oh, there! But that's only because there'd be nothing to see. Nothing but sand. There wouldn't be much fun in exploring that."

"No. I don't say there would. But who knows? If I were right when I said that no one has ever been there before, I dare say no one would want to go again when I should come back and say what I hadn't seen. But there's a doubt about that. Did you happen to notice a gigantic—well, not a Negro exactly—on the quay when you landed? He's not a man it's easy to overlook."

"You mean a man about six-feet-six, and big every way in proportion? A dark golden-brown colour? Yes, he wasn't one you could miss."

"Well, he was picked up in the desert about two years ago, dying of thirst. He couldn't explain anything, because he didn't seem able to speak any of the fifty languages of Northern or Central Africa. So they gave up trying at last, and found him work imitating what he saw others do, at which they say—of course, it was before I was here—that he was very willing and quick.

"He was quick also at learning the language here, and when he could talk he told an amazing tale of having run away from a city which lies in the heart of the desert, and has kept to itself for more years than he was able to count. It was a wild tale that no one really believed; but the District Commissioner, Beale, took an interest in it, and questioned him for a time, writing down as much of his answers as he could understand.

"I had a talk with Beale about it, and he said that he believed the man at first—Abrah they call him—but he found that the more he seemed willing to believe, the wilder Abrah's tales would become; and when he said that he had fled because he had been condemned as a weakling physically unfit to live, Beale thought he'd been making a fool of him long enough, and put the whole manuscript on the fire."

"It certainly sounds absurd."

"So it does. Beale thinks that he was probably one of a slave-raiding gang that was travelling along the edge of the desert, but sufficiently far away to avoid our patrols, and that he made up the tale to avoid confessing that he had been engaged in a criminal occupation."

"That sounds more likely. And it may have puzzled him to think of a more probable lie. But what did Beale make of his having been unable to talk?"

"He thinks he could have talked if he had liked. He preferred to make gibberish sounds for the same reason—that it saved him the trouble of explaining who he was, and how he came to be there."

"And you think there may be more in it than that?"

"I don't know. You could argue that the more unlikely the tale, the more unlikely it becomes that he would have made up something he couldn't expect anyone to believe. But it isn't only that. I've had just a vague scrap of confirmation, for what it's worth. You see that Scotsman, sitting away on the left?"

"The lank man with red hair where he isn't bald?"

"Yes. That's McGowd. He's a river pilot. He was an elephant-hunter up to ten years ago, when he got charged by a buffalo, and since then he's had something wrong with his inside. But in his young days—well, it's said there wasn't much between here and Timbuktu that he didn't know. I got talking to him once when he wasn't quite sober, and gave him another drink, and he told me that Abrah's tale is quite true."

"And when he got sober again?"

"Then he denied everything. When I reminded him of one or two details he'd given me, he got angry. But he didn't exactly say they weren't true. He asked me how long I thought he would keep his present job if a report got about that he was weak in the head? And did I know of another for him if he lost that? He may have meant that he knew something too queer to be believed, or only that he didn't want it known that he talked nonsense when he got drunk."

"What made you sound him about it?"

"Beale told me McGowd had once said he didn't doubt Abrah's tale, but when he heard that Beale himself thought it was lies he dried up."

"And you think he knows more than he's willing to say?"

"I don't know. I think I should like to find out."

"Well, good luck. I wish I could come too. It's queer that it was I who used to be fascinated by the great deserts. You remember how I once got all the books on the Gobi and the Sahara that I could find in the Liverpool library and was disappointed because they seemed to be more or less explored already?"

"Yes. You'll understand what the attraction is. But do you remember complaining that almost all the books were about the Western Sahara, and that the Libyan desert was hardly mentioned at all?"

"Yes. But I understood the explanation to be that there was nothing to be said about it: that there isn't even an oasis southeast of Kufra; nothing but barren sand and a great heat for the best part of a thousand miles, so that no one ever goes there at all."

"If no one goes, how does anyone know?"

"Yes. That sounds logical. But if there were oases, wouldn't they have been discovered ages ago, as they have been in the west? And wouldn't caravan routes have crossed?"

"No one says that there are oases scattered about. The idea is that there's one spot in the middle where some people live who keep to themselves."

"Do you think you could get Abrah for a guide?"

"I thought of asking him."

"Well, if he's told the truth, it'll only be a matter of price, and you won't mind that. But if he's unwilling, it will show he's cooked the tale, and doesn't want to be shown up."

"That's one way of looking at it. I thought rather the opposite, that if he'd made it all up he wouldn't mind leading me nowhere at a good price, and saying he'd missed the way, but if it's true that he had to run for his life he mightn't be anxious to look his relatives up."

"Yes, of course, if you believe that. For that matter, if they don't care to receive callers, it mayn't be very healthy for you. But if you mean to, I know it's no use saying that. So I'll say good luck again, and wish I were coming too…. By the way, when you were in Cairo, did you happen to meet a girl named Joselyn Wilde?"

"Yes. Why?"

"Not particularly?"

"I met her once at a dance. A dark, vivid girl? Keen on sports?"

Yes. He remembered her well. Once seen, she had returned to his mind a score of subsequent times, so that the thought of seeking her through the world had come to contend with this desert dream. It had been a definitely additional argument, however vaguely visualized, for the resignation of his commission. But he had seen her only once. Had talked with her for ten minutes after a single dance. What a longer acquaintance would have done it was simple to guess.

It had been a common fear of the twins that they might be drawn to the same girl, which had gone far to reconcile them to being parted by the separate careers which had been chosen for them rather by family tradition than by themselves. Leonard understood instantly the fear which that "Not particularly?" had implied. He buried his own vague impulse as he added: "I saw her for a few minutes only. Is it a case for congratulations?"

"Not yet. I wish it were. Perhaps if I'd been able to get rather more leave! But I understood that her stay in Cairo would not be long, and if you don't really need me here for any row that—"

"No. Of course not. If that's the idea, you'd better get back on the next train, and make what use you can of the leave you've got."

"Very well. Thanks. I'll go back tomorrow."

Denis spoke with a relief born of something more than a suspicion that that short meeting between his brother and Joselyn Wilde had been the commencement from which her attraction to himself, which had subsequently developed, had had its root—that she did not doubt that it was with himself, in the fancy dress that the occasion required, that she had had the single dance, the subsequent conversation in which mutual attraction had led to the first tentative self-revelations which are the opening tactics of the battle of love, as when the peacock shakes out his tail. Well, if Leonard were indifferent to her, what was the importance of that? But, if he had become free to wander about, the Libyan desert would be a better destination than the Cairo hotel where Joselyn Wilde might be on the next floor, and more accessible to him than to a lieutenant in Alexandria harbour, liable at any moment to be much farther away. Love between the brothers might be great, and their trust strong, but that was no reason that either should be put to so hard a test if matters would arrange themselves in another way.

Denis reverted to the previous subject to ask: "Do you think of taking McGowd along?"

"No. I don't know that he's physically fit. And, besides, he drinks more than he should. He may have been a good man twenty years back, but his day's gone. Anyway, I don't suppose that he'd entertain the idea. It's Abrah for me."

Next morning, Denis took the train back to Cairo. On his arrival, he learnt that Miss Wilde had left a few hours earlier on her way to Khartoum. He had some consolation two days later when a note addressed to the *Relief* reached his hands, making it plain that she

11

was no more willing than himself that their acquaintance should end because life led them for the moment by separate ways.

CHAPTER II.

THREE weeks later, Joselyn Wilde sat on the same veranda of the Paris Hotel where the Kinnear brothers had talked before. She had heard a report in Khartoum that a lieutenant of that name had set out with a single native servant to explore the unknown interior of the Libyan desert, and had stopped on her way back to Cairo with an object which she was now disclosing to Air-Pilot Jackman, a gaunt, hatchet-faced commercial aviator, with a reputation for being endowed with courage and skill and luck in about equally generous proportions.

"He took some camels," he said, "and those about the best string he could get. They've got enough water with them to float a raft. I don't see why you should think he'll have come to harm. Not yet, anyway."

"I don't think anything of the kind. I'm not proposing that we fly to relieve him, or bring him back. I thought I should just like to pay him a friendly call. I suppose you could do it, and be back the same night? What I asked was how much it would cost."

Air-Pilot Jackman avoided a direct reply. He said: "Yes might be back the same day, if you knew just where he is, and flew straight there. And if you could make a safe landing anywhere within ten miles."

"But the desert's all flat. I didn't think there'd be any difficulty about alighting or taking off."

The airman looked at his attractive but too persistent questioner with a humorous tolerance which he might not have shown to an equal masculine ignorance. "Flat, is it?" he asked. "I don't know why so many people have that idea. Why should a country be flat because there's an absence of rain? I don't say there isn't an answer even to that in the end, but it's a process that takes millions of years, and I doubt whether you'd wait the time. The Libyan desert is hills, and gorges, and black rocks, and the hollows of river beds that have been dry from the time of Adam, or long before, and rough plains, and sand dunes that rise and fall like a moving sea, only with waves that are ten times higher than any the water heaves. No, it's not over-easy to pick a landing that will let you get out alive, and harder still to find one where you can be sure that you won't damage the plane too much to take off again. You have to be careful when you know you can't get a pint of water anywhere for more than five hundred miles."

"But you've flown across it before?"

It was because of that fact that she had been advised to see Jackman, though perhaps less with the expectation that he would do what she required than that he would be able to persuade her of the plain folly it was. He had flown across the waterless desert, to Tunisia and back again, and he felt it to be a risk which a man may take once with good hope that his life will last, but to make it a habit would be suicidal mania in an acute form.

"Yes," he said, "I've crossed it both ways, and I'm here today. But I knew every minute for eight hundred miles that, if I were forced down, no one would ever see me alive again. And you ask me to fly round looking for a man who may be anywhere in about half a million square miles."

"That's not a fair way to put it. We know the direction in which he set out, and how long he's been gone, and when you're high up you must be able to see an immense distance in the clear air. I'll put it this way, if you like: suppose you agree to search for seven hours at not less than a hundred and fifty miles an hour—you know you can do more than that—and, come straight back if we've seen nothing by then. Say four hours in a bee-line back. That's eleven in all. There must be a price for which you'd be willing to do that, and I'm not asking you to say what it is."

"Well, that's fair enough." He thought he saw a way of ending a proposal which he was unwilling to entertain seriously. He named a price which he supposed to be beyond reasonable discussion.

Joselyn pulled a slender memorandum book from her bag, and wrote it down. "Five hundred pounds?" she said. "I suppose that's an inclusive figure? Well, it's a bit stiff, but I don't mind. Shall we say half an hour before tomorrow? I suppose it's an advantage to make an early start. You'll be satisfied if I give you a cheque on a London bank? I shall have to cable if you want actual cash"

He stared at her silently, taking the proposition seriously for the first time. Misreading his hesitation, she added: "I could let you have a hundred in cash, or a bit more, but I don't want to delay while I get the lot."

"I'm not worrying about that. You're not the sort to do me down with a dud cheque. Do you mind telling me why you're so keen on this flight?"

"I'm not wonderfully keen. It's just a fancy. Lieutenant Kinnear's a friend, and I thought I'd give him a call that he wouldn't expect. It's no more than a lark."

"Oh yes, it is. It's a very dangerous thing to attempt with no more object than that."

"That depends on what we consider to be worthwhile. And I don't think the danger's anything like you make out. Not with such a pilot as you. I know it would be all up if you were to crash in a desert place. But why should you? You don't expect to crash any day when you fly to Alexandria or Khartoum. But there's one thing I want to ask you particularly. You know it's said that Lieutenant Kinnear has gone in search of a lost city in the desert, and everyone thinks it's an utterly mad thing to expect to find. You've flown across it, and seen more, perhaps, than anyone else in a thousand years. Do you think it possible that such a place may really exist?"

"No. I don't. I'd go further than that. I'd bet a thousand to one that there's no such place. You were right when you said that, flying high, I could see an immense way, and I can tell you this: going and coming back—and I didn't take quite the same route—it was all the same. Southeast of the Kufra group of oases, there isn't a well, there isn't a sign of life, or a glimmer of green. It's a dead world, dead and dry. Why should men live there, or what would they live on? And shouldn't I have seen them, if they did? It's not a sensible thing to believe."

"Then, if that's so, I think we ought to find Lieutenant Kinnear, and let him know that he's wasting time. If we don't, he'll go on looking for something that isn't there till his water's gone. He's just the sort to keep on a day too long, and die of drought on the way back. I called it a game before, but I think now it's something we're bound to do. He's been misled by a silly tale, and you're the one man who's seen the truth with his own eyes, and can tell him to throw it up, so that he'll have to listen."

Air-Pilot Jackman made no further protest. "If it's to be half an hour before dawn tomorrow," he said, "I'd better have an overhaul now."

CHAPTER III.

LEONARD KINNEAR lay awake in the night, and considered stars—stars that were always there in the cloudless sky till the swift coming of dawn, and that shone with a brilliance never seen through the misty air of his native land. He was not depressed, which would have been a condition of mind not to be reached from a light cause in the pure dry air of that sunlit land. But he had become aware of the wildness of what he did. For nearly three weeks he had come on, with Abrah for guide, through the barrenness of the sun-baked land. He could not tell how far he had come, though he knew the pace had been much less than theory would have allowed, but he must have come far. And there had been no sign either of life, or that life had been from remotest time. Not so much as a whitened bone. Not a shrivelled cactus, a withered thorn, or a sand-lizard darting from stone to stone.

It had been a land, as tradition said, of absolute drought and death. And his water, on which life depended, was going fast. How much longer should he go on, risking life for so vain a goal, and with no plan of what he should do if he should find it to be more than mirage, or the invented tale of a cornered man? Surely for three days yet, or perhaps four, or perhaps five. He knew that he would be reluctant to say that the moment to turn had come. For it was a tale that he still believed.

As to that, he told himself that he had three reasons, slender enough, but still sufficient to lure him on. The one was that Abrah was leading him in a direct line. He had been able to check that, not only by sun and stars, but by a pocket-compass he carried, the use of which he doubted that Abrah knew.

"How do you know the way," he had asked "through this desert land?"

And Abrah had replied: "I watched the stars as I came. I had been taught the lore of the stars."

Well, he might have to rely on the same friends. Suppose his compass were broken or lost, and Abrah fled (a contingency that was never long out of his mind), he might find the cloudless sky would contain the only guides that would lead him backward the way he came.

But he knew that Abrah had led him straight, by whatever means. There had been times when they had bent aside to avoid high or difficult ground, but they had come back to the same course, as his compass showed, and there was a good presage in that.

The second reason had been Abrah's reluctance to come, and the reason he gave. He said he had a great fear. If he should return to his own people, they would surely kill him, and what sense was there in doing that? If Lieut. Kinnear should seek their gates, he did not know what they would do, but he expected it would be the same thing. Was the white lord anxious to die?

He had been induced to come at last by a great bribe, and on a bargain that he should lead to no more than a distant view of the city of which he told. He admitted that there were no camels or horses there, nor other means of a swift pursuit. If Leonard were to venture a nearer approach, it was to be alone, after giving him one of the swifter camels with which to fly and sufficient water to enable him to get back alive.

On that bargain he had reluctantly come, but Leonard knew that there may often be a faint or even a treacherous heart in a body of fine physique, and, remembering that first reluctance, he had a lively fear that Abrah's heart might fail and that he might wake any morning to find himself alone and the camels gone. It was an idea that gave him no better than broken and restless sleep, but it made a reality of the dangers that lay ahead.

The third reason was that he had used the opportunity of this solitary companionship to learn something of Abrah's own language, and had confirmed the fact that the man possessed a speech which was radically different from anything he knew—and he knew much—of Northern Africa's many tongues. Such a language could not be improvised. It was evidence of the existence of an isolated tribe, living in or beyond the desert, though it might not prove more than that. Abrah admitted that it had no written form, which suggested that the civilization of those who spoke it could not be high.

Yet if Abrah were to be classed as a savage, Leonard recognized that he was of a high type. His habits were cleanly, his voice pleasantly modulated; his obedience prompt and intelligent; his manner respectful, but without servility; and his physique was magnificent.

Leonard could not acquire a language completely in three weeks, but he learnt much, and that in a conversational form. He observed that its grammar had affinities to that of Latin, and that it had words that were derived from Latin or Greek, or that had come down from a common source. To those languages it was clearly a cousin, if not a child.

Now he lay awake till the sky was transfigured by a violet dawn, and he heard Abrah moving among the hobbled camels, and talking to them in that tongue, and he resolved that his search should not cease till the last pint of measured water had been consumed, leaving only the barest margin that would suffice for the homeward way. The wind rose with the dawn; the wind that plays with the desert sand like a giant child; that plays with it, as it flings the waters about when its wings beat upon the wide surface of sea. But the sand is a better toy.

Now it scooped hollows among the dunes, with smooth wide imprints therein, as though it were there that gigantic mammals had lain. It forced smooth gutters that were like the trails of immense snakes through the sand. It whirled round as a dog turns, treading the place where it will lie. The great dunes rolled like billows of running sand. On and on they rolled in the wind, and as they rolled they made mysterious sounds from the grinding of the myriad grains of the sand. They sounded at times like a giant snoring in sleep, and at others like the throbbing of distant drums.

Had this been a day on which the wind sought to display its ultimate rule of the desert and all it held, it would have increased its might till it tore up the dunes to their foundations of rock, filling the air for a hundred miles with a blind havoc of whirling sand, which it would lay at last in fantastic piles in another place at the caprice of its lordless will.

But today, as the sun came straight upward out of the east and increased its power, the wind sank, as though it were leaving the stage for another artist to take his turn. The heat increased with each hour as the little file of water-burdened camels padded over trackless routes which the wind had swept bare, and which had been smoothed and darkly polished by the age-long friction of flying sand. There were places where the whole surface had been polished until a foothold was hardly kept.

Before noon, the rocks had become so hot that they would burn an incautious hand, and when the sun rose to its midmost height there came a sound, fifty yards ahead, like the discharge of a six-inch gun, when a mass of igneous green-black rock, bursting from the intense heat, flung huge fragments into the air. It did no harm to the approaching caravan beyond that a camel's shoulder was streaked with red from where a flying splinter had torn its neck. But it demonstrated a second phase of the alchemy by which the action of sun and air was shattering and grinding the surface of a once-mountainous land, so that, at a distance of time that might be remote, but was no less sure, it would have reduced all to a common level of wind-blown sand.

As they advanced, they were confronted by a low ridge of jagged rock, smooth-polished and brightly black in the strong light of the midday sun, to which Abrah, who had been increasingly nervous and watchful during the last two days, pointed and said: "It is from there that you will see that I have told you that which is true, and it will be the farthest that we can go. If we see no man approach, we may venture to climb the ridge, so that we avoid to become separated from the camels by more than a few yards, for (as I have said before) they have no beasts which could make pursuit. But if we are seen, we must be instant to flee, for you may not believe how far they can throw their spears if you have not seen."

But they saw no man, nor any sign that there was human life in that barren place, until they had mounted the ridge. It was not high, but it was too steep at the last for the burdened camels, which they would not otherwise have wished to show on the rocky skyline to which they climbed. They hobbled them therefore in a little hollow where the afternoon shade began, though it was no more than a few inches as yet, and made a cautious finish of the ascent.

Lying flatly under the narrow shadow of a sharp-toothed pinnacle of up-jutting stone, Leonard Kinnear looked down on a wide level of sand, and beyond that to what looked like a gigantic mile-wide mushroom of rock, beneath which there was a long low vista of vivid green. Far off to the right, there was a grove of date palms rising high into open air, but, apart from that, whatever cultivation there might be was under the mushroom shadow, so that it would be invisible to the occupant of a high-flying plane.

It was a formation of rock which, on a smaller scale, had become familiar during the past weeks. For it would often be that a softer stratum of lower calcareous rock would be rubbed away by the incessant sand-papering of the wind, so that hollows would be formed, deep and wide, and destined to increase with a slow inexorable certainty, until a grain too many would fall, or be worn off, and the overhanging weight of the harder granite would collapse with a dull thunder of sound which would be audible many miles away, while high clouds of sand would be flung up and spread far to obscure the sun.

But this was hollowed to an extent and with a regularity which, though it might have been the wind's work at first, had become evidence of human brains, and of human hands, as was that ordered streak of vegetation below. The puzzle was how, if the rock had been cut away throughout, as Abrah's talk had implied, the higher stratum could be sustained, having become the roof of a lost support.

Abrah moved restlessly, "Effendi, you have seen? It would be safer to go."

Leonard heard, but was not quick to respond. He recognized fear in the voice of a man who would have been a match for any three of the mongrel Arab river men of the Nile, and who did not otherwise play the part of a coward. But there was, as yet, no menace in what he saw. If he should turn now, it would be with a meagre ill-founded to gain belief. He had not set eyes on a living man! Was he to say he had fled from the distant sign of a hanging rock and a grove of palms? There were the camels behind; there was a good rifle beneath his hand. But, by his bargain with Abrah, the man could go now any moment he would, and his service was not to be lightly lost.

"Have patience awhile," he said. "We are safe here, being hid. I would see more."

Abrah grumbled: "They will have our blood if they may. They can throw far."

But he kept his place, with no more words after that, until they heard that which drew their eyes to the sky.

CHAPTER IV.

JOSELYN sat at the pilot's side, and looked down on a barren waste that varied only in a monotonous way. So she had looked since dawn, and searchingly during the last four hours, till her eyes ached for that which she did not find.

They flew high. They had made wide circling sweeps in the air, as a dove will do till it sees the distant landmark that guides it home. But they had seen barren hills, or desert, and nothing more. Never the shine of water. Never a patch of oasis green. Never the sight of a living man.

They could not hear each other speak for the engine's roar, though it was a noise to which they had become so used that it was itself unheard. The pilot wrote on his pad, and passed her the slip: *I have done more than I undertook. You can see there is nothing here. I am going back now.*

She could not deny that he was within his right. And it certainly seemed that there could be no desert city such as the improbable tale had said. The ancient tradition was surely true that it was the most absolute desert, perhaps, that the world contained. But Denis Kinnear, she did not doubt, must be somewhere there. It would be bitter to go back, having failed in so large a way. She began to write. *But he must be somewhere. Won't you try?*—and stopped with a sudden realization that the roar of the engine had ceased, and that the propeller was slowing down. She was undisturbed by this, vaguely supposing it to have some connection with his purpose of turning back. But she left her writing for a verbal appeal. "Won't you try just— say another twenty minutes—more to the north than we've been yet? We don't want to go back beaten unless we must."

She wasted a pleading glance with the words, for he neither looked, nor made any answer to that which, in fact, he had not heard. His hands were busy among gadgets that had little meaning to her. Suddenly as it had ceased, the roar of the engine started again.

She must write now what she had spoken before. But he shook his head in reply. He wrote: *I thought it was all up when the engine stalled. We must get back while we can.*

She could make no protest to that, and remained silent, accepting the bitterness of defeat, but her eyes still continued to search the immense blank desert below.

The engine stopped—started—stopped—and resumed its rhythmic roar. The pilot's eyes and hands were on its controls, so that he had no spare thought or glance for the landscape below. But he must look when she reached over, touching his arm, and pointing far out to the left, and he nodded assent to the message her eyes conveyed, and which she spoke in words that he could not catch.

No water indeed, nor roof nor tent to indicate the dwellings of men, but far off, under the edge of what seemed to be, from that height, a slight change in the level of sandy plain, a grove of palms—an unmistakable grove, where he had thought that four hundred miles, right or left, would not have shown a grass-blade or a leaf of green. And then, moving out from the grove, a single upright figure, and a sudden glint as the sunlight was thrown back by a broad-bladed spear.

The pilot hesitated. He knew that she would have him descend. But, if he did, would he rise again? There was something wrong with the engine now. A fault of ignition, he supposed it to be. It made a large doubt that the long way back would be safely flown. And if he must fail in that, it would be better to go down where there was a prospect of succour, of food, of life, even though the engine had spent its power.

True, the men that were here might be of no sure friendship, yet that was a minor count when to be alone in the desert was certain death. But could he make a safe landing here? It was rough, rocky, much-broken ground. He did not see those who lay under the sheltering rock, nor the camels below the farther side of the little ridge, or his decision might have been sooner made. Perhaps, if he could make a safe landing for half an hour, he could patch up the engine to do that at which it might otherwise fail. While his mind hung irresolute he came round in a long descending curve, and as he did so he found that he need vex it no more with a decision already made. The engine stalled again, and could be coaxed to no further effort. The parachutes? But he was already low, and to abandon the plane was to lose hope that they would ever re-cross four hundred miles of unwatered desert that divided them from the civilization from which they came. With the impetus of his failing speed he came round into the wind, and searched the rough ground below for a landing-place that would be level and firm.

He said: "I'm going down. You can jump if you like. It may be the safer way." And then, as the seconds passed, and that chance of safety was lost: "No, don't move. You'd better sit where you are now."

The land rose up to meet them, looking worse at a nearer view. He did all that skill and coolness could, but he had seldom had more need of his reputed luck as the wheels struck an ice-smooth surface of rock and ran bumping across foot-high ridges to which ice would have been brittle and soft. But, as by a miracle, they kept their course until they ran into a narrow pocket of sand, when the plane swung sharply round, pitched over with a crumpling of metal wing, and lay still.

CHAPTER V.

LEONARD watched the approaching plane with a wonder which lessened as he formed a natural misconception of its significance in that lonely sky. Obviously those who dwelt in the oasis beneath the rock were not as isolated from the outside world as has been presumed from the fact that their existence was unknown to it. Probably they had made frequent secret excursions to civilization in earlier days, before the aeroplane had provided them with a means of communication that was not only secret but swift and sure. The plausibility of this interpretation increased as the plane turned from its course and came round on a lowering curve.

He saw no cause for alarm, supposing that the pilot knew where he should land, and that the engine had been deliberately shut off, but the fact of this contact with civilization, as he supposed it to be, gave him a perhaps illogical confidence in the character of these desert-dwellers, so that when he saw the machine bump perilously along the rocks, and then collapse in a sideward crash, he rose with no thought of caution, and ran in its direction with an impulse of rescue as natural and unrestrained as though he had witnessed the accident in an English field.

Abrah looked at it with different eyes. He had no opinion of what it meant, but he was sure that it had not come to earth unobserved by those into whose hands he would be reluctant to fall. He saw his white employer, who had been a stranger to him a month before, and whom by the bargain of his engagement he was now entitled to leave, jumping down the rocks and sliding in knee-deep sand with no thought of concealment in what he did. For a time he neither followed him nor retreated, watching him in an irresolute mood. He looked over the plain at the mushroom city he feared, from which there was, as yet, no sign of issuing life. With an angry frown, and a mutter of words in his native tongue, he followed his foolish master towards the place where the fallen aeroplane had now become a fiercely burning column of flame.

Sound-limbed still, but shaken and dazed, Joselyn had struggled up from the bed of sand upon which she had been shot out of the plane. Her hair was heavy with sand, and the sharp stones had scratched cheek and neck, giving her more pain than she would have felt from a deeper wound. Her ear bled. Beyond that, she was not injured at all. She looked at the wreck, and was aware of a mounting flame. At the sight, her mind cleared. Tales she had read of the horror of pilots trapped and burned in such wrecks caused her to hasten towards the plane, but she saw that Jackman, like herself, had been thrown clear. Only, less fortunately, he had been thrown a shorter distance and on a surface of rock. He lay five yards away, and even there the heat was hard to endure.

There was, indeed, heat enough on the surface of sun-baked rock without the addition of that petrol-fed pillar of flame. It scorched her hand when she touched it as she dragged him farther away.

When she had done this, she must consider whether it were a living man she had saved. He was insensible, but she did not think he was dead. There was the certainty of a broken leg. She saw that blood ran from his mouth, which might mean anything from a broken rib piercing his lungs to no more than a bitten tongue. She stood up, looking round for aid she was unlikely to find, and saw Leonard Kinnear twenty yards away, with Abrah (who could run faster than he) close at his back.

Joselyn looked at Leonard—Denis she supposed him to be—in a natural surprise that he had appeared thus from she knew not where, and Leonard looked with more amazement at her. Abrah's eyes looked a different way, and saw other things. He saw a group of men who ran fast towards where they stood, and there were spears in their hands. He exclaimed sharply, and next moment they were all looking at the same sight.

Leonard had a vain wish for the rifle which he had left lying beneath the rock from which they had watched, when he ran to the burning plane. But it was clearly not a case for a useless fight, even if they had had means of defence. The runners were still a long distance away. There should be time to get first to the place where the camels were.

But the air-pilot lay at their feet. Joselyn said desperately: "We can't leave him here. What are we to do?"

Leonard stood irresolute. It was hopeless to attempt to get him away. Were they to lose all for a dead man? Abrah had started to run. He came back. He understood Joselyn's gesture, if not her words. He lost no time in showing what he could do.

With the help of their urgent hands, the insensible body was taken upon his back. With that burden he could still run.

Leonard, unburdened, might have run faster than he, but Joselyn, though she ran well, made slower progress over the stones, for which she was less suitably shod.

They looked back at pursuers who were of a huge stature and strength, making Abrah's assertion that he had been a weakling among them a possible tale. There were nine in all, carrying broad-bladed spears that were of six-foot length, but which looked short in their hands, and which were, in fact, balanced to throw. One of the nine was well ahead, and running at such a pace as increased the distance between himself and his companions, while it was bringing him rapidly nearer to them.

Leonard saw this, but he still thought it to be a race which they would be likely to win, his thought being rather on the rifle upon the crest of the little ridge than the camels below. When he had that in hand, he had some confidence that he could check pursuit.

Joselyn could not tell whether the race would be lost or won, not knowing the goal in view, but she knew that she could do no more, though she saw that the men ran within their strength that they might not leave her behind.

But Abrah looked back, and in his eyes there was a definite fear. "Effendi," he asked, "could you drag her on? You do not understand how they can throw."

Leonard gave Joselyn a hand, but it was doubtful that they did better for that, being less able to choose their steps on difficult ground. He thought: "If I should run ahead, I could get the rifle in time, and could save us all," but it was a thing which, against reason, he was reluctant to try.

But Abrah's mind was relieved by a cunning thought. "It is best," he said to himself, "that it should be he, for I suppose he already knocks at the door of death." But he did not cast his burden away. He only ran less than before, so that he fell a little to the rear of the other two.

When he felt a hard blow on the back, so that he was thrown forward upon the ground, he was neither surprised nor annoyed. But he was very quick to rise, rolling the burden from off his back; and, as he did so, he was aware of a twitch of pain that told him that his plan had been near to fail. The spear, in spite of the distance that it had come, had driven completely through the air-pilot's body, and there was an inch of its point which was red with Abrah's blood rather than his.

26

Abrah had no time to consider that. The spear came from the hand of a man he knew, and one whom he had a special reason to hate. He meant that it should go back.

Jackman lay still. His luck must have been missing that day. He may have been dead already. Anyway, a blade that was four inches wide at its broadest point had gone through his body without waking a sign of life. Now Abrah pressed a heavy foot on his back and wrenched out the spear. Almost in the same action he had risen to his full height, and the spear was lifted and drawn backward to throw.

His pursuer saw what he would do, which there was a second's space to avoid as the weapon came. He dropped face-forward, so that the spear, already rising into the air, should go over his head. But Abrah had supposed that he would do that and had shortened the throw. The spear sank between a man's shoulders a second time. Abrah gave a bellow of laughter such as had not come from his mouth since he had left that place two years before with a goatskin of water upon his back.

They ran on again with the certainty that they would be first over the ridge, which was now only a short distance ahead, and would have been well content but for the sound of an appalling up-roar which came from where the camels had been concealed on the farther side.

CHAPTER VI.

THE Arab, desiring camel-meat on the next day, will slaughter the beast he dooms with a knife-thrust in at the lower end of the neck, precisely as a pork-eating Christian will stick a pig. It may be among the easiest of all methods of crossing the bridge of death, but it allows a vocal minute before consciousness falters and fails.

There was a man now who slaughtered the hobbled camels with his broad-bladed spear, and the resulting pandemonium could have been heard through the clear desert air three or four miles away. His was no object of meat, but to destroy the means by which unwelcome visitors might have got away to disclose a secret which had been kept for two thousand years. His work was soon done, and might have ended with safety for himself had it needed even ten seconds less than it did.

As it was, he came into Abrah's sight as he withdrew his spear from the last of the screaming beasts. There was no danger for him in that, for Abrah had no weapon which would cross the dividing space, but the man, seeing this, could not pass the occasion to try a throw.

He threw well enough, and had Abrah been new to the game he would have been likely to meet his death, but it was that which he had practised from boyhood days. He bent aside, and the spear whistled past his ribs with a clearance of six inches or eight, and became as near a danger to Leonard, who was a few paces behind, having paused to pick up the rifle.

The man who had cast the spear ran away, but in no panic of speed, thinking that before Abrah could reach it he would be out of range, and having the confidence of one whose friends are many and not far. He knew nothing of firearms, nor was he destined to learn, for the bullet came more quickly than sight or sound, and gave him an instant end. It took little time to see that the camels were done. Those that were not dead had fallen and were so far gone that their necks lay flat on the sand.

Leonard ran back to the top of the ridge, that he might meet the pursuit with the advantage that the position gave. He met Joselyn, who had been half-forgotten in the urgent effort to save the camels which were so vital for their return, and who had slackened her pace and then paused to look back as she gained the ridge. She said, in a breathless way, for she had run to the limit of muscles and lungs: "They are not coming on. They stopped where Mr. Jackman was left."

Cautiously, not to expose himself, for he had no desire to become a target for flying spears, Leonard looked back and saw that it was as she said.

There were eight in all, of whom one or two looked at the man of their own race whom Abrah had killed, and he thought they laughed. But most of them were in a curious group around the dead airman, whose appearance must have been very strange to them.

Bunched as they were, they would have been an easy mark at a longer range and in a worse light, and Leonard could have emptied his rifle with the certainty that he would have fewer foes when it was done; but what use was there in that? With the camels dead, they were trapped, and must find a way of parley, and then of peace, or there could be no comfort for them.

He asked Abrah, who had come to his side: "What will they do now?"

Abrah, who had funked it before, seemed, curiously enough, to be in better heart now that they were caught in a net that they could not break. Leonard wondered whether he could be so elated at the way the first encounters had gone that he did not see that, though they might have won a battle, they had lost a campaign. Now he said: "They will surround us to make an end. But they will not throw spears till they are so near that they cannot miss, for it would be to give them to us. When they are near, we can talk."

Leonard asked: "After what we have done, will they let us go?"

"I cannot say what they will do. But it will be no worse because two are dead. It may be better for that." This sounded unlikely enough, but they were a people apart, who might have unexpected ways. Certainly it would be well if they could be brought to the point of discussion in a peaceable mood. But even if they should be willing to let them go (which was much to hope) how was it to be done? The slaughter of the camels seemed to be an irrevocable obstacle, besides indicating that their departure was just what these people were determined to stop.

But it was already becoming clear that Abrah's first prophecy would be promptly fulfilled. Not less than two hundred spearmen were now spreading upon the plain, and bands of them were moving outward to east and west with the evident purpose of surrounding the little ridge. They were all men of a huge stature and fine physique, so that it might well be that Abrah had been esteemed a weakling among them rather than of exceptional strength. They wore a single, loosely belted garment of white, sufficient for such a climate, and intended rather to stave off the desert heat than to give warmth to those it covered, and they had white turbans upon their heads.

It was not a menace easily to be endured by those who were in the midst of the circle of flashing spears. It seemed a poor chance to let so many approach within talking range. Would they stop for words when, being so many, they had come so near? Leonard imagined that he might call for parley and be answered by a rush that would overwhelm, or the annihilating hail of a hundred spears.

He said to the girl: "I don't know whether you can shoot, or that it will serve any purpose to try, but there is a sporting rifle packed with other things in one of the camel's loads which there will be time to get before they arrive. If we should shoot from both sides it might serve to hold them back for a time, and perhaps till dark, though what use it would be in the end is not easy to see."

"I can shoot a little," she replied, "but it seems silly, placed as we are. We ought to make friends, if we can."

"I'm afraid, with their love of secrecy, and we having killed two of them, it isn't likely to be easy to do, but I agree that it's the best choice that we have."

"Effendi," Abrah interposed, "you should shoot one, if not more. It would be best to shoot a woman, if one were there, which there will not be, but we may hope that a man will do."

It was puzzling advice, and had the sound of wishing to kill the exact equivalent of themselves. Did Abrah think that their own deaths did not matter so long as they had been revenged in advance? It was a possible explanation, but Leonard felt that the advice must have a more reasonable basis than that, and Abrah knew the ways of these people, which should give wisdom to what he said.

Leonard levelled his rifle, and then paused with a scruple, not of the wisdom, but of the ethics of what he had been disposing himself to do. To kill for the defence of their own lives—yes, that was a natural impulse of self-protection. If it were to be a fight to the last, he would not delay to kill all he could. But to select one man, and kill him deliberately as a politic preliminary to the opening of peaceful negotiations, had a savour of murder which might have had power to delay his hand even had he been clearer as to the purpose of what he did.

"If I shoot," he thought, "even though I kill no one, it may warn them to approach in a more circumspect way, and may give more time for Abrah's voice to be heard." So he sent a random bullet over their heads.

But it had no such effect. They came on at the same pace as before, and with no effort to take cover at all. The distance was rapidly narrowing, and he saw that the time for scruples was gone.

As there was no one who had the appearance of a woman among them, the question of taking Abrah's advice literally did not arise. He took aim at one who flourished a spear in a particularly truculent manner, and had the satisfaction of seeing him pitch forward in his stride, and turn a somersault before he lay still.

The effect of this shot was different from that of the one before. Then there had been no more than a sudden noise. Now there was death. The runners halted. First around the dead man, and then farther away, until the whole advance stayed. They did not withdraw out of range, and Leonard could have picked them off where they stood, but his purpose had been warning rather than destruction, and now he waited to see what they would do. He had his reward when a man separated himself from a little knot of conference, and came forward alone, waving a white cloth over his head.

Abrah said at once: "Effendi, give me leave, and a white rag, and I will find out what they are willing to do."

It was evident that he had no doubt of the protective value of the ancient symbol of truce, or the good faith of those by whom it was now displayed. Leonard had a doubtful thought of whether he were worthy of so large a trust, or might be tempted to make his own peace at their cost, but if he should go with him he did not see that he would be better placed, nor perhaps even as well. His knowledge of their language, as he had gained it in the last three weeks, was not enough to encourage him to undertake such a negotiation himself, and an interpreter who is also a principal must be trusted perforce. He considered also that Abrah had acted with loyalty during the last hours, to the point which honour required, or even somewhat beyond.

"You can go," he said, "and find out what terms they will make, telling them that we desire nothing but peace, and if they had not killed our camels, and come at us with spears, we would have met them in a friendly way. You may tell them also that I have weapons which are pregnant with many deaths. And make it plain that you must return alone. I will have none of them here till we have come to a full accord. Are they men who will keep their word?"

Abrah did not appear to listen with care, acting like one who knew what he had to do, as perhaps he did, being concerned with his own kin. He answered the final question with: "There is no matter of that. They will do what they are told, as we all must."

With this cryptic reply, he went as one in some haste, so that he met the approaching envoy while he was still some distance away.

They watched the two stand for some minutes in talk, and then walk back together to the group from which the envoy had come. Here they conferred again, but when the group broke up Abrah did not return.

There was some calling, and waving of spears, and the whole of the two hundred warriors began to withdraw. Abrah went off with those to whom he had talked, and Leonard, who had his field-glasses directed upon him during this time, saw them all disappear into the city, if such it were, under the opposite rocks. He could not observe that there was compulsion in this. It appeared that it was all done in a friendly accord. It might be well enough, or even better than that, but it was not simple to understand, and could be interpreted in several ways, some of which were less pleasant than others. And it would be dark in four hours, and their defence be less easy than in the day.

CHAPTER VII.

THE CRISIS being in suspense, if it were not past, the two who were left alone became conscious of each other, and of the enigma of how they met.

Leonard looked at his companion in a natural wonder. He asked: "How on earth did you come to be flying here?"

"I thought," she said frankly, "that you might be glad if I looked you up. Of course, I didn't expect to crash, and I didn't know what a mess I should find you in."

He was too chivalrous to say that, if her plane had not appeared, the worst part of the mess, and, in particular, the loss of the camels, would not have occurred; but she saw that he still looked puzzled, as at an inadequacy in her reply. She added: "I heard a report in Khartoum that you were trying to find this place, though everyone said it didn't exist, and I thought—you'd be glad to see me."

As she ended, the confidence of her first explanation had left her voice. She thought him distant and strange. Was he angry that she had come? Even if he were more puzzled than the occasion seemed to require, he might still say he was glad! When she thought of how Denis and she had parted last month, and of the letter which had missed her at the hotel, and followed her up the Nile—well, there was a coldness in this reception hard to condone. Was he too concerned for the peril of the position to have thoughts for her? Or for the love he had protested before? With a sure instinct she felt the explanation to be other than that, but it had a baffling quality she could not define.

He answered kindly enough, but still with that friendly distance so hard to understand or endure: "It was a sporting thing for you to try, and of course I'm glad that you came. At least, I should be if I knew how to get you out of the mess we're in. I'd give something to hear—and to understand—what Abrah's saying now, and what they're saying to him! But even if he makes peace, and they're willing to leave us alone, I don't see how we're to get away now that we've lost the camels and your plane's burnt. And it's hard to think that they'll be willing for us to go. Do you think that there'll be any search for you, when they find that you don't return?"

"I don't know," she replied, but with an indifference as puzzling to him as his coldness had been to her, her mind still being rather on the manner than the matter of what he said. "I don't see why there should. I told Mr. Jackman that I didn't want it to get about. I thought it was just a matter—between ourselves. Of course, I didn't expect it would end like this."

He was bewildered again by the expression "between ourselves," and this feeling caused him to regard the problem with a more direct attention than it had had from him before, so that the light of truth came to his mind. "Who," he asked abruptly, "do you suppose that I am?"

She started at this question, inconsequent in itself, and having the sound of inexplicable insult from him to her. "Of course," she answered coldly, "I know who you are. You're Lieutenant Kinnear. Why do you ask?"

"Attached to the *Relief?*"

"Yes, of course. At least, I heard something about your having resigned." (Was there, she wondered, some mystery about that, perhaps some scandal which he felt that he must confess before assuming that their past relations could be maintained?)

"I'm not that Lieutenant Kinnear, and it wasn't he who resigned. I'm his brother. People don't often tell us apart."

She looked at him in a doubting silence. It was hard to believe, though it seemed an unlikely lie. Was it some queer old-fashioned chivalry which prompted him to deny that he was himself, so that their relations might be on a footing of uncompromising formality until they should return to more conventional ways? If so, she would brush such nonsense aside with a firm hand. Surely, if ever, it was a time for realities, being in the peril they were!

Her look of doubt changed to an incredulous smile. "Yes," she said, "you certainly are alike! But if you want me to swallow that, perhaps you'll tell me first how you knew my name?"

"I met you at a fancy-dress ball in Cairo two or three months ago. You're not the sort that anyone would forget."

"But you—" she began. "But it was then—" She had almost said that it was then that she had fallen in love with him, even before his own feelings had been revealed. But had there been two to whom she had felt in that way, without knowing which was which? And this one, whom she had sought as her lover, was not he whom she had accepted, and to whom she was pledged—and was yet the one to whom she was attached by that tender memory of her first meeting, as she had afterwards supposed, with Denis Kinnear? Well, if that were so, she must be clear for the future, whatever had been before!

She saw that, although she might be unable to tell them clearly apart, there was the vital distinction that one had fallen in love with her. It was he to whom her kisses had been given in the past months. It was to him that her faith was due. And she believed at last that he was not here. How soon, and how, could she get away? As to that, there might be an answer, bad or good, approaching them now. For Leonard (as she now understood him to be), who was using his field-glasses again, said: "Abrah's coming back. He seems to be coming alone. There ought to be a good meaning in that."

CHAPTER VIII.

As Joselyn's puzzled resentment at what she had taken to be her lover's inexplicable aloofness died out of her mind, it gave freer place to realization of the sharp peril in which she stood; and while knowledge of the unlikely truth drew her apart from one who was no more than the brother of him she had learned to love, it drew them closer than they had been before, on a different plane, as sharers of common dangers, and allied against them in a place most barren of other friends. It is better, at such a pass, as she had cause to perceive, to be with a true friend than with a lover who seems untrue. So that it was with a sense of comradeship better established than it had been at any time up to a few minutes before that they waited Abrah's return.

When he had left them, he had carried the spear which had been thrown at him by the first man whom Leonard had shot, having used it as a staff to which to bind the white rag which had been his warrant of safety among those from whom he had fled two years before. Now the spear was still in his hand (which might be a better omen even than the fact that he had been allowed to return), but the white rag that it bore was gone, and that was a fact harder to read.

"It looks," Leonard said, "as though he has made so close a peace for himself that its need is done. That may be for himself alone, so that he may come and go as he will; but it may be different for us."

"What shall you do," Joselyn asked, "if he says that he has gone over to them, or if you have reason to think him false?"

"I don't think he will say that. He will either be loyal to us, or he will attempt to persuade us that he is, so that he may lead us into whatever trap they have laid. But I think we must trust him, if we can; or, if we have a doubt, it should not be shown. For he is our only hope, and the only means—beyond the few words that I have—of communicating with those without whose friendship we shall be unable to live longer than the month that our food would last."

"Well, we shall soon hear what he has to say."

Abrah came to them with a face content, as one who had done well and expected praise. He said at once: "It is all agreed. They will accept our lives—mine and yours—for two of those who were slain, and they may take the woman's life also, as for the third man, though that may not so easily be arranged. But even of that there is good reason to hope.

"By that bargain, we have twelve months of a good life, and after that we must endure or fail, as the laws require."

"They will not help us to return?"

"They cannot do that through which they would be overwhelmed by the world. But that is no loss, for there is a much better life here than can be found in your land; and when you have seen what it is you will not wish to be away."

"Yet you fled?"

"It was to save my life. But having seen what life beyond the desert is like, I am not sure that I should do it again, even at the same need."

Joselyn, who could not understand what was said, interposed to ask: "Are we safe? Will they let us go?"

"It seems that we are to be safe, for a time at least, if we choose to stay, about which they would say that our choice is nil. If you will have a moment's more patience, I may be able to understand better myself before I try to explain."

He talked to Abrah for a few minutes further, and then turned to Joselyn to say: "It is a queer tale, which it would be less easy to understand if I had not heard most of it from Abrah before, though I had doubted that much of it could be true, and had not always followed what he said with complete understanding, or as carefully as I should have done had I known where we should be today.

"But—as briefly as I can put it—his tale is this: there is a community dwelling here from remote time, descended from an ancient race which had dominion over a wide land, which may be Egypt or not—I have not learnt on which side of the desert it lay—until they were conquered and massacred by hordes of savages who broke out upon them from a barbarous land. But a few fled to what may then have been no more than an oasis here, where they remained in safety, because no one but themselves knew that it existed, or was tempted to search so far in a barren waterless place. Their descendants, recognizing that, if they should reveal themselves to the world, they would be no more than a few score among nations of alien men, have relied upon the security that isolation gives, and this the more as they have gradually developed a higher standard of life, such as—they have supposed—would make them a tempting prey.

"Because they can support only a limited population, they have adopted a method of elimination by annual contests or competitions, in which either lives are lost, or the losers are subsequently put to death until the total population is reduced to the permanent maximum which they allow. Abrah fled across the desert when his life had been forfeited by this rule, he being defeated in a contest of speed by the man he killed when he pursued us as we came from the plane. He crossed the desert with no more than a bag of dates and a goatskin of water, which, to one of their physique, would have been held to be an impossible feat; and it is one that, he says himself, he would not try to repeat, at whatever need. As it was, he collapsed when he was within twenty miles of safety, and was picked up by a Sudanese desert patrol.

"He says that his people, or those who rule them, have no quarrel with us, and as to those we have killed, their deaths have simplified the position, as he hinted before that they would be likely to do. So long as we are content to observe their laws, it seems that we can remain here, taking the places of those who are dead, by which rule we shall have life for about a year, and after that we must keep ourselves by proving from time to time that we are of sufficient relative value to be retained."

"You haven't agreed to that?"

"I haven't agreed to anything. I'm just telling you what Abrah says. It isn't easy to see what better—indeed, what else there is for us to do."

"We must find some way of escape."

"We shouldn't differ about that. But the present question is: are we to go back with Abrah, or remain here and probably be massacred during the night?"

"I don't see how they could expect you to get the best of any of them. Most of them seem to be about seven feet high."

"Yes," he agreed, "And as strong as bullocks and as active as boys. But Abrah says that all the contests are not of strength, but of excellences of different kinds. And there would be a year in which to decide in what class enter, and how we should prepare. The real question is, if we agree, can we be worse off than we are now?"

"We should be, if we made a promise to stay. At least, I don't see how anything could be much more ghastly than that. Do they have these competitions for women as well as men?"

"So I understand, though I don't know of what descriptions they are. But I don't understand that we are asked for any pledge that we shall stay. They assume that we have no choice. We are simply told that we can remain, providing that we observe the laws of the community to which we have come. In fact, that is no more than every civilized state requires aliens to do."

"But they don't have such horrible laws."

"Perhaps not. Though it might be said that these people show better results than we who spend all our resources to save the weak and diseased, and to make sure that criminals don't feel the cold."

Joselyn did not discuss this, her mind having no vacancy for considering abstractions at such a time. She said: "Well, if we've got to!" She tried to reach a courageous gaiety as she added: "It ought to be an adventure worth having, if we come out safe at the other end."

"I'd better ask Abrah first," he said, "whether it's understood that we can keep our own possessions."

"That's a good idea. But it will be enough if you say yours. I've got none to lose."

She wondered silently in what manner her feminine needs would be supplied in that alien place, divided, she supposed, by a millennium of isolation from the civilization from which she came. But he made no reply, the major question which he had to discuss with Abrah being one which he would not mention to her, and beside which there was triviality in the salving of goods.

"Abrah," he said, "you have our trust, and though we would have preferred to return to our own people, I must thank you for what you have done. We will come with you now, as you propose, if I can be more clear on one point than I am yet. You said that our lives—yours and mine—would be secure for the next year, but you spoke about Miss Wilde with less definite words. I will agree to nothing by which her safety is left unsure."

Abrah was silent for a time, giving consideration to his reply. "I cannot promise," he said, at last, "of myself, for what advantage would that be to you? I said what I was told, and it is a question of how it should be taken, for ill or good."

"Which you can judge better than I?"

"Then I tell you it may be heard with a quiet mind. Its meaning was that a way will be found, but it is not yet concluded what it will be."

"I must have something better than that. I must be sure, or I will not move."

"Then you will choose death for both, that one (and she the woman!) be saved a shadow of risk which may never fall."

There was reason in this, but Leonard had noticed a subtle difference in Abrah's manner, and in his words, which he did not like.

Since he had returned, he had spoken without actual rudeness, but in a different tone from that of the quayside labourer whom he had hired on the Nile bank. It was as though, being back with his people, and come to accord with them, he was already forgetting the obligations of less prosperous days. He spoke as an equal now, who had been a servant two hours before. Well, it was natural enough! It would be foolish to notice that. But it made his master, with doubtful logic more resolved than before that Joselyn should not be persuaded to yield herself to his people while exposed to a danger she did not know, and with which he was unwilling to disturb her mind.

"Yet," he said, "I am so resolved."

Abrah did not appear to resent this, nor to take it as rejecting the offer of peace which he had brought. He considered it in a grave way, as of a difficulty to be overcome. "I can promise this," he said, "as not being beyond the discretion I am allowed. If this matter be not arranged as you require, you shall be returned here, with the freedom you now have, and so that you shall not be worse placed than you are."

Leonard saw that, in reason, he could ask no more, and that it would, in any case, be useless to press Abrah for pledges beyond his power to fulfil. In fact, the offer exposed how utterly he was at the mercy of those who proposed that which he might take or leave, but the loss of refusal would be entirely his.

"That," he said, "is sufficient for me. I will ask one thing more: will my possessions be left in my own hands?"

"Do you think us thieves? You are not here among uncivilized men."

The difference in Abrah's tone was more evident than before. Being one of his own people again, the two years of menial service among those who cultivated dirt and disease, and various vices which he had not previously known, was ended now, to be no more than a bitter dream if he could re-establish himself as one fit for membership of that limited community.

Leonard took no notice of that. He said: "Well, it is what I am glad to hear."

CHAPTER IX.

THEY went down to where the camels sprawled flaccidly with outstretched necks on the blood-drenched sands, and made a hurried choice from their loads of such things as they would be most likely to need before morning should come, or beyond that, in the incalculable strangeness of the place where they were to be—guests, or what?—for a period which they could but fearfully guess, but which had the look of a long time.

The position of Abrah, who had been a willing servant at noon, had changed so much in the last hours that it was rather as one who solicits favours than as giving command that Leonard asked him to lend his aid to carry a portion of the articles he was anxious to take. But Abrah showed no reluctance to that, and his strength more than doubled the total that they were able to bear.

Certainly it seemed a quiet and desolate place where the camels lay. The scent of their blood had not called a hyena out of the rocks, or a vulture from the bare sky.

"I wonder," Leonard said, "that no birds of prey have come to so great a feast. Are there none in the desert here?"

"On what would they feed? There is nothing here but the barren rocks. I had not seen such a bird until I came to the river land."

"But you must have refuse that you throw out? Have you no creatures that lurk round you to find a meal?"

"We have nothing that we treat in such a fashion as that. What we would destroy, we cast into the water that bears it away."

"There is a river here?" Leonard asked, in a natural surprise.

"There is a stream that flows underground."

The sun was low now, and the sand had ceased to dance in the cooler air, as they made their burdened way across a rough plain that seemed wider to tread than it had been to their eyes in the glaring light. As they neared the mushroom rock, it grew broader, higher, blacker in the sunset light, with a greater marvel in the green cincture dividing it from the plain, which it overhung like a roof without apparent support.

Joselyn faced this strange approach to the vaguely imagined subterranean city with a determination of courage which she found hard to sustain. She had become physically and emotionally exhausted by the prolonged strain of her experiences since she had entered the aeroplane when the dawn had been no more than a faint light in the eastern sky. Vaguely, but no less acutely, she feared the ordeal of meeting the strange people to whose unproved faith her life and honour were now so utterly surrendered. What reception, what hospitality, would they be likely to meet? Would she be separated from the protector who was her lover's likeness, if not himself? Or would they be obtusely confined together, as though assumed to be intimately at one? Would Abrah continue to be with them, or would they be left to the mercy of these strangers of alien speech, without means of request or protest beyond the point to which signs might avail?

From these doubts her words came: "I wish we'd stayed where we were, for this night at least."

"Oh, I don't know," he answered, from a more buoyant mood, "we may as well see at once what we've got to face."

He had the satisfaction of feeling that a loaded automatic was in his pocket: a loaded rifle beneath his arm. There was not only the sense of power that the weapons gave, there was the significance of their being left in his hands. Their use might not have been fully understood, but there had been Abrah to explain, and two deaths to demonstrate the potentialities of that which was in his hands. Optimistically, he concluded that he would not have been allowed to bring them with him had there been hostile or treacherous purpose concealed beneath the verbal compact to which he had given choiceless consent.

Apart from that, he had a most lively curiosity to explore this hidden city which he had found, and of which he might still hope to tell an astonished world. And when his thoughts turned to the girl at his side—well, he had no wish to betray a twin brother he loved, and who trusted him, but suppose the worst, suppose they were doomed to remain here for the future years, surely that would be a special circumstance which would justify much from which honour must otherwise turn aside? As he looked at her, the attraction he had first felt revived with recruited vigour, and he was not without reasonable hope that, if the occasion should fairly come, he could persuade her to a similar mind. He had met her first! She had confessed, only an hour before, to the common difficulty in distinguishing between him and the man she loved.

Was it unreasonable to expect that propinquity and comradeship in this alien place would establish a living bond, of strength to overcome whatever of preference or obligation she might feel towards a distant duplicate whom she might never see? Certainly, if they were to be prisoned here, Providence had shown a rare consideration in the companion who had been sent to him out of the sky. But now to both of them the moment came when fears and hopes and fatigues alike were forgotten in the wonder of what they saw.

During the past weeks, Leonard Kinnear had seen no change above him from the infinite dome of sky—an unclouded dome which would become brilliant at night with its countless stars—and around him the tawny desert, that would become emphatic only in blacks and yellows and reds. But now he looked ahead to a wide vista of freshest green, overhung by a black roof of basaltic rock, and lighted by the in-driving rays of the setting sun.

It was easy to see that the original formation of the rocky plateau, which they approached from beneath, had been of a kind familiar to all who have studied the geology of the Libyan desert. An outcrop of shelving strata had exposed a soft calcareous rock beneath a layer of basalt too hard to be worn away, even by the incessant toil of the desert wind and its tool of corroding sand.

But the lower, softer stratum would crumble into a deeper cavity so long as the harder rock above could support its own weight, a question of centuries, to be decided at last by its thickness and density, and the firmness of its unfissured unity with the sustaining mass. But, soon or late, it must fall. That was the desert law, which had brought huge masses of rock to ground as the ages passed, with thunders that could be heard for scores of miles in the clear air, and columns of dust that rose into high pyramids on a still day, or would be caught by a twisting wind, and dragged far through the darkened sky.

But here the slow natural process which levelled the desert crags had been stayed and controlled by the hands of men. The soft stratum, ten or twenty feet in height from the level plain, had been worn away, first no doubt by the wind's action, and then more deeply by excavation, but the basaltic roof had not fallen, being sustained by huge pillars, the centres of which may have consisted of softer rock, but which had been faced with granite blocks so that they had become strong to resist the wind, even had its power to penetrate deeply among them not been checked by the vegetation which now filled the wide space below.

For here was now a green hothouse, mile-wide, shallow-roofed, open on three sides to the wind, and such evening and morning light as could penetrate its cool green shadows, and brighten the grape-clusters of the vines that festooned its roof.

Cool it was in comparison with the hot air that danced between the sun and the burning sand. The two who were led into the shade of a long green corridor felt a sudden chill as they encountered its humid heat. But it was far from cold, and its greater difference was in that humidity which would render it less tolerable to endure than the dry torridity of the sand and sun.

They passed no gate. The green subterranean garden was fence-less to a desert that bred no foe beyond the invading sand, and this must have been controlled and carried away by various narrow channels of water, and many fountains among the leaves.

Meeting no man, Abrah led them far along the straight corridor, which grew dimmer as they left the light of a sun which was itself leaving the desert sky, until they were surprised by light from an-other source. Not in lamps or bulbs, but in a thin continuous streak, like a fine-drawn wire, a line of electricity shone along the rock-roof of the corridor, partly obscured at times by the hanging vines, but sufficiently strong and continuous to illuminate the high, narrow, leaf-walled passage, and make plain the way they should go.

It was a new surprise to find knowledge and use of electricity among this isolated people, and required a further adjustment of mind towards the problem of what they were, but Leonard reflected reasonably that it did not follow that they had stagnated in ignorance because they had dwelt apart, and light, to those who lived more or less underground, must be a primary necessity. Beyond that, he could only guess how complete the isolation might be, or what means they might have of learning the discoveries of the wider world.

They came at last to a metal gate, and the first sign of a guarded way. Two men held the gate, and the light from above flickered on the blades of spears. They were alert now to an uncommon event, but their presence there may have been as perfunctory as that of sen-tries who give dignity to a palace door.

Now the gate opened without demur, or the need for words, and the three went on by a passage that was of the same width, though of less height than before, but was now walled as well as roofed by the solid rock. Also, it was no longer level. It sloped steadily downward. At its end, they came to another gate, metal as before, but more heavily made. It opened on to a bridge of stone which crossed a chasm, black and deep, from which rose the sound of a river which flowed far below in a rocky bed. Then there came a third gate, upon which converged three passages, right and left and ahead.

It might seem a wonderful thing to find this subterranean city in the midst of the most barren desert in all the world, but Leonard knew enough to see that, to the geologist at least, it would all be a credible, almost a natural thing. The fault of strata, the consequent outcrop of rocks of different solidity, the presence of subterranean water—it was all no more than the Western Sahara illustrates a hundred times on a smaller scale, where green oases have resulted, and men have sunk wells to find that abundant water will rise so long as it be kept clear of the choking sand.

Here there were guards again, and there was also an unarmed man who was much the smallest they had yet seen, though tall enough to look down on them. He was thinner, with a more sharply featured face, and a lighter skin, as though of a different race. Also, he had a slight stoop. He looked to be one who would be of less use with a spear than any they had yet seen, but might hold a pen in a better grip. Leonard had a moment's wonder of how he had contrived to survive those who had condemned Abrah as one to be weeded out.

The guards opened and closed the gate with the same indifference as before, while the smaller man spoke to Abrah in words that Leonard was only partly able to understand. But it was clear that he spoke as having authority, either of himself or as the messenger of one who ruled, and that Abrah made some protest, though rather as pointing out a difficulty that should be observed than of a matter in which he was himself greatly concerned.

But the man did not give way. He said at last, in words that Leonard had learned enough of their language to follow: "Well, there need be no trouble in that. You tell him now."

Abrah turned to say, in the language which was native to neither, but which they had both learned in the last two years: "It is ordered that I leave you now. But I am first to explain that you will be guided to a room where you can leave all that you have, knowing that it will be touched by none, and where you can rest. But that will not be for more than four hours, after which there will come one—probably he who is now here—who will guide you to the presence of our lord Hulah himself."

"He is chief here?"

"He is King of all."

"Will he wish to see me during the night?"

"Is there night or day under the ground? Our lord Hulah wakes when he will."

45

"But, if you are not there, how will he be able to understand what I say?"

Abrah put this to the messenger, who appeared to be curt and admonitory in his reply. Abrah translated: "Would you propose that there is aught that our lord Hulah does not understand?"

Leonard thought that even this might be possible. But he had sufficient discretion to frame his answer another way: "It is not that he would not understand. It is my own ignorance that I fear. How shall I understand him?"

"Doubtless you will learn that in his own time."

"I suppose the interview can't be deferred until I have had a reasonable night's sleep?"

"Men do not question the King's will. It will be well to remember that, now you are here."

"I suppose they are allowed to be tired when they have done a day's—or whatever you call it—work?"

"They are not tired if the King calls."

"Very well. I'll say no more about that." He spoke to Abrah personally, not as interpreter, to add: "If you're leaving us, perhaps you'll tell me who's going to carry what you've got now. Our friend here hardly looks equal to it."

It was a difficulty already apparent to those concerned. Confronted with it, the messenger, whose muscles would certainly have been unequal to a burden which Abrah had borne with ease, proposed that the guard should take it, even at the cost of leaving the gate.

There was an altercation on this, the guard questioning the messenger's authority to require him to leave his post, and there being a strict etiquette which forbade Abrah entering the precincts to which they went, but in the end it was agreed that the orders under which they were acting implied that this must be done, and they went on as before.

The way proved to be long, through passages which were narrow, and not very high, but in which the air was still fresh enough to show that there must be an efficient system of ventilation in these subterranean warrens. They were lighted by a thin continuous line of electricity which was embedded in the polished stone of the roof.

The sides of the passages, like the roofs, were of black polished granite, but whereas the roofs appeared to be all of one piece, the sides were of evident blocks. It seemed that the excavations had been immediately beneath the stratum of harder rock, so that its under surface formed a natural ceiling, and the softer sides had, for their own preservation, been faced with the harder stone.

It was evident that they were going deeper underground, though at a very gradual slant. They passed doors at times which were closed. These were formed of single sheets of bronze, giving them an aspect of sombre strength, but it was easy to think that there might be no meaning in that, for where should there be wood in this desert land? The origin of the metal was less easy to guess.

They came at length to a door at which their guide paused. He opened it, without entering. He spoke to Abrah, who went in, laying his burdens down. He made signs that the room was theirs, and went off, as one whose mission was done.

The floor of the chamber was about twelve feet square, and its height not less than seven. These might be considered good dimensions for rooms which were not made by the mere building of walls, but must be hewn from a solid rock. In the ceiling there was a round halo of light.

The room was furnished with a metal table and stools, and a pallet bed, covered with a single goat-hair sheet.

The door had a simple latch, but no lock or bolt either outside or in. It seemed that they could not be confined there, neither could they secure themselves.

They did not see all this at once. Leonard heard Abrah repeat the message that he had been given before. He asked: "Is it for both, or for me alone?"

"It is for you alone. How else should it be? The King sees no women, except it be for one use, or that they are of his own blood."

Leonard received this information without objection. He had heard of Eastern monarchs of quite different habits with which strangers might be less certainly pleased. He was reluctant for Abrah to go, feeling that their isolation would be increased. If there were anything they required, any information they should have, now was the time to speak. He asked: "We shall not be left without food?"

Abrah drew his attention to a gutter which was raised to a convenient height along the farther side of the room. A stream of water ran along it, narrow and clear. "You can drink here," he said, "when you will; and you can use it to wash, or to cast refuse away. It will not flow into other rooms. It is drained off."

He showed also a recess in the wall, where there were a bunch of grapes and some dates. There was also a small goat's horn, such as would serve for a cup. "You will find all you need here," he said. "You are not now among the squalor of those who live on the Nile banks, but in a more civilized place."

Leonard hoped he might find it to be no worse. He asked, repeating a question that Joselyn was addressing to him: "Is there no more than this chamber for both?"

"Can I answer that? I have no right to be here. I stay talking too long."

With these words he was gone, and they stood facing each other in the midst of a scattered litter of the arms and clothes and other impedimenta that they had thought useful to bring.

CHAPTER X.

"I HOPE," Joselyn said, as the door closed, "they don't expect us both to stay here."

She looked round with some consternation and some contempt at the meagre size of the windowless room, ventilated, as it seemed, by no more than some holes along the top of the bronze door, and furnished with the narrow pallet bed, which could certainly not have been intended for more than a single use, unless these people slept in succession in a place so independent of night or day. It was a position which would arouse most women to some indignation of protest, even though it might be mitigated by a degree of congeniality in the enforced companionship.

"Abrah couldn't say. He didn't seem to know much. I'm to be ready to see the boss of the show—King, he called him—in three or four hours; so the programme doesn't seem to include going to bed for me."

"And I'm to stay here?"

"That seems to be implied. The King doesn't make a habit of receiving women who are not of his own family."

"Doesn't he? Well, I don't know that I particularly want to see him. But you might mention that we could do with another room. I hope you won't forget the way back, all the same. How shall you make him understand what you want to say? I suppose Abrah'll be there?

"I believe not. It was implied that the King—Hulah they called him—would be superior to such difficulties."

"It sounds likely! But I expect you'll find some way of making him see sense. You'd better start on these grapes before I finish the lot. They're about the best I remember tasting. Quite the best thing we've come across in these dungeons yet. I wonder," she added, with more gravity, "whether we are at the end of the mess, or is it beginning now?"

He answered with the vague optimism that the occasion clearly required. Both being too restlessly excited for sleep, they sat side by side at the low bronze table, and ate the simple fare provided, wondering whether they had come to a place where the full menu would always consist of fruit and water. They talked of many things, but mostly of themselves, as youth will be ready to do, and keeping mainly to the past, for the present was of an ambiguous kind, and the future a threat that they would not face, or an enigma they could not read.

In much less than four hours (or so it seemed) the messenger came again, and with a motion of his hand, making no effort of words, he signalled Leonard to come.

Leonard had already put the automatic in his pocket, with no clear thought of any advantage it could be, and wondering whether he would be searched before being introduced to the presence of this monarch of (as he lightly described it) an oasis and a hole in the ground. He gained the sense of confidence, of equality, that such a weapon gives by its power of death, but he was not foolish enough to think that he could shoot his way to freedom from where was. And, if he should, what life would the desert give?

Joselyn let him go with a cheerful word, "It's just as well," she said, "that there should be someone left to stand by all this junk that we've hauled here. And while I'm sitting on it I shall be pretty sure that you won't bolt."

When she had been left alone, she walked restlessly up and down the little room for a time, trying to adjust her mind to the crowded events of the past day, and the wonder of where she was. After a time, she yawned. She looked at the bed. She considered the unboltable door. She picked up the heavy rifle, and then the lighter sporting weapon, which she found more to her mind. She yawned again. She said aloud: "I wonder how much longer he'll be." She considered: "I can't stand forever. And if I sit on one of those wretched stools I shall go to sleep and fall off."

Without removing her clothes, she lay down, with the lighter weapon beside her hand.

She was wakened by a light touch. Her eyes opened to see a woman bending above her, who rose, and moved towards the door, beckoning her to follow. She was dazed with sleep, and thought stirred reluctantly. It would be foolish to object, to refuse. It might be that she was being led to the room for which Leonard had successfully petitioned on her behalf. It might be that she was being taken to him. Anyway, there was some comfort in the fact that it was another woman who summoned her from a room where it was plain that she should not be.

CHAPTER XI.

KING HULAH XCII came of a race of kings who had endured for much more than two thousand years in that lonely rule, keeping to one name and one pattern in all they did. They were long-lived, and having followed the ancient custom of Egypt, by which brother and sister would always wed, and the royal line be kept pure from any various blood, they had become so alike, from generation to generation, that the old king, and his heir who might be in the prime of life, and the youthful prince who would follow him, could be told apart by no more than the differences belonging to change of years. Only once, and that less than a year before, had an event come which had drawn that dynasty to perdition's edge and made its ancient custom a broken dream. Hulah XC, of the pure blood of his race, had unaccountably been of a disposition to change the long-founded things. He had had a vision of converting the world; of persuading it to transform itself from the sewer-like filth and muddle in which it quarrelled and starved and bred, to follow the example which he would reveal.

For, in the small kingdom they ruled so long, the line of Hulahs had not imposed the custom by which they had fixed their own race to so close a pattern that it might have been said until then that it had had but one king who had never changed. Rather they had sought (the numbers of those they ruled being limited by the slender resources the desert gave) to improve quality, as other monarchs might seek to increase the numbers of the people who called them king. Surely, Hulah XC had thought, if he should show to the world the splendid fruits of this ancient policy, it would be moved to imitation, and to reverence those who had been first to discover the possibilities latent in the human race, if it be controlled with no more forethought and wisdom than was given to the breeding of the goats which were the only domestic animals that they had—a small herd being maintained on the herbage which had been taught to grow under the oasis palms.

In the enthusiasm of this belief, Hulah had taken confident counsel both with his sister-wife, and with his son, who would be Hulah XCI at his death, and with his daughter who was wedded to that prince, and who already had adult children to sustain the integrity of the sacred line.

But he had found it to be a dream that they would not share. There had been quarrelling, fierce and long. He had been told alike by sister and children that he had imagined a folly which would bring his people to destruction and himself to shame. From generation to generation, something had been cautiously, furtively learned of events in the outer world, and of the conditions under which mankind was content to live. Did the king realize that they were no more than a rabble of many peoples and changing rules? That they were still subject to scores of diseases, one or other of which would be sure to destroy his own long-isolated people if they should be brought into such pernicious contacts? That they were not of a level of intelligence to appreciate the doctrine that he would expound? That they were not controlled by monarchs of authority to enforce their wills, even if they should have better judgment than the vulgar crowd could be expected to show? That even this lonely spot where his ancestors had ruled for much more than two thousand years, might be claimed as the rightful possession of some country that had never set eyes upon it—by Italy, Egypt, France, or the Sudan—and that the whole world would approve their right?

Bitterness grew when he would not yield. Finally, to save their people, their dynasty, and themselves, his assassination had been proposed. His sister-wife had hesitated, reluctantly agreed, repented, and betrayed the plot. By her action, what would have been no more than the destruction of one man—the thrust of a single knife—had become an uproar of violent strife in a narrow room.

It had been seen by none but themselves, and known (or even guessed at first) by none but the eunuchs, who surely would not reveal it to those who dwelt without the interior gates which shut apart the apartment in which those of the royal race were accustomed to live. It had ended with none living except the King's son and grandson, and of these Hulah XCI had been so hurt that he had resigned some weeks before his body was committed secretly to the subterranean flood by which the others had already been swept away.

After that, Hulah XCII, a young man of no more than twenty-three years, had found himself upon a throne which there was no woman to share—a fact that he had not been willing that his people should quickly know.

But he had already taken steps to provide a remedy for that catastrophic position, and as he sat pondering while he waited for the white stranger to be brought before him, he wondered whether he had done well. Should he have waited for the gods to move, as it had been likely that they would do, for the remedy of such disaster as that? Had he had the required patience, he saw that the coming of this woman today would have appeared to him—would surely have been—their interposition on his behalf. Was it less so because he had already secured one in another most secret way, intending that she should become his wife and the mother of future kings? Well, he would talk to the foreign man who had come to a place that he could not leave now that the camels were dead, and to whom he had given a precarious tenure of life, less for his own sake than for that of the woman, who might have been injured had she fought at his side among flying spears, but who yet might be useful to him in another way, in the crisis which he knew to be nearly come. As he mused thus, Leonard Kinnear was led into the room.

Leonard saw one who was plainly dressed, his power being too real, too absolute, to require the trappings and ritual which are the safety of more precarious kings. Mystery and aloofness from common men were the tricks that had for so long a time sustained the power of his ancient throne, and there were few, if any, of those he ruled, except the half-bred eunuchs, who had entered that room, or even passed the interior gates which divided the royal apartment from the accommodations of lesser men.

Leonard saw a man who was young in years, but with the look of one to whom youth had not, and would never, come. His appearance was bleakly austere. His butter-coloured skin was drawn tightly over the high bones of a fleshless face. His thin nose was out-curved like a vulture's beak. His mouth was tightly closed, but when he spoke there was an expressive mobility in the movement of thin sensitive lips. His eyes, palely brown, had a cool searching intelligence which might not be easy for either liar or fool to meet in a confident mood.

He sat solitary at a table of beaten copper, beautiful in a weird way, and in a chair of the same design. It was straight-backed, uncushioned, undraped, showing that comfort was not the deity which had allegiance from him. On the table there was an inkhorn, a metal pen, a goatskin parchment, which may have been for the making of notes, but which, in the event, he had no occasion to use. On the floor was a goatskin rug.

Rooms might be expected to be small where they must be hewn from the solid rock, but this was not only almost as small as that from which Leonard had come, it seemed to him to be strangely bleak and austere for the reception-room of one who claimed the state of an ancient king. Yet behind this bareness of outer show he felt that there was a cold and purposeful power, of very formidable if not sinister kind, and of which he would do well to beware.

Hulah XCII motioned him to take a seat of a plainer pattern, but otherwise not unlike his own, on the other side of the table. With a second movement of his hand, he dismissed the messenger from the room. Leonard found himself to be alone with the King. He had not been searched. No one appeared to be interested in any weapon that he might bear. Here was evidence of unsuspecting goodwill, or a great assurance of power, or perhaps contempt which might be of a too arrogant mood.

The King looked at him in a cold silence which was equally destitute of hostility or kindly regard. It simply searched him for what he was. Suddenly the King asked: "Why have you come here?"

Leonard understood the question by no more than a good guess. He tried a halting reply, and the King changed to another tongue, of which he knew nothing at all. He expressed his ignorance in English, lest silence should be misconstrued, and it was to be expected that Hulah would not understand.

Leonard had some knowledge both of ancient and modern tongues. It was by them that his college honours had been gained. Since he had joined the army, and especially since his regiment had been stationed in the Sudan, he had concentrated upon Arabic, both as a modern colloquial tongue, and to gain access to one of the most poetic literatures of the world.

Hulah, showing no sign of annoyance at the deadlock to which they had come, paused for a thoughtful moment, and asked the question again in a different speech. His slow deliberate words, strangely accented, and having an unfamiliar construction, were yet plainly to be recognized as Arabic of an archaic kind.

Leonard replied in the same language: "I was curious to see what the desert held."

He had spoken as deliberately as the King, and it was clear that he was understood. Yet the King did not respond, neither did he regard the substance of the reply. It became evident that he desired to test to the full the points where their knowledge of language met.

When he spoke next, it was in words that Leonard guessed to be ancient Greek, to which he made a stammered reply in what he supposed to be the pronunciation of that obsolete language. Hulah, observing the quality of his response in the same impassive manner, paused again, and then spoke in Latin, which was more easy to understand.

He listened to Leonard's reply, and for the next half-minute sat motionless and as though his thoughts had wandered to other things. But he must have signalled in some way that Leonard did not observe, for after that short interval an attendant entered the room bringing a shallow oblong tray of fine sand, which he placed on the table before the King.

Hulah took a stylus from a groove at its side. He wrote some Latin words in the sand. Then he turned the tray towards Leonard, pointing to them in succession, for him to pronounce in his own manner. Having listened to these, he smoothed the sand with a roller at the foot of the tray, and wrote more. After this process had been twice repeated, he said: "It is enough." He commenced to question in Latin, using so closely the pronunciation that he had heard that Leonard could understand without difficulty, neither did the King appear to find difficulty in following his replies. Once or twice, a doubtful phrase was resolved by writing upon the tray. Once or twice, one or other would substitute Arabic, when hindered by a limitation of Latin vocabulary, but otherwise the conversation proceeded without difficulty on either side.

Leonard recognized the intellectual feat which had so rapidly grasped and adopted a different system of pronunciation from that which Hulah had evidently been accustomed to use. He realized that he was confronted by a most formidable mind, and he met the interrogation to which he was subjected with, to the limit of his own ability, the combination of finesse and frankness which he felt that the occasion required.

"Did Abrah tell you of this place?"

"He did."

"And tell others?"

"No one believed."

"Except you?"

"I had a doubt, so I came to see."

"Others will come?"

"I cannot say. I suppose not."

"Why did the woman come?"

"She followed me. It was a mistake."

"She is your wife?"

"No. It was my brother she sought. She thought it he who had come."

"She is his wife?"

"Not yet."

"Will he follow her here?"

"I suppose not. No one knew where she had come."

"But some knew the route you had taken?"

"They knew I came into the desert."

"Then how did she find you?"

"She took a chance. Her bird-machine could fly far."

"You will be content to remain here?"

"I do not see how I could leave."

"You would certainly die."

"I prefer to live."

"You are wise. If you deserve life, you may find it yours."

"How can I deserve life?"

"By excellence either in strength, or in some service or art. But you will be instructed in that. Answer me now. You learnt something of the language that Abrah speaks?"

"Yes. But not much."

"You will learn no more. It is not for you."

"Am I to speak Latin to all?"

"You will speak to one. He is versed in this tongue, and will tell you all you should know. If it prove that you have more knowledge than he, it may be your gain, though it may be your part to seek life by another way. You will go back now, taking some sleep, after which you will learn more of my will."

"May I make a request?"

"Speak."

"They have put the girl and myself together. May we have separate rooms, as is the custom in our own land?"

"It was needless to ask, being that which is already done."

It was a reply that had a satisfactory sound, but also raised a vague fear. He was assured that he had what he asked, but might it not prove to be even more? He would have inquired further, but Hulah recognized his intention, and checked the unspoken words. "It is enough. I do not answer. I ask."

And with that word, the messenger who had guided Leonard to the room entered and led him away.

CHAPTER XII.

LEONARD was led back to an empty place, as he had been told to expect. He looked round, and observed that his possessions were undisturbed. Only, the bed had been used, and the sporting rifle lay by its side, where it had not been before.

There was no sign of a struggle, of disorder. Probably she had gone willingly, though guided by those with whom she could have no speech. She might not be far. She might be in the next room! He delayed his guide with an attempt to question him upon this, but the man was either ignorant or unwilling or unable to understand.

Well, of what did he complain? They must either be left together or put apart. His request had been granted before he asked. Was he to make trouble of that? But he wished he knew where she was, and how and where he might see her again. For the time, he could do nothing better than sleep, as the King had said.

But sleep, which he needed, was slow to come. He considered the interview he had had. Did he like this strange ruler, who could think and speak in old tongues that had become silent in their own lands? Not at all. Yet he would not say he disliked. The man was cold, inhuman. He did not appear to be one who would easily be moved by any emotion. Not by love, nor perhaps by anger or hate. He might be just, by a strange code, and in a most ruthless way. He might be even better than that. But he was not easy to read.

Leonard judged him to be wise, implacable, practising neither kindness nor cruelty for themselves, but with the single purpose of maintaining this solitary rule in its ancient mode, for which no price would be called too high.

He slept at last, and for long hours, and was undisturbed. He waked to find that a meal had been already laid out for him, of a plain kind, but with more variety than the fruit of the night before. He ate with appetite, turning his mind resolutely from the fear that he had come to a place which he could not leave. He must take the present chance, learning all he could of the strange life he had discovered; and doubtless a way of leaving would come at last. For the present, he told himself that he was not anxious to go.

It was true that he could have imagined a meal more to his mind. But those who explore the remote parts of the earth cannot expect to find the comforts of home. And he could mend even that, for the time, if he could get the loads that the camels bore, which it had been promised that he should have. If he could obtain them, and know that Joselyn Wilde were content and near, he felt that he would confront the adventure with confidence that it might be worse, and hope of a good end.

While he was in this mood, a man entered whom he had not seen previously. He was old, though he still moved with some ease and vigour. He had an ascetic scholarly face, with more of humanity in it than could be seen in that of the King, to which it yet bore a faint resemblance, as of a man having a portion at least of a kindred blood. It was noticeable that, though the men Leonard had seen since he passed the guards of the interior gates might not be deficient in health or in bodily vigour, yet they had no excellence of physique, such as had been conspicuous in Abrah, and in the two hundred spearmen who had issued out to the desert at the sight of the circling plane.

It was a simple guess that there were other tests than that of physical strength by which they were allowed to endure, but the difference was more than such an explanation would meet, for they appeared to be of another breed.

The man who entered now spoke in the Latin tongue, which he had already learned to accent in the manner which made it easy for Leonard to understand. He said: "It is my lord Hulah's will that I should transfer you from here to a better place. But you must first give me a pledge,"

Leonard had a fear that he would be asked to undertake not to leave, which, though it might appear to be an impossible thing, he would have been reluctant to do. But he answered only: "If you would say what it is?"

"It is one that it is vital to understand, and to break it would be a short passage to death; but it is hard neither to give nor to keep.

"You must know that we who wait on the King are few in number, and have contact with many things that are not for the privity of those who do not enter the inner gates. You must give your word in a solemn way that you will talk to none without of that which you may learn here, and to no woman at all; nor, indeed, to any except myself and the King. On that pledge, I would consult with you on much in a free way, both to impart and to learn."

This did not sound either an unreasonable or a too onerous pledge, but Leonard caught at one word, the implications of which he was quick to probe.

"Why do you say: 'to no woman at all'?"

"That will not be hard to observe, for none is allowed within the interior gates, excepting one of an aged sort who waits on the King's suite."

"So that the girl who came with me will not be here?"

"The King has made exception for her."

"I shall see her?"

"That, I suppose, will depend largely upon yourself, and the degree to which you may gain the confidence of the King."

"Then, Miss Wilde being excepted, I give my word."

The man hesitated at this, but after a moment's pause he said no more than: "That is well. It is also our lord Hulah's will that you learn no more of the common tongue which is spoken here, which there should be no present occasion to do."

"I will accept your assurance of that."

"Then I will guide you to the place which will be yours from this day."

"And these things I have here will be brought?"

"They will be brought, and also those you left with the dead beasts. Excepting only that the water-skins will not be required, and the beasts themselves have been used already for food; for flesh, as you will know, does not long endure in the desert heat."

"It is a pity that they were killed. They could have been of much use alive. If not to me, then to you."

"Do you think that? Do you suppose that we should have been secure here for more than two thousand years bad there been less than a rigid law that no beast should live having longer legs than a goat? We have been ruled, as you will agree when you know more, by those who allow no slackness, from which failure is bred."

Leonard said nothing to this, which was poor hearing for one whose ultimate purpose was to find some means of crossing that desert space which had been held an inviolate barrier for so long a time. But it was not a subject on which it would be wise to make further remark. He picked up the firearms, less from any desire to have them at hand than fear of accident if they should be moved by those who would not understand the danger of what they did, and followed Olah (which was the sage's name), finding, as he went, no lack of subjects on which to talk to the one man with whom he would be able, as it was agreed, to speak in future with a free tongue.

"I was surprised," he said, looking upwards to the thread of light in the roof of the passage along which he was led, "that you should have such a light here, you having so little contact with the outside world; for even there it has not been long in use."

"But it has been used here for a thousand years. You must not judge us by the backwardness of the savage peoples from which you come."

"Would you call us that? There may be other things we have which it would be to your advantage to know."

"So it may. It is of such we look to you to tell."

"It must have been a great labour to excavate these dwellings beneath the rocks."

"So it has been. But you must know—as, indeed, you will shortly see—that we have more space than the pick would win, but for which we must have remained less than we are. That which you first saw was the wind's work, which those who came to this place on an ancient day drove deeper, and pillared up. After that, they cut rooms in the rock in a patient way, so that each generation had more space than before. But it was when they came to the great caves that their numbers grew, and their wealth began."

"That was long ago?"

"It was longer than I can say. For you must understand that it was no work of our hands, but was done by a folk who were driven out, or rather destroyed, when our ancestors came here. It was they also who worked the mines, which are very rich, both in copper and tin."

Leonard exclaimed with surprise: "You work mines here!"

"So we do, though not much. For even when the ancient people were driven out they had metal here, ready for use, in a great store, which was ample to serve our needs. For metal endures long, and our occasions for it are no more than you will be able to see."

"It is an easy guess that it was for this metal that men first opened the rocks."

"It may be an easy guess, but I should suppose it to be wrong. It is more likely that they sought water, seeing the palms, and it being an old tale, as you are likely to know, that where the rocks outcrop, as they do here, water will not be too far below to be reached by the toil of men. But they may have found more than they sought, both of water and other things."

"Such mines would bring you a great wealth, if you should trade with the world of men."

"They would bring servitude, if they should become known; or destruction, as it was to those who were here before we came." As

61

they talked, they had come to a passage upon the left hand, to which Olah pointed, saying: "That is the direct way which leads downward to the great caves, and the lake, and the river level. It was by that passage—which is of no great length till the caves begin—that penetration was first made. But there is another way which was opened later, which will become more familiar to you."

"Is that," Leonard asked, "the main passage that is in general use?"

"Yes. It is the only one, except for those who have the right of the King's way."

"Shall I tell you what is puzzling to me, even though it may show me to be foolish in what I fail to observe, or in the deductions I draw?"

"It is the way by which you will learn most quickly, where many things must be different from the life you have lived before."

"I am puzzled that we have seen no men or women who pass either in or out."

"That is simply told. They have different hours."

Leonard considered this, and saw that he might have said less if he had thought more; for had not Abrah pointed out to him previously that there was neither night nor day in these recesses to which sunlight could never come? It was mere assumption that all men, under such conditions, would wake or sleep at the same hours, and there might be good reason for a different order of life.

"Yes," he said, "it was foolishly asked." And after that he became silent as he was led by a passage he had not traversed before, to a chamber larger than that he had left, though of a similar design, but which had long shelves cut into the walls, on which there were piles of manuscripts, papyri and parchments, both rolled and flat, showing that it had been a library to some man of an older day, but beside these it was little furnished, and had the look of a place which had been unused for a long time.

"I will order," Olah said, "that this chamber be better furnished, and also cleansed in the next hour, and that it be supplied with a new bed. It has been long unused, but we are little troubled by dust in these upper rooms which were hewn from the harder rock, and they would remain dry for a thousand years. There is a chamber beyond this, in which you may sleep, or which you may use for storage of what you have."

"Before you go," Leonard replied, "you must let me know how I can see you again, and how far I may move abroad, for if I go far I may either become lost in caves that I do not know, or blunder among those to whom I may be strange, and to whom I shall be unable to speak."

"You will have no trouble for that if you will keep within the interior gates, which shut off the whole apartment which is reserved for the Royal House, and do not enter the King's own suite, the entrance to which is not guarded, but is closed by a gate which, when I have once shown it, you cannot mistake. You should not go as yet beyond the interior gates, nor, in particular, should you venture to cross the lake, which you may be little tempted to do. But I am not leaving you yet, for all this it is my purpose to show you now."

CHAPTER XIII.

IT was some hours later—but whether night or day there was nothing to show—when Leonard was left alone to consider what he had seen and heard.

He had learnt much concerning this strange community, both on its politic and economic sides, and enough to see how difficult it might be for him to adapt himself to it, or for it to accept him as a permanent member. He supposed that he would be allowed to live only if he had some knowledge or craft which it would be useful to them to acquire, and only so long as would be necessary for him to communicate what it was. And under the laws that prevailed here, it was not necessary that he should be charged with any treason or transgression against custom or rule. He could be condemned to elimination as a redundant or inferior member of a society which must be continually reduced to a fixed maximum. To defend himself against such a fate, he must be able to show not merely that he was fit to exist, but that he was more so than others who would be in competition for prolongation of life; and it was easy to see that, under such a test, he would not endure long, unless, as he had had more than one hint, he could be of some private use to the King in connection with political trouble which was anticipated to arise. He might have realized that he held his life on an even more precarious tenure had he known that the King would not have issued the order which had enabled him to survive at all had he not heard that a strange woman was with him, and feared that she might come to harm among flying spears.

He had learnt that he was now lodged in the most ancient part of the excavations, which consisted of a suite of chambers reserved for the royal family—of the almost total destruction of which he was unaware, for Olah could be discreet in silence as well as speech—and an outer suite for the officials, among whom he was now placed, and the twelve guards of the royal gates.

To the whole apartment of the King there were three exits only. One through the main interior gates, which was that by which he had first come; one by a descent of precipitous steps in a black cavity to the side of the deep lake which the subterranean river fed; and a third, known as the Queen's Gate, leading to a twilight garden in the open rock-roofed excavations through which Abrah had brought him at first—though to a different and separated part—which issued from the royal suite, and could only be used by the King's leave.

He had learnt of the long descent of the line of Hulahs, and how they had kept it pure by intermarriage among themselves, and how the eunuchs who formed the official occupants of the outer suite of the royal apartment were also of their blood, being begotten by them upon women selected for that purpose, so that they were blended of common folk and the royal house. It followed naturally that these half-bred people (of whom Olah was one), had the characteristics and physique of their mothers, greatly modified by that of the royal parent from whom they came. They were in number less than two score, and were sterilized so that they should not become the parents of a mixed race, their numbers being renewed, from generation to generation, in the same way.

The twelve guards were chosen, after other eliminations, by physical competition, being those of the greatest strength and skill in arms of the whole tribe, and their position was therefore coveted and honoured, though it was no more than a ceremonial occupation. There were four for each of the three exits, each two having twelve-hour duties. They had certain much-valued privileges with the women, as their physical qualities deserved, and their children were freed by custom from preliminary tests as to their fitness to live, and were likely to show a high percentage of survival in the sports of boyhood, which were literal competitions of life or death.

All this had been very freely explained, but when Leonard had spoken casually of the Queen, he had observed that Olah put the question aside in what had seemed to him to be an awkward manner, so that he had reverted to it in another form, only to be foiled again. And when he had spoken more generally of the living members of the royal house, he had seen a blank expression upon the old man's face, and received so irrelevant a reply that he had not only judged that there was a limit to the confidences which he was to receive, but had become vaguely aware of something sinister and concealed, some secret trouble which threatened the hoary stability of that ancient throne.

But among a confusion of information, not yet ordered in his own mind, and some of it not fully understood, there was one dis-

65

covery which had made him willing, or even impatient, for Olah to leave him alone, though he had been far from indifferent to the importance of the information which he was gaining.

"This chamber," Olah had said, "was occupied at one time by an outlandish man, who had become lost in the desert and wandered here, of whom it is said—for it was long before the time of my own birth—that he was most skilful in ancient tongues, though his own was of a barbarous kind.

"There are writings here"—Olah drew out some most ancient papyri as he spoke—"which were left by those who opened and worked the mines, among which there are some that even we have not been able to read, and on which he was set to labour, with little gain that he would admit, though he wrote much in his own tongue, which was as useless to us. They must also be, I must fear, beyond any skill that you are able to direct upon them?"

Leonard said that the writing was beyond his knowledge to read. He set his eyes upon the papyri as he spoke, and so far, it was true. The words were no more to him than unmeaning signs, to which he held no possible key. But he had seen the neat rather cramped handwriting of the "outlandish man," and it was an unmistakable English script.

"Doubtless," he had asked, "he is long since dead?"

"He destroyed himself by attempting flight in a foolish way, showing that those who come here are wise if they decide to remain content."

He had turned the subject to ask, in as casual a voice as he could assume, if the lady who had come with him were lodged near, or when and how she could be most easily seen.

Olah's tone had, he thought, some reticence in his reply which he did not like. "She is lodged, as I have said, in the King's suite, to which those do not intrude who are not so honoured by his command, unless they be of the royal race. She may come forth, as I suppose, at her own or the King's will, but I cannot say what she will do."

"Will she know I am here?"

"She will be told if she asks. Is she much to you?"

"She is my brother's affianced wife."

"She was not wed? Then you may call that a past dream, which should be no trouble to her, and the less to you."

"You say that I may not enter the royal suite. Yet you have said that the way to the gardens is through it. Are we denied the sight of a green leaf?"

"I did not say that. I did not call it the only way. It is for the royal use, and there is, in fact, a garden reserved. But you may go out by the main gate, and arrive nearly at the same spot, though it will be a much longer road."

"Are we forbidden the shorter route?"

"No. We may enter the Queen's garden at times, and may go there by the royal way, for we are not meant to mix too much with the common folk. But it must be at times that are fitly arranged."

"And when we may suppose that the Queen or her ladies will not be there?" The question seemed to cause the momentary disconcertion which he had noticed before, but Olah controlled it instantly to reply: "How should I answer that? Kings and queens may go as they will."

He showed that he had not been blind to the object with which the last questions had been put, when he went on to ask: "Have you a special cause for wishing to speak to the woman?"

Leonard was quick to use the idea which this question held. He answered readily: "There are things among my baggage that she should have."

Olah looked faintly surprised. "I had heard that she came by another way, and not being expected by you."

"That is so. I did not say that I had anything which is hers. But I have things that, being detained here, it will be useful for her to have."

Olah appeared to accept this, and, if he were free from guile, became helpful in his reply.

"There is the woman who waits on her, and also on you. She might take what you have to send."

Leonard thanked him in an indifferent tone, and turned the conversation to other things, as though they were of more importance to him.

CHAPTER XIV.

I go a way [Leonard read] *by which there may be doubt if I live or die, but from which it is most sure I shall not return. I leave here the diary that I have writ, and other records that I have made, where they may endure unto other days, and come at last, by good hap, to eyes that will be acquaint with the English tongue. For the little that I can bear, except my sword, must be for the belly's need.*

Peter Brisco
Sunday, August 15, 1684
(by the best count I can make)

Postscriptum: There is a Sappho, complete, as it doth appear, hid away in the far corner of the low shelf, which may be called the greatest gain in the world. Would that I might but risk to bear it away!

For the next two hours Leonard remained absorbed in the diary of Peter Brisco, one who, it became clear, had been scholar and adventurer, a man both of sword and pen, such as were bred in his days, and who had died at last (if Olah were right) in a fantastic effort to escape, his preparations for which may have been watched by those around in the assurance that they need not trouble to destroy one who was contriving his own end. So he must have died, one of the nameless thousands of his wandering race who laid the foundations of the Empire that was to come.

Leonard read of how he had resolved to attempt flight by way of the subterranean river, the details of which were not easy to understand, nor did Peter's own reflections thereupon suggest that it was better than a most desperate chance—the bold resolve of a cornered man who would not resign himself to death while there was a passage, however dark, that might still be tried.

> *For I can see* [he had written] *that they mean my death, having had the use of me which they designed, and no further will to slaughter one of their own blood that I may live to a later day. So I will commit myself to a Better Hand, being that of the high mercy of God, and say farewell to them and their bloody ways, for I have come to think that they are devils in all they do.*

Beside the forecast of this intended escape, to which Leonard had most eagerly turned, he read much for wonder, much for warning, much which checked or amplified the information which Olah had given him, and left some things which were still far from simple to understand.

He observed, both from occasional passages in the diary, and when he turned over the loose leaves which had lain beneath it, that Peter Brisco had some claim to add the title of poet to his other accomplisments. There were fragmentary attempts at translation from the discovered Sappho.

> *Athos, loved once, and once to love denied,*

had been abandoned after the rhyme *triéd* had failed to provide a satisfactory termination to the following line.

A second attempt, commencing:

> *Athos, loved once, so vainly loved, and now*

had been continued for two or three much-altered stanzas, and abandoned with a despairing note:

> *I cannot English this to my own content, so that it would be like to be but for the laughter of other men. It is, in my conceit, beyond human wit, so that it must lie hid in its own tongue.*

Leonard paused again over the papyri to which Olah had first directed his attention, or rather—for its hieroglyphics could have no meaning for him—upon the notes which Peter Brisco had made upon it.

This [he had written] *is almost wholly beyond my skill, though it hath words which are sister to those which the Arabs write (which I may read, though I cannot speak). But after I have studied it long, and resolved it with other tongues, I have gained so much that I conceive it to have been writ by one of an older race, the most of whom had been either slain or thrust forth by these who are now here, and he kept by them for some use he had, and so writing this, not in his own tongue, but in one that was ancient to him, which he was assured that they did not know. And its substance is that there would others come in the fullness of many days who would bring these people to sorer wreck even than they had caused to those of his kindly blood.*

It is all writ in verse of the Arab kind, but whether it be good or else bad I am a scholar too poor to say.

As with the Sappho, Peter had used his solitary leisure in attempts at metrical translations, but these were even more fragmentary and tentative, being from a manuscript that he could not easily read.

When he meet her (face to face?)
In the peril-hearted place—

The word "peril-hearted" appeared to have given some satisfaction to the translator, for he had tried it in several variations, but always breaking off at the same point, as though the words that followed were beyond his skill to construe.

Another effort read:

(closer?) yet
When the spears are red and wet.

Well, be it devil's foresight or idle dream, it is nought to me, for it is, if I read aright, at the coming of three, of whom two are maids, and I came alone, as a man would be more likely to do.

Leonard put this aside with no further thought till a later time. It would need more than an old prophecy from the hand of a bitter slave to get him free from the hazard in which he lay. And the objection that Peter had observed applied to himself also. For one maid is not two.

He was interrupted by the entrance of the woman of whom Olah had spoken, who brought a meal on a tray. She entered quietly and without ceremony through the boltless door, and went without appearing to give any attention to him, or to what he did.

He observed that he could have no privacy, being subject to such intrusion at any time, and in a place where there was no distinction between night and day that he could yet understand. Yet he supposed that there must be a procession of regular periods, though they might have no direct relation to those of the rising and setting sun. The fact that his room was furnished with sand-measures, large and small, in which the sand was not controlled by a turned glass, but was set to run down a narrow chute, was evidence in support of this otherwise natural conclusion. Possibly the woman was regarded as too inferior to be esteemed as more than a piece of moving furniture in the room. Probably it was the etiquette of her occupation that she should appear oblivious of what she saw. If that were the standard of excellence in an attendant, she would be likely to practise it well, knowing, perhaps, that the number of actual or potential chamber-maids had become one more than the community required, and that the least efficient would be eliminated at a coming date.

The woman was past her youth, and quiet in manner and movement, though somewhat heavily made, being doubtless one of the crossbred sterilized children of the royal house and the physically finer plebeian race that they controlled. She wore a loose garment covering all but her face, which was unveiled.

The meal consisted of two small fish of the catfish kind—which he supposed must have come from the subterranean river, they having eyes in no more than a rudimentary form—a wheaten cake, and six dates. Eating it, he considered how vital, in this desert place, must be the problems of population and food. He was puzzled, from his incomplete knowledge, as to why more had not been done to irrigate the desert from the water supplies that appeared to be available, and supposed (which was much less than the whole truth) that it had been found too difficult to extend cultivation over the barren roughness of basalt rocks, or to overcome the assaults of the blowing sand, or, perhaps, that it might have been considered inexpedient, at the time when this community first settled into the rigidity of its present custom, to extend far beyond the protection the caves supplied, and the limit of the ancient oasis, though that had been allowed to remain for its crop of essential dates, and the pasturage it afforded for the flock of goats which must be source not only of flesh and milk, but also of clothing from hair and skin.

He supposed the woman would soon return to remove the tray of curiously hammered bronze on which she had brought the meal, and considered how best he could approach her to establish contact with Joselyn Wilde.

CHAPTER XV.

WHATEVER cause there might be for Peter Brisco's opinion that these people—or rather their ancestors—had been devils in all they did, it appeared that theft, at least in its cruder forms, was not practised among themselves, or even towards the unwelcome stranger who had intruded upon them, and who, he was fair enough to observe, must either be destroyed, or allowed to return to his own people—and so reveal the secret the keeping of which was regarded as vital to their own existence—or fed from the limited resources which were already insufficient to support the natural increase of their own population.

Investigating, after he had finished his meal, he found that the adjoining chamber contained all his recent possessions, short of the actual camels—even their bridles, and the ropes by which they had been strung together, having been scrupulously delivered. He supposed he owed this to the fact that the King had made no order depriving him of their use, and that in the absence of such instructions no one would care to be first to pilfer. He reflected that honesty is largely a matter of habit, and that theft, among that small and isolated community, must be singularly purposeless and its fruits difficult to both enjoy and conceal. He saw also that, if theft were definitely discountenanced, that attitude would be alone sufficient to make it a very unpopular recreation. The law that kept the population down, not by limitation of natural births, but by the annual destruction of its less desirable members, would be potent in discouragement alike of illegal practice and unpopular vice.

Now he searched his luggage for any articles which might be welcome to a girl who found herself suddenly deprived of the necessities and luxuries of her civilized life, and dependent upon the charity and understanding of an alien race, or at least such as would not appear to be sent with other than that natural purpose. Some soap—some pieces of linen cloth—a pair of scissors—a brush and comb—a few nondescript articles of less certain utility—a selection from the contents of a first-aid cabinet—he could do no better than that. But they, were enough for the purpose he had in view. He wrote a short note to be included among them, in which he informally omitted commencement or signature, hesitating a moment over the manner of address which their rather exceptionally close and yet limited intimacy would require or allow, and concluding reasonably that, if it should reach her hands, she would be in no doubt of from whom it came.

> *Can you let me know* [he wrote] *if you are being looked after properly, and if we can meet safely, and, if so, where and how. I'll do anything you like, or come anywhere, but don't want to cause any possible trouble to you.*
>
> *But I'm anxious to see you, if there's any way that I can.*
>
> *We've got to decide whether we shall try to settle down, or make a desperate effort to get away; but if anyone asks what this letter is, you can say that it's to urge you to be content to remain here, and you can be sure that I shall say the same thing.*

He read this over, and crossed out "desperate," and then wrote the whole again, so that the deletion should not appear. He felt that he had chosen the right tone—striking no note of alarm if she were safe and content, and yet giving assurance that he was at hand and would be ready for her support if she were threatened with danger or indignity, even to the extremity of attempting a flight which he could see no way to survive.

He had this parcel packed when the woman returned, and though she seemed faintly surprised at the efforts he made to explain his wishes, or perhaps that he should address her at all, and though his slight knowledge of her language made the explanation a difficult process, yet, when it appeared that she understood, she accepted the mission with the docile willingness of a dog that may find comprehension hard, but has no thought but obedience if he can grasp the intentions of those above.

She might, he knew, accept only to betray; but he judged her to be of a simpler mind, and had a thought, as she went, that the exactness with which she had been trained and subordinated to the special offices she performed might be his protection, and the vulnerability of those whose captive he was. There might be very few conceivable circumstances under which she would open a conversation with those she served, and not many in which they would speak to her. He saw himself in this long-stabilized community as an element of incalculably disintegrating quality, from which there came a vague hope of what he might be able to do, if he could maintain his life, and act with the difficult wisdom that coming occasions might require. It was a colder thought that the King might have the wit to regard him in the same way, in which case that essential maintenance might be very difficult to secure.

In his talk with Olah he had omitted, amidst a hundred contending subjects of conversation, to ask him how the hours of activity or sleep were regulated in these caves where no daylight came. Now he might guess the use of the sand-measures upon the shelves, but, without knowing when they should be set in motion, or the periods they were designed to cover, they were useless to him. Vaguely, he supposed that a diurnal period must be nearly done, and mind and eye being wearied by the novelties they had heard and seen, he might have lain down to rest, had not a man entered whom he had not previously seen, and who now, in a single Latin phrase, summoned him to the King.

The man's eyes regarded him blankly when he answered in the same tongue, for it was no more than a phrase he had been instructed to say, and, beside that, as Leonard made a right guess, he was not of the status of Olah, but rather of that of the woman who had just left—a male servitor, who did not expect to be addressed in a personal manner.

Tired or not, Leonard knew that it would be well to go when the King called, and for the next two hours he found himself subjected to a series of questions concerning the civilization from which he came, which touched it at many points, but turned at last, after he had stated his own occupation, to a detailed inquiry into the organization and weapons of the Sudanese army, with obvious reference to their possible direction against the little kingdom he ruled. Leonard's replies, given with a discreet accuracy, involved mention of the offensive arms of the infantry soldier, and, by a natural sequence, to a question as to the nature of the weapon he had brought with him, and used, to fatal result, when he had been attacked. He had the sense to answer these also with accuracy, at least to the mention of the two rifles, though he supposed that it might lead to their surrender, leaving him with only the automatic his pocket held. But the King said no more than: "You shall show me their use on another day," making as he spoke one of the brief notes, a hieroglyphic rather than words, by which he would occasionally record a vital item of information.

At the end of two hours, Leonard was dismissed without indication of the impression he had made on the King's mind, or to what extent he might be considered useful for further examination. The King had spoken no word of satisfaction or thanks, closing the interview with a curt: "*Jam satis*," and meeting one or two attempts at counter-question with a blank disregard, as though he were deaf to anything but the answers that he required. It was evident that questions must be directed to Olah's ears, and that he must be content to be the giver of information when he was seated before the King.

He was led back to his own room feeling that he had come to the end of a long day, but he had not failed to use his eyes to better purpose than when he had first been taken to the King's presence. He had the advantage now of the information that Olah had given, and of what he had already observed of the topography of these subterranean passages. He had the incentive of knowing definitely that Joselyn was located somewhere within the King's suite. He did not think that this—nor, indeed, the whole of the interior city, which was within the three gates, and inhabited by the half-bred eunuchs—could be of great extent. That was contradicted both by the information that Olah had given him regarding the number of its inhabitants, and by the immense labour which must, at some time, have been required to hew out these passages and chambers from granite rock. He knew now that the whole occupied area was divided into five parts—the open oasis, the covered cultivated ground open on three sides under its low rock-roof, the inner passages and chambers of softer rock inhabited by the general body of the community, the separate interior chambers reserved for the royal house and their attendants, almost on a level with the others, but hewn mainly from the harder rock, and finally, behind these last two, and at a much lower level, the great caves which, formed by the fracture which had broken the continuity of the strata, gave access to the mines, the lake, and the subterranean river by which it was fed and drained.

Of these, he had only to give immediate consideration to the third, which was itself subdivided between the royal suite of chambers to which he understood that Joselyn had been taken, and those inhabited by the King's attendants in which he was himself located, but he was pleased to observe that the door between these was not locked or guarded in any visible manner. The guards were stationed at the three gates of exit from the King's apartment, but this dividing door was protected only by the etiquette of custom, or the fear of penalty that an unauthorized trespass might entail.

Whether extensive or not, Leonard was puzzled by an apparent absence of life in the royal suite, to which Olah had denied him the clue when he had avoided mention of the tragedy of the past year, which had left Hulah XCII the sole living member of the royal house, its continuance dependant on his own life, and its marriage custom, after more than two thousand years, irretrievably wrecked.

Now, as Leonard followed his guide along a passage that was narrow and straight, he counted the sheet-metal doors in the left-hand wall, and concluded reasonably, from there being none on the other side, that he was at an extremity of the excavations. He supposed, from the experience he had had, that those doors were un-barred, and would give way to a pressing hand, but it was not one that it would be sane for him to apply without knowing more as to what he would find therein, or a more evident need. Behind any one of them, Joselyn Wilde might be located, under circumstances that he could not guess, or she might be some distance away. All he could observe was that they remained closed, and he could hear no sound come through them, either of movement or voice.

The passage turned twice. He noticed also that two others branched off. It was important to memorize these turnings with care, for the passages were all alike. Floor and walls and ceiling were all of green-black basaltic rock, polished so highly that the figures of those who passed were reflected, on either side and beneath, from the line of light that shone lengthwise above. The metal doors bore no numbers nor signs, nor had they any distinction of pattern suffi-cient to differentiate them at a passing glance. He went out through the dividing door, and along two similar passages to his own cham-ber. Well, he had gained one thing. He knew the way now to the room in which the King interviewed him. He could find it at any hour of the day or—but there was no night here. He could find it at any time.

On his table a paper lay. It was his own note to Joselyn Wilde. Seeing it, he had a quick fear that the parcel he sent had been opened by other hands, and the letter therein returned as a contemp-tuous gesture, indicating the uselessness of attempting communica-tion with her. There was time, before he took it up, for a swift cur-rent of angry fear to disturb his heart. If she were in peril now! If they had wronged her in any way that it might already be too late to avert! He thought of the bullets his pistol held. There should be some who would come to a swift death, let the sequel be what it might. That bloodless, inhuman King!

He raised the paper in an unsteady hand, and saw that it had been used for reply. On the reverse side, in a somewhat round femi-nine hand, was a longer note than his own. Like his, it had ignored the conventionalities of address or signature, and the writing was unfamiliar. But there was nothing disconcerting in that. Until that moment, he had not had an opportunity of observing Miss Wilde's handwriting, and she might well feel as sure as himself that he would have no doubt of whom his correspondent might be. But he was puzzled by what he read.

> *Say, stranger, but you're the goods! If you're another that's pickled here, and you'll get me away, I guess it's more dollars for you than you'd think to ask, and then some.*
>
> *If you know how to get anywhere near the Chief's room, you can come about three hours after you get this. I suppose it's night by that time, but anyway it's all as silent as sin. I'm in the third door along, and it won't lock. I'll open it before then, so that you won't make a stir in the wrong place. But I don't believe there's anyone about here, except that yellow monkey himself and the woman who brings you this, and she makes herself scarce in the night.*

Leonard read this twice and again, with a bewilderment which did not lessen. On the face of it, it was written by an American woman who was a stranger to him, as he was to her, and who was a fellow-captive in this impossible place. But was such a proposition sense? Apart from the fact that Olah had made no mention of such a woman, which was not in itself conclusive, there was the immense improbability that another expedition, of which he had never heard, would have adventured the Libyan desert, and would have come so far, with the result that another woman had fallen into these people's hands at the same time as Joselyn and himself. An improbability, however remote, is not impossible. They sometimes occur. But Leonard felt that the explanation must be more—or less—simple than that.

Was it no more than an attempt on the part of Miss Wilde to write in a disguised manner? The explanation seemed insufficient: the occasion wanting. Writing as she did, in a language known only to themselves, it seemed a pointless subterfuge to attempt. Whom could she think to deceive, and to what result?

He thought next that it might be a mere playful whim, but this also seemed an improbable explanation. As an effort of humour, it was not much, and it was an occasion on which humour was unlikely to obtrude. It was not until he had observed that there was little that was distinctly un-English beyond the first paragraph that he came to the conclusion that she had attempted to adopt an American idiom—perhaps to indicate that she was not too depressed by her present circumstances to write in a playful mood—and that the pose had lapsed after the opening sentences, as her mind had settled upon the serious question of how their meeting should be contrived.

Anyhow, he was likely to know before long. The vital fact was that she was well, and saw no obstacle to their meeting during the hour of quietude. The directions she gave were incomplete, but were not likely to cause him much trouble, knowing what he already did, and with the added sign of the open door. The time could be no more than a guess, for he did not know how long it was since the letter had been delivered, but it was certainly too early yet, he having only just come from the King. It was mere prudence to allow two or three hours for sleep to come to those who were probably awake now, and better to be late than too soon.

He ate some fruit which the woman had left, and which seemed to be the only item supplied for the last meal of the day—it was, in fact, intended for the hour of waking—and endeavoured to exercise such patience as he could, and such ability as he possessed to judge of the passage of time.

CHAPTER XVI.

LEONARD picked up the rifle, and put it down. If he should be stopped and questioned—if he should have to explain to the cold eyes of the King what he did during the hours of rest in his private suite—if by some unlikely chance he should intrude into a wrong room—it might be a good argument for his peaceful intention that he had not taken a weapon the fatal nature of which he had already demonstrated. And, at close quarters, the automatic was the handier, deadlier pattern.

He went out as quietly as he could, and returned after a few paces when he found that, however carefully he might tread, his steps would be loud on the stone. Silence being a vital prudence, he took off his shoes, and started again.

He passed along the lighted corridors with some confidence, until he came to the entrance to the King's suite. After all, to that point, he did nothing wrong. He had not been required to remain in his own rooms. Might it not be his own national custom to walk smooth floors in feet that were softly shod, and save leather for rougher ways? It was true that, if he should meet anyone, he would not be able to defend himself or explain with intelligible fluency, but there might be gain even in that. An explanation in a foreign tongue may be beyond understanding, but it is equally beyond criticism, and is likely to lead to a deferred judgment at worst. Doubtless, before Olah could be summoned to deal with the event in the Latin tongue, he would have invented sufficient explanation to suit the case.

But, as he entered the King's apartment, he knew that he trod a more dangerous way, for Olah had been explicit in his warning that none but those of the royal blood were allowed therein, except by the King's word; and the double door, though it was not bolted nor locked, had a large, elaborately wrought latch, too heavy to be lifted with ease without the use of both hands. It was not a door through which he could say that he had strolled in a casual manner, or by mistaking the turn he took. The very gentleness with which he handled the latch, the slow movement with which he drew back the door, were evidences of furtive purpose and fear to anyone who might have observed them unseen. But the door was well-hinged, and came open with little noise. The passage ahead was empty and quiet. The door he sought should be easy to find. The "third door along." Along what? It was near to "the Chief's," which should surely mean the King's room. That should be direction enough, and he knew the way. So there he went, very silent himself, and hearing no sound from the closed doors. From the King's room, he tried each direction without result. First the doors that were three away upon either hand. Then those that were three away from the two ends of that passage. Then he explored other passages further off. But the result was the same. The metal doors were all closed. He listened at those which, from their situations, were the most probable chances, but heard no sounds from within.

Perhaps he had come too soon? To his impatience two hours, or perhaps less, had seemed three? Joselyn would not be fool enough to open her door too soon. She would wait the hour which is said to be that of the deepest sleep. Had he been more certain of the door, he would have settled down to wait with what patience he could. As it was, he must migrate continually from passage to passage, looking with recurrent disappointment for open doors which were not there. It was a method of spending the midnight hours which, after the twentieth rotation, is likely to lose its charm, even without the knowledge that it cannot be done much longer without resulting catastrophe.

When at last he must admit to his own mind that the time of the appointment was passed, and that there must be some other explanation of the delay than Joselyn's cautious punctuality, a natural reluctance either to venture the opening of doubtful doors, or to retire defeated from an enterprise to which he had been so clearly invited, stirred his imagination to a belated recognition of the fact that a King may have several rooms, and that the one in which Hulah XCII had interviewed him might not be that to which Joselyn had been introduced, possibly in a more social manner.

There was no guidance in this idea beyond the obvious suggestion that he should investigate a wider area, but when he considered the probability that the King would occupy contiguous rooms, and reflected upon the positions of passages with which he had become more than sufficiently familiar during the last two hours, and the sides on which their doors lay, he had no difficulty in recognizing the most promising area of exploration, and it was within less than five minutes that he stood before a door that was certainly not closed, though there was no means of ascertaining whether or not it occupied the position that the letter had indicated.

For one minute of caution he paused before its forbidding silence. Other doors than Joselyn's might have been left open during the night. It would be a mistake of the first magnitude to intrude into the wrong room. This might, for all he knew, be that of the Queen herself. He made a slight shuffling noise. If he should be discovered by those he would rather miss, he had decided to rely upon protestations that he had meant no more than to take a short walk, being unable to sleep, and had become lost. What should he do, under such circumstances, but look for someone to guide him back? How, in these subterranean vaults, should he distinguish between night and day?

The noise he made having no result, he called "Olah" in a low voice, but one that should have been audible on the other side of the door. Having gained assurance that anyone listening could not have failed to hear that name, he added: "Joselyn—Miss Wilde—are you there?" The words, he knew, could have no meaning for the wrong ears. But there came no sign that they were heard by any, either right or wrong. Well, he was tired of these furtive ways! He would know the fact without more delay. He pushed open the door.

He looked into a larger chamber than he had yet seen, appointed similarly to his own, but with more of comfort, and more ornately furnished. The table and two stools were of metal, as was usual in this place where timber did not exist, but a couch of the same material was piled with cushions, above a draping of goatskin rugs. Subtly, it gave him the impression of a feminine room.

He looked round by the light of the thin-drawn halo in the roof, which seemed to be a universal feature of these subterranean chambers. The room appeared to be vacant, and it occurred to him that it might be prudent to withdraw before the owner should return. The idea recurred that he might have blundered into the Queen's room. Perhaps she had joined the King during the night, and might any moment return! It might be the etiquette of this brother-and-sister union that the Queen went to the King, rather than he to her.

However that might be, he had no difficulty in anticipating that, if he should be found in the Queen's room, he would have graduated either for immediate decease, or for the same fate at the next annual elimination, though he lacked sufficiently detailed knowledge of the customs of this strange people to judge which it would more probably be.

But while he weighed these possibilities in a mind that advised flight, the natural obstinacy of his disposition, which had led him into many previous difficulties (and assisted him to survive them), made him reluctant to retreat without gaining more certain proof that he had not entered the room he sought.

He advanced towards the couch on the farther side, and as he did so became aware of two things that offered warning and encouragement with conflicting emphasis.

The first was that there was a recess at the end of the room, opening upon a further, smaller chamber, so excavated that the light of the one in which he stood would only shine in upon one side, leaving the major part in a partial darkness; the second was that a lady's handbag lay on the couch, thrown down with a carelessness which had emptied a portion of its contents among the cushions, including an open leaflet which boldly advertised the kiss-proof quality of a lipstick vended by a world-famous Old Bond Street firm.

He did not recognize the bag, though he remembered that Joselyn had had one of these companions, essential to all her kind, clasped in one hand, while he had pulled her along by the other in flight from the burning plane, but he saw the improbability of it being owned by the consort of Hulah XCII. Emboldened by its presence to the belief that he had found the chamber to which he had been directed, he advanced to inspection of the recess, and stood motionless within it, paralysed between an instinctive inclination to retire from a place where he had no business to be, and a blank amazement at what he saw.

CHAPTER XVII.

UNDER the shadowed wall of the inner chamber was a low bed, and on the bed was a sleeping girl. She was fully dressed, and lay stretched across the goatskin rug in the careless attitude of one who had leaned back in an indolent waiting mood, and been overtaken by sleep. She had one foot still on the floor.

The light was dim, but it might have been less and still been sufficient to disclose that this was not Joselyn Wilde. Neither would it be easy to believe that she was of Hulah's household. The small, high-heeled shoe, and the silk stocking alone! And yet, who else? Leonard had already felt moments of doubt as to whether the isolation of this desert community were as absolute as it professed. And the first things to be brought from a far land, be they spoil of sack or that which the merchant bears, will ever be women's clothing and gauds. He might have retired even then, had he not seen the contents of the parcel which he had been at such pains to collect thrown carelessly down on the floor, at the bed's foot. He saw proof enough that his letter had been wrongly delivered, and answered by the girl who was now before him.

Obviously this was not a case for retreat. He was on the threshold of the unexpected, of something that it was necessary to know, even though it might augment difficulties which were already more than enough. Also, directly or indirectly, there might be a means here of learning something of Joselyn, by whom, as it now appeared, his letter had not been received.

But it would be foolish to wake her—to commence to talk— while the door stood as it did. He went quietly back to the outer room to close it, and as he did so Helen Vincent, roused perhaps by the slight noise it made, opened eyes of the most innocent blue that have ever been used for the deluding of foolish men.

"Gee!" she said, with the slight American accent which, from a girl's lips, can be attractive to English ears, "but I went off!"

The words reached his ears, and he paused in the outer room, making sufficient movement to disclose his presence, and next moment Miss Vincent appeared, a small slim blonde, dressed in an obviously European travelling suit of tussore silk, the fineness of its original quality sufficiently evident despite the disfigurement of some carefully mended rents. Certainly she could not be mistaken for Joselyn Wilde! Four inches shorter, and smaller, slimmer in all dimensions. Softer also, giving the impression of one who would look for protection rather than be a companion in dangerous hours. Yet there was no lack of self-possession in voice or manner as she addressed the stranger who, presumably at her own invitation, had made this midnight intrusion upon her.

"I reckon," she said, observing Leonard with approving and smiling eyes, "you'll be the guy who's going to get me out of this; and you can't do it too quick." She looked at a watch on her wrist, and added: "Well, I'm glad you're here now, but I can't say you've made the run within schedule" (she called it schedule) "time."

"I had some difficulty in finding the room."

"I'll say you had! But we'd better talk fast, now you are here. I reckon we've got two hours, or a bit more, before anyone comes awake. If you don't belong to this gang, you might tell me first who you are, and how you knew I was here." As she spoke, she picked up the bag from the couch, carelessly stuffing back its effluent contents, threw it on to the table, and adjusted the cushions for him to sit beside her.

"I didn't know it," he answered, willingly taking the proffered seat. "The fact is, I meant the letter for another lady. But," he hastened to add, "it was a fortunate mistake, as it's been the means of letting us know that you are here."

"That's real nice of you to say that! But you don't mean that he's got more, beside me? He must be in a big way! I reckon even Al Capone—though I don't say he was ever in the kidnapping racket: I wouldn't call him that mean—but I'd say he'd think he'd got mouthful enough if he'd got me!"

Leonard's bewilderment was increased by a note of petulance, faint but unmistakable, in her voice, as though she felt the presence of another woman to be intrusion upon a stage which she should have been considered sufficient to fill.

"I wish," he said, "you'd tell me how you came here."

"Don't I wish I could! If I knew that, I'd know a bit more about the way back than I do now."

"I'm not sure that that would be very much help. But if you'd tell me what you can, it might be clearer to me than it is to you."

"You want it all from the start? Well, I was in the train, I can't say where, except that we'd left Cairo about—"

A sudden memory of a newspaper "sensation" of the past month caused him to interrupt sharply: "You're not going to tell me that you're Miss Helen Vincent?"

"That's the baby I am! They tried kidnapping me twice at home, but it didn't click. You wouldn't think that the darkies here—"

"You mean that you were kidnapped off the Egyptian train, and brought here?"

"You've said it in one. And if you didn't get here the same way—?"

"Not exactly. But if you'll tell me how you were brought, it may be just what I need to know."

Amazing as the statement was, and fundamentally as it shook his previous conception of the position, and of the nature of those among whom he had become captive or guest, he could not doubt the truth either of the tale to which he listened, or of the obvious, and apparently the only, reasonable deduction therefrom. Olah having withheld from him any knowledge of the catastrophe which had gone near to total destruction of the line of Hulah, it was not likely that Leonard would guess that the richest of American heiresses had been abducted, not for ransom, but to become the bride of a desert king.

But this misconception did not alter the importance of the fact that there was a method of contact with the outer world which was known and used. And the channel of this contact was clearly indicated as being the subterranean river. But on the essential point of where and how access had been obtained to it in the far Egyptian desert, Helen Vincent had nothing helpful to say. She had been, she believed, drugged, so that her memories of the first days of her captors' flight, during which she had been veiled and bound to a camel's back, were both fragmentary and vague. She knew only that the road had been very rough. Her description was not of such a desert as Leonard had crossed, but of great ridges of igneous rock following one another like an ocean which had been petrified on a day of storm, a land of black sterile rifts, and rocks that burnt the incautious hand; and it was not difficult for anyone who knew the place at which she had been removed from the train, and had a general knowledge of the conformation of Egypt and the Sudan in their relations with the Libyan desert, to see that she must have crossed its northeastern barrier, where, perhaps because it has been bereft of rain for a shorter time, it is still fissured by deep valleys, and ridged by hills that the blowing sand has not corroded away.

Somewhere, in the 20,000 square miles of that monstrous and repellent wilderness, there must be access to the subterranean river. But this was a point on which Miss Vincent could give no guidance at all. She had not only been drugged. She had been blindfolded during the descent to the water, and for some hours before, although they had been travelling through the night. All she knew was that, after they had taken to the water, they had rowed against the current for many days, journeying on a raft, and the rowers standing upright (except when they had to stoop, owing to the lowness of the cavern roof), and facing the way they went. The sides of the cavern, during the latter part of the voyage, had often been so near that it would have been possible to touch them on either hand. During the last days, the roof had seemed to descend upon them, probably owing to the river rising, and, as this condition had become worse, the rowers had toiled in a desperate ceaseless effort, as men might who were racing death.

She said that she had been treated as well as the circumstances had allowed, the unpleasantness of the ordeal among aliens with whom she had been unable to exchange an intelligible word being mitigated by the services of a woman—the one, in fact, who was now waiting upon her—and who had delivered the letter by which they met. So she had come to the journey's end, and had been brought up from the river's level to this room where she now was. Here there had been no restrictions upon her liberty, beyond the fact that she was not allowed to pass the sentries who guarded the three exits from the royal apartment. When she had discovered the limits of this restraint, she had found no pleasure in walking passages which led nowhere for her, and had remained in her own room.

She had been visited on several occasions by a man whom she had regarded as the chief of the kidnapping gang, and whom Leonard had no difficulty in identifying as Hulah XCII, and by Olah, who had been at pains to teach her certain words of his own language, which she had resolutely refused to learn, having affected a density of wit which was certainly not hers. But she had formed a quite natural though erroneous opinion that her captors wished her to write a letter which would assist them in securing the ransom for which she presumed that they were blackmailing a distracted parent, and she recognized the absence of any common language as a difficulty which she did not intend to assist them to overcome.

During the last forty-eight hours she had been left entirely alone, except for the ministrations of the woman servant, a circumstance which Leonard rightly connected with Joselyn's appearance upon the scene, and which increased his anxiety to ascertain her welfare—an anxiety which might have been further augmented had he had any clue to the truth, that the King was disposed to regret the haste which had resulted in the purloining of the choicest and most luxuriously provided feminine morsel that could be found in the Egyptian mail-train, when it had been halted during the night by inexplicable damage upon the line, and to prefer the thought of Joselyn Wilde as a potential mother for the ninety-third of the royal race, and of the sister that the more orthodox nuptials of the next generation would ultimately require.

Leonard repaid this narrative with a brief account of the circumstances of his own and Joselyn's appearance upon the scene, and Helen, content to conclude that the King had been satisfied with the importance of her own kidnapping, and had not attempted to complicate the position with what could have been no more than a minor coup, became actively sympathetic in consideration of where Joselyn could now be.

"I don't believe," she said, there's a live soul inside what you say they call the King's suite, except me and the skunk himself, unless Miss Wilde's here. I don't know why Olah kidded you about the whole family being about, but you can call it a thumping lie. I know where the King, if that's what he calls himself, spends his time in what goes for the night here, and I know a dozen doors that I'd risk an oath haven't been opened or shut for the last two days, and I'm as sure that there hasn't been a step along this passage or the next that I haven't known; but if Olah's right that Miss Wilde is located here, it won't be many hours before I'll find out. And if you'll come back, as soon as you safely can—I don't know what time it is, for my watch stopped while I had the dope, and I started it at my own guess, but about eighteen hours from now—I'll have a bit more to say."

She added: "And you can tell me then how you've figured out to get us away. But you'd better quit now, or you'll open the door to find someone else on the mat."

Miss Vincent raised innocently trustful eyes, the simplicity of which was somewhat negatived by her gift of incisive speech, as she implied her confidence in masculine ability to rescue her from her present captivity.

Leonard, more conscious of the difficulties of such an enterprise than of any method by which they could be overcome, had a separate doubt of whether it would be right to encourage her to face the ordeal it must involve, if she were right in her belief that she had only to wait to be more safely returned when the amount of her ransom should have been handed over. "If," he asked, "we could find a way of getting off by the river during the night, you'd take the risk of a try?"

"Why, sure," she answered, on a note of surprise, "I'd not leave Pop to pay out, and the skin-faced devil to crow over the pile, if I could see a way to give him the slip. Get away?" she laughed lightly. "But that's what I sure would!"

"It's a pity," he said, "that you weren't able to notice more about where you got down to the river—though I don't say it would have helped us much if you had. It ought to be easier to find the way out, and we can't be far wrong if we keep due east after that."

He saw that while it would have been an impracticable task to search for the entrance of the river-tunnel among twenty thousand square miles of granite ridges and sharp ravines, it should be much simpler to follow the river's course, and to observe the place at which the tunnel gave possibility of exit to the sunlit surface above. And when that surface had been reached, though it might be a desperate chance that they would survive the scourges of drought and heat on so hard a way, yet of their direction there would be no doubt—to go due east must be to reach the fertility of the Nile valley at last.

But he saw also that, even if he could overcome the sentries at the gate that led to the caves (and for himself alone, he had not understood that they had instructions to interfere with his movements either out or in), and could find raft or boat that he could control on the black flood, and if he could get the three of them away unobserved or beyond pursuit, and with the large store of provisions that such a flight would require, there would still be the danger of a rise in the river-level, such as Helen Vincent's narrative had implied, that would swell at any time to a volume which would reach the roof of the cavern, giving them a gradual gasping death, as the lifted raft would bump and perhaps jam in the narrowing arch, and the air-space would become less, till the rising flood would close with the roof, and their drowned bodies would be swept on to swirl in some inky pit, or blunder out to the light again, and the ultimate sea.

Or suppose they should fail to observe, and be carried past the place of escape, to what end could it be? They could turn back when they realized the error that they had made? But would they have opportunity for that? Suppose the flood should rush on by rapids that would tumble their feeble craft to irretrievable wreck in the hollow dark, or sweep them upon a current too strong to stem, to be cast over the brink of some precipitous chasm? Or if, by improbable chance, they should struggle up again to the light of the torrid day, what possibility would there be that they would traverse the unknown distance across the burning waterless hills? From these thought-swift imaginations a question came: "How were you lighted upon the raft?"

"They had lamps, electric lamps, I believe. They seem to understand that."

"Well, we should have to understand too—I mean, we couldn't take that way in the dark."

Helen Vincent said nothing to that. Her manner implied faintly that it was his matter rather than hers. She had become clearly and reasonably anxious for him to go, which at last he did. He went quietly back, his mind becoming more bewildered rather than less as he considered what he had learned, and what it actually did, or seemed to, imply.

He passed the heavy door that closed the King's suite without interference, or observing evidence of human life, and was nearing his own room again when he observed Olah to be coming from it, having evidently been to give him an early call, and found no more than an empty couch.

CHAPTER XVIII.

REMARKING complaisantly to herself that she reckoned that that had dropped some grit in the mill, and with the memory of an English face that she liked better than most she had seen before to console her dreams, Helen Vincent went back to bed. She knew that beauty and long hours of vigil are open foes, and she valued her childlike freshness of cheeks and eyes at far more than the ransom that she supposed that her father would have to pay.

Yet when she had said that she would adventure again the black terrors of the water-tunnel, and the dangers of desert ways, if she could thereby frustrate her captors' plans, she had made no higher boast than she would be likely to equal if the occasion should come.

She might be the half-spoiled child of fortune today, but she was the child also of hardy, straight-speaking, straight-shooting, pioneering ancestors, and of her first ten years of motherless self-fending life, before a gush of oil almost in the "yard" of her Oklahoma home had put more dollars into her father's hands than he would have been careful to count, even though those that he failed to sum should be swept away.

She slept as lightly as though she had not been in a place of alien foes, with an unbarred door, and no more than a single new-found friend whose willingness to give her aid might be much more than his power. It is true that she did not guess the full extent or the nature of the peril in which she lay. The three wordless interviews, or rather inspections, she had had from Hulah XCII had passed without the thought entering her mind that she was being considered, not as a hostage so valuable that she must be carefully kept and fed, but as a mother of future kings. Had she known it, there may be doubt, though not much, whether her spirit would have quailed before the shadow of such a fate, or risen to resolution that would have held promise of little joy to him who would attempt to wed her against her will; but there is an even smaller doubt of the flaming anger she would have felt had she known that Hulah had surveyed her with deprecatory lustless eyes, contrasting her in thought that was near to contempt to the large-scale, physically perfect specimen women of his own people on whom it was his routine custom to procreate the half-bred eunuchs who were the satellites of the Hulah throne.

Having refreshed herself with sufficient sleep, and satisfied the clamour of a healthy appetite, she addressed a lively and sanguine mind to consideration of the problems the night had raised.

Towards Hulah XCII, whom she still regarded less as a king than as the head of a kidnapping gang of exceptional audacity and resource, and as having the advantage of a hiding-hole beside which the Arizona desert might be compared to a backyard two blocks away, she had conceived a most active hatred, embittered by an undercurrent of fear which she was unwilling to entertain; and this made the thought of escaping before he would have received the reward of her abduction particularly pleasant, even beyond the ordinary desire of an affectionate daughter to protect the paternal wad. She did not overlook the apparent certainty that, if her ransom should be arranged, she would be returned to civilization by the subterranean route she already knew, and, if it must be traversed again, she was conscious that there would be more pleasure in the company of this Perseus who had appeared so opportunely to break her chains, than in that of the alien captors with whom she had made the journey before.

Her thoughts turned to the girl whom she had not seen, but had undertaken to find, and she considered her in a different mood, with a quick frown, and a bitten lip. She was sure that she would be of an objectionable kind. Perhaps the sort who would treat her with a kindly tolerance due to her difference of nationality—much as she herself would be too liable to treat an otherwise attractive girl who had the stigma of a dubious past. Probably also, she would treat—it was silly not to have asked his name, but it had not seemed to matter while he was there—would treat him as though he were equal and friend, if not something much closer than that, and she herself would be no more than an outside third whom they were kindly bringing along. The thought of flight down the black flood became of an altered colour. "I can't think," she said, half aloud, "why she came muscling in." But she could think very well, and it was an idea that she did not like.

Yet these reflections, though they caused a shoe to fly across the room from a petulant foot, did not deviate her from the fulfilment of her promise to discover where Joselyn Wilde had been lodged, nor even a genuine feminine sympathy being aroused as her eyes encountered the sundry articles which Leonard had sent, and which now lay tumbled half-opened upon the floor. "Hell's bells!" she thought, using one of the two-score of her father's more frequent oaths, "she'd be better off in a good gaol, if she'd thank him for dumping that." Her own presence of mind at the moment of her abduction, joined to the willingness of her captors to bring such of her belongings as could be readily borne away, had saved her from such privations as would find relief in the gift of a masculine hairbrush, or a cake of soap of an unknown name; and the resources of the room to which she had come, which had been previously occupied by a princess of the royal line, had been of a quite interesting, and in some instances most useful, character.

Somewhat illogically stirred by the sight of that despised parcel to realization of the possible extremities of a sister-woman, Helen put on a nominally stouter pair of shoes than those she had kicked away, and set out boldly on the path of rescue. Within the limits set by the sentries at the three gates, she had not found that her movements had been obstructed previously, and the absence of common language had rendered it impossible for any pledge to be required, or any warning or prohibition received.

It was a problem of silent passages and closed doors, which she saw no means of solving unless she should open each in turn as quietly as latch and hinge would allow, in the hope that any inmates they might contain would be sunk in sleep, until she should look down at last upon the face of a woman of kindred blood.

Had she not refused so stubbornly to learn the simpler elements of the language these people talked, she might possibly have made shift, by means of words and signs and a nimble wit, to gain some guidance from the woman who waited upon her. As it was, she must depend on fortune and on herself, and on the fact that, as she rightly supposed, though for a reason she did not guess, she was of a value not likely to be abused without more evident cause than that she should push open unbolted doors.

She had sufficient discretion to avoid those which were contiguous to that from which she had seen the King come, and she had a disposition at first to pass those also which, she was convinced, had not been open or shut within recent days, but a second thought suggested that it might be useful to practice upon them, and curiosity urged her to discover what secrets they might conceal. She looked at her watch, which still enabled her to measure diurnal periods, though her times might differ from those which the world preferred, and knew by experience that she had less than an hour before the woman might come to her own room, and, for all she knew, others within the rooms, who might still sleep, would be alert and about.

She trod quietly enough, though she had too much respect for the height which her heels gave to go shoeless over the stone floor, and she pushed open one door after another along her own corridor with an ever-lessening caution and increasing surprise.

Had she looked in upon rooms for storage, there might have been no cause for wonder, and had they been merely vacant and empty there might have been little more. But they were rooms like her own, in which men and women had lived, and which appeared to have been undisturbed since their owners left—she thought at first on a recent day. But the closer attention she gave when this scene had repeated itself half a dozen times showed of dust in these granite caverns while they were undisturbed by human movements, but she saw that it was spread, in a fine film, over articles that lay disordered as though their owner had expected to return in the next hour; and as these scenes were repeated, doubt and wonder were submerged in a growing fear.

She might have turned back with some excuse of the shortening time, had not this fear in the blood of her self-indulgent body reacted to a fighting mood which was fundamental to what she was. She might be turned aside by a word, a light desire, or a mere indolent or petulant whim, but the thrill of fear roused her to a stubborn persistence in what she did. And so she went on till she came to a room which was like her own in its signs of occupation, and like it also in having an inner chamber which concealed the bed and whoever might be upon it.

There were less conclusive evidences that a European woman had been there than had been those at which Leonard Kinnear had hesitated, for Joselyn's handbag was beneath her pillow, and her fewer possessions were more neatly and reticently arranged, but Helen gave the room no more than one instant's glance before she turned and noiselessly closed the door. Then she walked softly into the inner room, and looked down on a sleeping girl who, though she had not expected a visitor during the night, was as fully dressed as she herself had been when Leonard had looked down upon her. But there was a difference in that where she had trailed a foot on the ground, Joselyn's hand hung over the side of the low bed, and her hand, on the floor, held a revolver in a firm grip.

The weapon was small, but Helen knew enough of such matters to be aware that it was capable of inflicting a fatal wound. "If she saw me here," she thought, attributing a celerity of homicidal action less characteristic of English habits than those of her own land, "she might drill me before I'd had time to do more than squeal." She remained very still for a few moments, in view of this sinister possibility, while she considered the physical attractions of the girl whom she was already disposed to regard as her rival for the one eligible male the horizon showed.

"If we'd started from scratch," she considered, "I wouldn't say I'd have had all that much to fear!" Even as it appeared to be, she felt that she could give battle with not less than a buoyant mind.

In cautious silence, she withdrew to the outer room, and having taken up a strategic position well out of direct range of bullets which might be fired by one who had not become fully conscious of what she did, she called, in a discreetly modulated voice: "Miss Wilde, are you awake?"

CHAPTER XIX.

JOSELYN, being called from sleep to an interview for which she was less prepared, had an excuse that she looked surprised. Yet though she had had no previous knowledge that Helen Vincent was there, she understood the general position much better than she, and though there were some things that Leonard had learnt that she did not know, there were others in which she was better informed even than he, and some deductions she had made therefrom came near to understanding that which he had not guessed, and they had not been such as to leave her a quiet mind.

She had had visits from Olah, who had made similar efforts to establish conversational contacts with her to those which the King had first made with Leonard, and these had met with partial success. Joselyn lacked Leonard's extensive knowledge of languages, but, unlike Helen, she had been genuinely anxious to learn, and, in the end, it had been found that she remembered sufficient of the Latin in which she had taken a college course to maintain a halting conversation, and to understand much more of the written word.

She had been twice inspected by Hulah, who had gazed at her on the first occasion with coldly critical contemplative eyes, and on the second with more open approval, which had ended in some qualified praise in the Latin tongue, which he had intended her to understand, and had thought to be as approbatory as such a woman could reasonably expect to hear. After further reflection, he had instructed Olah to inform her during the previous evening that she was being considered for the high honour of becoming the consort of Hulah's throne, and to require her to prepare herself for the physical inspection which, to do him justice, it may be observed that he assumed would be required in every country, civilized or savage, before she could expect to be elevated to such a status.

In fulfilment of this mission, Olah had written sentences which she had been less willing than able to understand. *Uxor* is a simple unequivocal word, which she could not profess that she did not

96

know. But being afterwards on the alert, she had met the specific proposals that followed with a capacity for misunderstanding and irrelevant reply which had temporarily baffled the patient diligence with which Olah had striven to bring her to a comprehending and disciplined mind.

He had returned to the King to indicate in discreet words the necessity for a further session on the next day, when he would no doubt have constructed simple sentences which would not lack clarity in conveying the royal will; and Hulah, who had the wit to understand more than was said, and who was influenced by other information that had come to him during the day, decided, though it did not occur to him to doubt that the foreign girl would accept his will, that it might be best to develop the event from another angle.

He had talked to Olah for some time, informing him of matters which had only come to his knowledge during the day, or with which he had not thought it necessary to acquaint him previously, and instructing him to see Leonard with certain proposals, before proceeding with the wooing which it would have been beneath the royal dignity to pursue in a more direct or conciliatory manner.

Joselyn had been left in a confusion of doubt, anger, and fear, which had resulted in reluctance to remove her clothes for the ease of rest, and in the firm grip of a loaded weapon to guard her sleep. She did not know how definite or serious the King's proposal might be, nor what penalty, if any, might attend its rejection; but it was, at least, a new factor of trouble in a position already sufficiently bad. She knew even less of Leonard Kinnear's whereabouts than he of hers, for questions which she had addressed to Olah on that subject had been met by answers which, whether by his intention or her own ignorance, she had been unable to understand. And if she should establish communication with him who (as she must remind herself with continual reluctance) was not her lover, though he lived in her lover's form, and spoke his voice, of what possible use could he be in this place where they had no strength to resist, and from which flight was a futile dream?

"I suppose," Helen said, "you are Miss Wilde?"

"Yes. I don't know how you come to be here, but it's pleasant to hear an English voice."

"I'd say it is. But I'm not that. I'm American," Miss Vincent replied, explaining the slight accent which, in that unexpected locality, Joselyn had, for a moment, been unable to understand. "I've got a message for you from—the gentleman didn't mention his name."

"Lieutenant Kinnear, I suppose."

"If you figure that, I'd call it a safe bet. I got a note that was meant for you. He wants us to be ready to clear."

"You mean he's got a plan for getting away?"

"I wouldn't say that yet. I'd say he's nosing round for a safe hole where he can slip us through. But I put him wise to the way I came, which was one that he didn't know, and I reckon the market's gone up since he heard that."

"If you know a way to get out of here...," Joselyn began eagerly.

"Well, we got in," Helen replied, with a combination of reason and optimism very cheerful to hear. "I don't see why we should call it a one-way street."

"Neither do I. But they killed the camels that brought us here, and that has made it a rather more difficult problem to get away. At least, I shouldn't say us. I came in a plane that crashed."

"Yes, he told me about that. You must have been scared stiff when they came howling 'round you on every side."

"I don't know that I was. Somehow, it didn't seem real. It all happened so suddenly from when I had been flying high overhead. And, as a matter of fact, they didn't howl. I'm sure Leonard Kinnear didn't tell you that."

"No, I put in the sound. But I don't suppose it would have been much odds if they'd yelled till their lungs split. You Britishers never seem to wake up enough to get a real scare."

The words were said with a smile that disarmed them of any rudeness they might have held, and Joselyn answered without thought of offence: "Oh, but we do! I'm scared now. I'd give about all I've got to be the right side of the desert that it seems we can never cross."

Helen regarded her new acquaintance critically. She did not look to be one who would be frightened beyond reasonable cause, but you never knew! She answered: "I can t say I'm feeling that bad. But I'll get a break if I can."

Joselyn noticed the subtle alteration of tone, and her own voice became cooler as she replied: "I'm not scared without cause. If you'd tell me how you come to be here yourself, and of what way of escape you know...."

"Well, I'll do that. If they find me here I don't see why they should make a dust, nor that I shall care if they do. I didn't promise to stay put. And it's my belief that we're about the only people alive in the cells now, besides that hook-nosed guy that you call the King."

Joselyn made no answer to this, not yet having heard of the inspection of empty chambers that her visitor had just made, but she knew enough to guess that if they should pool the different knowledge they had, its total might be much more than the sum of its simple addition, and she listened with few interruptions until Helen concluded the narrative with her invasion of the succession of empty rooms. Then she asked: "You feel sure that you've been kidnapped, and brought here to get your father to pay a ransom for your release? You haven't thought that there might be any other possible explanation?"

"No. I'd have said a baby could see that."

"Well, I think you may be quite wrong"

Helen opened surprised eyes, but she was too sensible not to realize that the very improbability of the statement itself made it the more unlikely that it would have been randomly uttered. "Why," she exclaimed, "if they aren't after Pop's wad? Say, they must have spilt a grand, if not more, getting me here!"

"They may have thought you were worth that—though I'm not sure how much it is!—or a bit more. They haven't made you understand that the King's wanting a wife?"

Helen gazed at her with amazed incredulity, as she adjusted her mind to entertain this monstrously impudent explanation, and she recalled the way in which the head gangster, as she had considered him to be, had inspected her, before—for the last two days—his silent visits had ceased. With a sudden intuition she guessed that he had had a new specimen to appraise, and that Joselyn spoke with some personal knowledge to support the theory she had advanced, though speculation did not go sufficiently forward upon the accurate track to guess how decidedly her own charms had been discounted in favour of the more recent comer.

"You mean," she asked, "he's a guy who's collecting wives? Gee, if I thought that!" She looked lovingly at the revolver that Joselyn had laid on the table as this conversation proceeded, and which was now nearer to her own hand as they sat on the couch together. "Miss Wilde, if I hadn't got one of those, I'd be tempted to grab it up."

"I'm afraid I can't spare it," Joselyn replied, rather surprised by the hard note in the voice she heard, which seemed curiously at variance with the soft femininity of her visitor's exterior attractions, "but I'll tell you one thing—I think, at the moment, I'm in more danger than you. From what Olah was explaining yesterday, and I wasn't admitting I understood, I don't think the King wants more than one wife; and for some reason he seems to think that I shall be ready to take it on."

"I don't know," Helen answered doubtfully. "If you'd seen all those empty rooms!" She shivered at the recollection, and at a vague memory of the Bluebeard fable that came back from her childhood days. "It looks more likely to me that the beast grabs all he can, and does them in when he gets hold of a fresh supply. I'd a lot rather think he's the blackmailer that I guessed, him first."

"Well, it's no use thinking that if it isn't true. And I can tell you another reason that makes it unlikely: it must be three weeks, if not four, since they took you out of that train?"

"Yes. I'd say that. They took a good while getting me here."

"And up to three days ago I can tell you there was no idea—certainly none that was publicly known—of where you were. Only the day before I left your father was increasing the reward he was offering from ten to fifty thousand dollars."

The look with which Miss Vincent received this information was not entirely melancholy, though her brows wrinkled in thought. "Gee," she said, "but he bid up! But I see what you mean. Poor Pop! He'd not have done that if he'd had a gangster's note saying how much he'd have to put up, and how to pass it across. I reckon there was some noise in the press?"

"Yes, there certainly was. But I don't think, unless the police knew more than they let out, that anyone guessed in the least what had occurred. All that was published was that the train was stopped in the night by some accident to the permanent way, and it was afterwards found that you had left the train, taking some of your luggage with you."

"What did they think had happened?"

"There was a suggestion in the papers at first that you had joined an American friend. A Mr. Abe something, if I remember—"

"Oh, Abe Fisher? They thought I'd done that!" Miss Vincent's cheeks dimpled with laughter at the idea. "Wouldn't Pop be just wild! My, but he'll be glad when he gets me back!"

"It was understood that Mr. Abe was also rather indignant. I believe there was something about a threat of—" But at this point the conversation was interrupted by a sound of approaching steps, and Leonard Kinnear and Olah entered the room together.

CHAPTER XX.

WHEN Leonard met Olah, as he was returning on shoeless feet to his own room, at an hour which was still somewhat earlier than that of general movement within the interior gates, he naturally expected that there would be at least some display of curiosity as to where, and with what purpose, he had been abroad during the night. He imagined, as they approached each other, that Olah might have been waiting for him there during the whole of his absent hours, and considered what degree of truth or reticence would be wisest to use for an explanation which, he supposed, would be passed on to the King, with consequences not possible to foresee.

But events will rarely move as our fears or our hopes forecast. Olah asked no questions at all. He did not appear to give any attention to Leonard's movements, or what he wore. He said: "I have come to you at an early hour, having been charged by the King to inform you of certain things, and to make proposals thereon, and when he wakes, he may not be long before he ask if I have done this, and had your reply, after which he may wish to see you without delay, for he is not one who will dally in what he does."

Leonard thought that this had a good sound. The more that Olah's mind, and that of the King, were busy in proposing to make use of him, the less attention they might give to his own projects of an opposite kind. He had had no time as yet for detailed consideration of what Helen Vincent had told him, but a vague determination to adventure escape from this sinister place had already hardened as he had walked back to his own room. If Joselyn should be free and able to join them, he must contrive to find some time, some chance, for the three to escape with a sufficient supply of food and—well, not water. There would be enough of that at first, but there must be receptacles in which they could carry it over the hills in the burning drought. He had roused himself from these thoughts to meet Olah in a cool way. Now he said: "I shall be glad to hear what the King has to offer. I suppose I may be able to tell some things that it will be useful for him to know."

"So," Olah replied, "I have no doubt that you could, and so in future days he may ask you to do; but what he proposes now is present action, and for your help to be sure, if there be need on a near day, as you will understand when I have told you some things of which you may not yet be aware."

"Well," Leonard replied, "it is hard to discuss that of which I have not heard. Come in and sit down, and tell me what I may need to know."

Olah came in at that word, and settled himself to share the morning meal of water and fruit, while he explained the tragedy which had destroyed the family of the King, and other things that he had hidden before, including the abduction of Helen Vincent and the object with which it had been done.

"For," he said, "you must understand that the King rules not by force—for what have we here, even for defence of our own lives, if the folk should be moved to refuse his will?—but by most ancient traditions that none may break. And if we admit change, though it should be no more than the size of a seed that the wind may bear, how can we say to what height it will grow, or what will remain with a watered root when its own seed will have been scattered abroad, and come to a further crop?

"Yet when the King died who was father to him whom we now serve, and with him all the women who were of the royal race, it was clear that some change must be, and the King's wisdom resolved that it would be a less certain harm if this change were from the outside rather than in ourselves, and should be unknown by those whom it was his duty to rule.

"He therefore resolved that he would not raise one of his own people to share his throne, and to become the mother of future kings, but that, as the Sabine women were raped of old (as must ever be at sufficient cause), he would capture one from another land who would fill the need, and after that brother and sister might wed again in the old way, and there would be no more adulteration of changeful blood.

"For this purpose he sent by a secret path which had not been used from an old day, and which was only known to exist by those of the royal blood, of whom the King lived and none else—it is approached by the river beneath the ground, which I need not gloss, for, I have told it not, you would surely hear it from her—and gave command that one should be seized who had the look of a virgin, of a fair form, and who, by her state and attire, would be accounted of good blood in her own land.

"They therefore took this girl of whom I have told (and whom you will soon see), who was young and fair, though not large, and from the state in which she was furnished and garbed must have been of great account in her own land; but I must tell you that the King looked at her, and there was no desire in his eyes, neither did his wisdom approve. She is small, which he does not like, and of a dull wit, so that no patience will prevail to teach her our common tongue, and she has not the look either of courage or will to rule which a king's mother should have,"

Leonard listened to this, and thought that Hulah, in his judgment of the girl he had seized, had shown no more wisdom than is required for a bad guess, but it was an opinion to keep, so he only answered: "I can follow what you tell me with ease, having seen Miss Vincent (which is the girl's name in our tongue); but what is all this to me?"

"I am coming to that. But I must first tell you another thing, which you are less likely to guess. The trouble which became death to all but one of the royal race is not wholly past. It is latent, and like to stir, but this time from below, though it has not yet ventured to raise a rebellious head.

"Of the death of those of the royal race, we believe that there is nothing certainly known outside the gates of the King, for it has been hid with a great care, but there have been whispers, we know not from whence, of the coming of the girl to whom you have given a name (which we had not had), and even of the channel by which she came."

"I suppose that would be more than you could expect to conceal, there having been so much known by those who brought her away, and perhaps others who handled the raft."

"It is not through them. You shall not think us so clumsy as that. There were some of trust, and others who did not live a sufficient time. But, be its source what it may, there is a whisper that does not die.

"I have told you that this unrest is not new. There was a plan last year of which there was much talk, and which was only stilled when those who extolled it most were eliminated on other grounds. By this plan, those who, in the routine that our custom has, had been appointed to die, would have been given a chance of life, though not much; for they would have been made the servants of an expedition which would have sought to cross the desert to other lands. Bearing goatskins of water upon their backs, they would have been slain as the water lessened, and the need for bearers decreased. But this would have been done strictly by lot, so that, it was calculated, some even of the water-bearers would have come alive to the fertile land."

"And," Leonard conjectured, "the return of Abrah, with the tale of having crossed the desert and lived, has given such ideas a new life?"

"So it may have done to some minds. But I would not hang too much on that peg. Indeed, as to him, it was the King's thought that it might be best for him to live, not only for the tale he would tell of his bitter thirst and travail in desert ways, but even more for the life he must have lived in an alien world, being serf to those who were neither great of heart nor comely of form, and for his first seeing of dirt and sores, and living men who were crippled or halt or blind, the telling of which must show how much better are they who remain here; while the numbers and strength of those of the rivered land should warn them that, if this place shall become known, their last day of freedom will be here at a short wait." Olah changed his tone to ask abruptly: "Am I wrong in that? Is there no power that would claim to be lord of this desert land?"

Leonard considered this, and it was a possibility he could not deny. He was not clear as to where the imagined boundaries of the great powers met in this unvisited waste, but he supposed that Egypt or Great Britain, Italy or France, would be allowed by their neighbours to be its lord, and that it would not be of much avail for any feeble people to say that they could have no right at all to a place where they had not been.

He knew also that liberty, which had been to his fathers no more than an uncertain flickering light, had now lost even the service the lips will give. Elaborately organized slaveries were said to provide most comfort of life for those who would wear their chain in a docile way, and comfort had now become the more dominant god. No, he could not truly assert that Hulah would be left to his own ways, especially if it should become known that there were rich mines here of copper and tin, and a subterranean river which, as it seemed, would be able to bear them far towards the Egyptian rail.

"I cannot say," he replied, "by whom a claim would be made, but I must agree that, if you would keep the customs you have, you would be wise to remain unknown."

"That is what we suppose. And it is therefore a vital need that the stir of unrest should still, and that all men should accept the settled order of life which has endured so long, and which has brought them to what they are."

"That may be true, but still I do not see how I can be concerned," Leonard replied; "or at least not beyond this, that the King may wish me to pledge my word that I will not say or do anything to foster unrest while I am here, and that word I am willing to give; for I think (if you value your ancient order of life) there may be wisdom in what you say. But if the King thinks that my being here may remind men of what he would have them forget; would it not be wiser to let me go, as, by the river way of which you have now told, I might be able to do?"

Olah heard this suggestion with an expressionless face, and ignored the question with which it closed, replying only to that which had gone before.

"The King asks much more of you than that. He would have your word that you will be faithful to him if this treason should come to head, and he will give you much in return."

Leonard saw that this offer was natural enough, and might be made in good faith. It was evident that, if he should become a permanent member of this strange community, he would be questioned concerning the alien life from which he had come, and that his replies, and his own attitude, might be influential in what would follow. It might also appear probable to the King that he would be more inclined to encourage than to allay such discontents, as opening a likely way to his own escape.

This being so, the King might have thought it prudent to put an end to a dangerous life, as he could have found pretexts to do, and the fact that that solution was in his power made it the more probable that any proposal of service that might be made would be of a genuine kind. Yet the fate which, as Olah had plainly implied, had fallen upon those who had handled the river raft would have been sufficient alone to show him that the King would be ruthless in what he did, where his own safety or that of his narrow kingdom were in the scale; and he saw that any bargain which might be made would not be sealed by honour or goodwill, and its conditions would be likely to last so long as common interest should endure, but no more than that. So he said: "Well, I will hear what you propose."

"That is soon told. He will offer you the command, on very good conditions for you, of the two hundred spearmen who form the army we have kept from an ancient time. These men, whom you have seen, are also engaged, with their wives, in the cultivation of the crops, both in the oasis and within, and in other ways, but are a caste apart from those who work underground, whether at the water-mills, or in fishing, or mining, or at the arts of metal-working, and the forging of tools. These men, who see most of the sun, and are trained for war, are the best we have, and if they be loyal, the miners may sulk or chatter the most they will, bringing no trouble to any except themselves."

"I suppose those who work below could cut off the light?"

Olah looked surprised at this suggestion, as though it were one which had not previously entered his mind. But it was still one that he could not deny. He said: "Yes. So they could. But—beside that it is a thing that they dare not do—would it be greater harm to us, or more gain to them? For we could still feel a way to retreat by the Queen's Gate, to where we should soon reach to the light of day, which they would find it harder to do."

"Well, we need not consider that at the present time. But I suppose your warriors have a leader now, whom they may prefer. How would you incline them to give him up, and to be more loyal to me?"

"You will first meet him in single combat, and he will die, so that that question will not remain."

"It would be a strife that I might not win."

"On the contrary, it would be so arranged that you would have no trouble at all. For you would use the deadly weapon you have, against which no other would avail."

"So I am to make myself popular with these men by shooting their leader under conditions that would allow him no possibility of victory or escape?"

"That is how it would be. For Ebah is an arrogant and most truculent man. At the times of elimination he has sent others to death whom have been better liked, he being of a great strength, and of a skill both in throwing and dodging spears against which none may prevail. If you say that you can kill him in a new way, an opportunity will be found, and there will be great laughter to see him die."

Leonard had listened to a proposal he did not like, but he saw that it was one which must be declined, if at all, in a discreet way. It might be well to ask time for consideration. He recalled that Olah had said that the offer was made on good conditions for him. He supposed that this must imply something more than the privilege of shooting a truculent man. He asked: "Am I to answer this first, or is there more for me to hear?"

"There is much more. The King offers that you shall have one of the white women, of which he and you will make choice in turn."

"Should I choose first, or he?"

"He would choose first, being king. You would expect that."

"Then my choice would be none."

Olah protested at that. He said there would be choice either to take or to leave. He played on the word in the Latin tongue. "Why should it be put in the worst way? You would have one who is choice. One who would have been queen had the other not been here, as we may surely suppose. Besides, why should you presume that there will be one that you both prefer? There will be points, it is a sure guess, that you will not weigh in the same scale."

Leonard had some reason to think, from the neglect of Helen during the last two days, that the King's choice was already made, but whether or not that choice would have suited him, he saw that it was an argument that it could be no gain to pursue. He saw also an implication that Joselyn was still safe, and that her honour was unassailed, which he was glad to think; but, beyond that he reminded himself that he was not making a bargain, but listening to a proposal that it must be well that he should understand fully.

"It is likely enough," he answered, "and, be that as it may, you must give me the King's offer as you had it from him. Is there still more?"

"The King will make a new law that, though you are not of the royal blood, yet you may dwell within the interior gates, both you and your wife, and the children that you may have; and these children will not be eunuchs, as are we of the half-blood, but they will be a new order between the people and the family of the King. You will see that when the King gives, it is with a most open hand. He would have you more than content, that you may be at his side in a very resolute way."

Leonard saw that, from the King's standpoint, that might be true. Indeed, the offer was of such a character as to raise a doubt of whether it were made in good faith. If this trouble from which it came should be ended, how much longer would it endure?

But there was a more urgent question of what the position would be if the offer should be declined. He answered: "Yes, I can see that. How soon will the King expect an answer to this?"

"I suppose that he waits now. It would be unwise to delay a most grateful reply."

"I do not wish to delay. But you said yourself that it is the King's object that I shall be fully content, and take his side in a resolute mood. You will see therefore that it is important that I should give something better than a random reply. If you put it thus to the King, he may be more than content. I will ask for one day, and no more."

Olah did not dispute this, but he stood irresolute, as one who was much less than sure, and, as he did so, Leonard had a thought that he was quick to speak.

"Before I decide, I may have something to say to one of these ladies, and perhaps both. Where can Miss Wilde—the one who came with me—be seen?"

Olah looked puzzled, and in more doubt than before. "I do not see," he said, "why you should require that."

"But I do. For, among other reasons which I need not detail now that you are in some haste to be gone, if she were willing for this, it might set me on the same path with quicker feet."

"The King will not understand that. It is a matter on which the women should not be asked. There are honours here to which they should be both humble and glad. It is enough that they be told what they will be expected to do."

"But you must observe that these women are not of your race, and that they may not regard it in that light. If I could make a way smooth, would you have it rough? Or have you the King's order to keep us apart?"

"No. You must not think that. I have no order at all. If you wish to see her you can, and it should be now, so that the King may understand that there is action without delay. But as to why you do this, there may come an hour when he will ask you what purpose it had, when you should be prepared to explain."

"Well," Leonard replied, with more show of confidence than he was able to feel, "I suppose that I could do that."

He saw that his immediate object was won, which was no more than to gain an interview with Joselyn, so that they might agree on a common front, whether of resistance or the revising of terms to their own minds, or on a bold attempt to escape the perils which were closing them in.

Olah rose. He said no more than: "We had better go," and led the way to Joselyn's room.

CHAPTER XXI.

OLAH stood listening to words that had no meaning for him, and had the more leisure for observation, and for consideration of what he saw.

He observed that Leonard spoke first to Helen, which he approved, for he knew enough of the King's mind to have made a confident guess that Joselyn was cast for the Queen's part. He noticed that they spoke as being already familiar with each another, at which he was the less surprised as he remembered the remark that Leonard had made, which he had passed at the time. He saw that, after those first brief words, Leonard turned to Joselyn, and spoke somewhat longer to her, which he liked less; and that a conversation then developed at which they all took part as having an assured understanding among themselves. The thought came that these people might not be easy to subordinate to the King's will, and to laws and customs which might be antipathetic to their own traditions; but he did not doubt that Hulah's wisdom would be sufficient to control the event. He remembered that the King would be waiting to hear what he had done. It might be well also to make a prompt report of their meeting, which the King might prefer to know. He said: "I am not needed here. I must go to the King." He went on, and they closed the door, and sat down, having enough to discuss.

Leonard had said already: "I have things to tell you which I have only just learnt, and which may not be pleasant to hear. But I must caution you first not to show your thoughts, for Olah knows what I shall be likely to say, and will report all to the King."

Now, as Olah withdrew, he could speak without fear of his observation, and they could respond naturally. He told them all that Olah had said in the last hour, and much that he had learnt during the previous day that showed what manner of life the King asked them to share, holding nothing back, for they were faced by an issue too serious to put aside. They must understand what had be resolved before the next morning should come.

As he spoke, he had a memory of the prophecy, if such it were, that Peter Brisco had tried to read. Two women and one man! They had become that. *"When the spears are red and wet."* To what horror might they be coming now in this place which was never reached by the light of the cheerful day? Not that the sunlight was friend to them. Its dreadful heat was the menace that held them bound.

Joselyn had listened in silence, or next to that, till the tale was told. She saw that she would be the one whom Hulah would choose, and, though she was of good courage and had the sanguine spirit of youth, she could have been sick—physically sick with loathing and fear. She felt that death was a path which it would be more easeful to tread. But would Leonard—would this girl whom she had known for no more than the last hour—look at it in the same way? They (so she thought) might have no less to lose, but would they not be offered better parts in the coming play?

It made it worse that this man who might, in his next words, be telling her that they had no avenue of likely escape, and that she must reconcile her mind to this hateful end; he would look at her with her lover's eyes, and speak with the voice she knew, so that she must continually remind herself that it was not to him that she should turn for comfort and love—that to do so, which had the delusion of all that fidelity could expect and require, would be subtle treason to him to whom her faith was already pledged. But she would say nothing yet. Perhaps to the others it all had a sound of safety, even of honour, putting peril aside, and giving them more than they could have expected to get, and that in a pleasant way. She would hear what they meant to do.

As to Helen, Joselyn was so far right that she was less moved, either by fear of the perils of flight, or loathing of the terms on which they were invited to stay.

That was natural enough, for the thought of being united to Leonard Kinnear stirred her blood to no more than a pleasant thrill, and she shared Helen's guess of what the allocation would be likely to be. Beyond that, she had a toughness of original core, and an acquired habit of relying upon those around her to make her bed soft, which united to give resilience to her mood of reaction to this amazing tale, for which she had been partly prepared by the conversation which Leonard's coming had interrupted.

But she was never one whom it would be easy to drive, and her very confidence in her friends and her own wit were an armour disinclining her to be stampeded to a course which was not of her own selection.

She looked at Joselyn, whose eyes did not meet hers, and saw that her lips were white. It was an impulse of natural generosity which decided her—though it is likely enough that she would otherwise have arrived at the same point by another path—that the King's offer was not for them. She did not discuss the unions proposed for Joselyn or herself, but attacked it from a different angle.

"He wants you to shoot a man," she said, "with whom you've got no quarrel at all, and who wouldn't be able to get near enough to you to have a chance? It sounds lousy to me."

Leonard said: "That's about the right word. But it seems right to them. I suppose they'd call it a political necessity. I expect we should find points on which we shouldn't agree about twice a week, if I were fool enough to take on the job. I don't suppose it's I whom the King wants so much as the rifles. They've seen what they can do, and they're weapons that no one here but we would be able to use."

Joselyn sighed relief, as one who came out of the shadow of a great fear. She looked at those whose words had made them her friends to say: "I felt sure you'd look at it like that. But what are we to do? We seem to be only sure of today."

Leonard felt that the eyes of the girls were on him, and he was not quick to reply. He understood how Joselyn felt, and whether he loved her for her own or his brother's sake, he was not prepared for any bargain that would put her into the King's power without her consent. But the trouble was that she—that they all—apart from some almost miraculous deliverance, appeared to be in that position already. He considered the possibility of moving the King by an appeal to his generosity, or by offering him the support of the rifles on terms more satisfactory to themselves. But he feared that such a bargain, if it could be made, would be kept for no more than a short day. He would make himself the mercenary of the King—assassin would be a blunter, but perhaps no less accurate, word—on condition that the two girls would be left in safety and honour, and that the King should look elsewhere for the bride that his throne required, and any day, if the fear of unrest should cease, or he should have done his part, he might be required to prove his own fitness to live by a test, the failure of which would be equally certain and prearranged. And they had the day! Presumably they would be left in unrestricted freedom for that transient time. Feeling that his silence might be misunderstood, he spoke, thinking aloud: "We can't spend the day inspecting the river, and looking round for a raft. It would be too evident what we mean to do."

"It looks," Helen agreed, "as though Hulah's got the drop on us right enough, when you put it so. But I'll back you," she added confidently, "to put a snake in his bed."

Leonard wished that he could feel equal confidence in himself, though her words gave him an idea which he did not like, but would not instantly thrust away. Not that he could literally put a snake in the royal bed.

He supposed himself to be in a place where snakes were not to be found. But the facts which they had so far learned of the regimen of the royal apartment appeared to indicate that the King slept unguarded, and quite alone. There were guards at his three gates, but they had been admitted within these precincts. To attack—to destroy—the King in the night appeared to be so simple that it was not easy to conclude that it could be what it looked. To kidnap him appeared equally simple, but to what end? Where should he be taken? Should he be held prisoner in his own chamber? How long—to what purpose—could such a position continue? How could any treaty result, the terms of which would be honoured so that they would be able to get away? For desperate positions, desperate remedies may be tried. Yet he felt, if he were to deserve the confidence expressed in Helen's vividly objective speech, and in her innocently trustful eyes, he must think of something better than that.

"I think," Joselyn said, "that we've been forgetting one thing. It wouldn't be day, if that's the right word to use, down at the river, or in the mines. You said they work different hours. There might be nobody there."

"That's an idea," Leonard allowed doubtfully. "But unfortunately it doesn't get us very far. Even if we should reach the river unobserved, and a raft should be tied up there ready to start—which isn't sense, when you remember how very secret this river passage has been kept, and that it has possibly not been used more than once in a thousand years—even then we should be no better off unless we should find means of provisioning it. It would be mere suicide to start such a journey without a supply of food."

"Of course," Joselyn admitted, "we shouldn't want to do that. But," she went on, with a stubborn reluctance to yield to any difficulty that might hinder escape, "we should float down with the current. We mightn't have to paddle at all. We could just lie down and be carried along. And we should have all the water we needed. I should think any one could remain alive a good while under such conditions as that."

"There would be the desert after the river were left."

"We might take enough food for that time, if we should keep it untouched till then. We could each save something from the meals that are brought to us during the day."

"We might try that, though it wouldn't be much, and I've some stores that came off the camels' backs," Leonard half agreed. He did not wish to appear unwilling to face hardship or take a risk which was not daunting to her, but he saw the futility of the idea—and all based upon finding a raft that almost certainly was not there!

Joselyn, thinking him willing to yield, pressed the plan further. "You say we can't go straight down to the river and look about for a raft, but why should we? Why not go first to the gardens of the queens, or whatever you call them, that we haven't seen yet, and just wander round?"

"Well, we might try that, though—" His doubt—or more than a doubt whether they, and especially Helen, would be permitted to pass the guard at the Queen's Gate—was left unspoken, for Olah entered the room.

"The King," Olah said at once, "will see you tomorrow at this time, that he may receive your assent, and that you may have your orders from him."

Leonard saw that, though his assent was assumed, he had gained the respite for which he asked. He was quick and bold to take advantage of the opportunity that Olah's appearance gave. If the following hours were to be spent in exploration of possibilities of escape, it might be a vital protection to have first obtained his approval of what they did.

"I shall be ready to meet the King," he replied, "at that time; and for today we propose to see as much as we can of this place where he would have us remain, so that, when I answer him, I may speak of that which we know."

Olah looked perturbed. "You may go," he said, "where you will, but for the women—"

"That is what they are anxious to know. If they accept the life which the King proposes, will they be closely confined, or free to wander about, so far as this place extends or the desert drought will allow?"

"The King's offer," Olah replied, with a note of obstinacy in his voice, "is not to them, but to you. They must take that which the King's bounty provides, which they may find to be more than they should expect."

"That may be; but it is for myself I asked, rather than them. I may prefer a wife who is well content."

113

Olah still hesitated, but he remembered some general instructions which he had received from the King a few minutes before. He was to do everything possible to win Leonard's support, which the King wished to obtain in a spirit of genuine loyalty. It was to gain that that he had, as he considered, already bid a very high price. This being so, Hulah might not be pleased if they should be thwarted in what was, in itself, but a small thing, though the need for it might seem to be even less.

In this dilemma Olah compromised, as most men would be likely to do.

"You can go where you will," he replied, "as I have said; and so, I suppose, can the woman you brought, for her existence is known, and what harm would it be likely to do? But the other woman must remain here, as you can see, for her existence must not be guessed."

"Are the Queen's gardens closed to her, which she is anxious to see?"

"I can give orders that they shall be vacant, as the custom was when a queen walked."

"I shall be grateful for that. Do I understand that we can all walk therein, but that Miss Wilde and I only may go further abroad, so that I can show her what I saw yesterday when with you? And will you give instructions to the sentries at the three gates, so that I shall have no need to talk in a language in which, at the King's own wish, I make no study to learn?"

"That will be different now, as I suppose. But I will give them instructions as you desire. You will pardon me now, for I am engaged on other affairs."

This conversation having been carried on in Latin, with some excursions into Olah's own tongue when, on one side or other, its resources failed, had had little meaning for Joselyn, and none at all for the American girl.

As Olah left, Leonard repeated what its substance had been, and added: "It is less than I hoped, but all that I could expect to arrange. To inspect the gardens can be of no use to us, but it must be done first, so that our real object may not become too easy to guess, and after that we—or at least two of us—will be able to investigate in the other direction."

"I don't see much to shout over in that," Helen said with a discontent for which there was some occasion. "I seem to be in the soup worse than before."

It was not only that she disliked the idea of her new companions wandering off on an exploration she did not share, she was quick to see that the same difficulty might recur to obstruct a plan of actual flight at a later hour. Leonard and Joselyn might be able to pass the guards with an unchallenged right, but for her—? Would they leave her in that dilemma, saying that it would be absurd for two to remain because the third could not escape? Or that Joselyn's cause for flight was even greater than hers? But if Joselyn were not here, her own position would be no better! She would step, so to speak, into the firing line from which Joselyn withdrew. Well, suppose they should be generous enough to recognize that? Suppose they should decide to shoot their way through the guards, if they would not allow her also a free passage when the time for escape should come? It did not seem a very hopeful prelude to such an attempt, the further difficulties of which she could only vaguely conceive. She may be excused if she looked vexed.

But to Leonard the whole plan was so desperate, and as yet so nebulous, that this potential future difficulty was of little relative size. He felt rather a momentary satisfaction in the advantage he had taken of Olah's unexpected return, and the qualified permission which he had obtained. He said: "Oh, well! We may find a way round that, if there's no worse difficulty to overcome. Anyhow, it's something to be sure of the next thing we've got to do, and there's no doubt about that. We've got to give Olah time enough to give the sentries the instructions he promised, and then go to look at the gardens as though there's nothing else on our minds."

"There's no reason," Joselyn suggested, "that we shouldn't walk about the inside passages before then. There's no harm in knowing as much as possible about where we are, and we never know what use it might be."

There was general agreement with this proposal. They were in a position in which any form of activity appeared preferable to the passive acceptance of fate which was the implication of sitting still. They spent the next hour in systematic examination of the passages within the King's apartment, both within and without the heavy doors which closed off the royal suite, turning back only when these explorations approached one or another of the three guarded exits.

They were twice passed by the woman who waited upon themselves, and who, for all they knew, might be the only menial attendant upon the King, now that he had become the sole survivor of his ancient race. They met, also, two men whom they had not seen previously, coming from the audience-room of the King. They were both larger than Olah, and one of them would not have been many inches less either in girth or height than Abrah, or any of the spearmen whom they had first seen, but it was easy to guess that they also were of the half-bred eunuchs who alone had access to the King's apartment, and were the mediums through whom he ruled. Curiosity there must have been on both sides, but discretion ruled, and they passed each other, going singly, as they must in passages which would take two abreast but no more, without a direct glance from either party.

When they felt that they had learned sufficiently of the geometry of the monotonously similar corridors, with the rows of closed metal doors in their polished walls, and with the relative positions of their own various rooms, they sought the exit to the gardens which had been the resort of so many queens and their brother-kings in the relaxations of their strange, secluded, unchanging rules during two if not three thousand of previous years.

CHAPTER XXII.

THE two guards, who had been sitting on metal chairs, with short broad-bladed spears lying across their knees, rose as they approached. Right and left, each swung back a heavy copper door. They did not appear to look at those they let through, acting more like automata than sentient men.

Leonard, asking himself by what signal they should claim return through the heavy doors to men sitting inside with whose speech they had so little familiarity, looked back and observed that they had not closed them again, but now stood, one on each side, with a spear advanced in a ready hand. Their huge bodies, only lightly and partly clad in this long tradition of peace, and the equable warmth of the subterranean place, gleamed with a hue akin to that of the copper doors, so that it might have seemed that they were cast in the same metal. Doubtless it was the etiquette of the occasion that they should stand thus at watch till those who used the gardens should return.

It occurred to him that these two, and the other ten of the twelve warders, even though they might constitute a guard which was never changed, must be a dozen witnesses to the fact that not a queen only, but half a score, more or less, of the royal family, had been accustomed to pass the gates, and that this custom had ceased abruptly, and silence fallen upon the rooms of the royal suite, except only for the presence of one who had been the King's grandson before, and had suddenly become King. He wondered also by whose hands, and with what possible maximum of secrecy, the bodies of those who fell in that fatal brawl had been hurried down during the night hours, to be cast and carried away on the subterranean flood. Was it wonderful, however carefully the truth had been suppressed, however hardily it had been denied, however loyal and dumb the eunuch household might have proved to be, that doubtful disturbing rumours had spread through gardens and mines? That there had been a whisper that the immemorial customs must alter now? That there would even be change in the succession of kings who had been mere incarnations in thought and will of a hundred who ruled before?

Even Abrah's return, looked at in a correct perspective, might be of less significance or result than the fact that he had attempted flight rather than submit to that ordeal of elimination by which the population had been regulated without resistance for so many previous centuries, and which had weeded it out to the standard of physical perfection, and exact adaptation to its various activities, which it had now reached.

He saw that, though the iconoclast of his race had died, probably thinking in his last moments that he had lost his life for no more than a beaten dream, yet, in fact, for good or evil, the harvest of his intention was still to come. It was through him—though there might be no thanks to him therefore—that the three of them were there. For surely he would not have come, nor Joselyn followed, had not the idea of crossing the desert first come to Abrah's rebellious mind. And certainly Helen Vincent would not have been there had not that King's mind turned as it did against the age-hardened traditions from which it had seemed to the other members of his inbred race an impossible folly to break away, so that the issue had been resolved in flurry of bloody strife. Such was Leonard Kinnear's thought, until it was obliterated in the next moment by the strange exotic beauty of what he saw.

The garden of many queens was neither a hothouse enclosed, nor was it bare to the sun and sky. It was roofed with rock, at a height of twenty feet, or at places no more than ten, and might seem less than it was where the roof was festooned with vines and with hanging plants of a hundred kinds, or would be much more where the ground had been excavated into deep hollows, at the bottoms of which would be quiet broad-lilied pools, or a running stream.

The low morning sun—for they found that it was the point of dawn in the open world—shone in as far as the foliage would permit, and the winds entered at will. There were places where the sun's light, for the short morning hour during which it could enter below the far overhanging roof, was cunningly caught by hidden reflectors, and cast about; and there were others where artificial light, buried in the rocky ceiling or embowered in leaves, made independence of the retarded light of the sun. There were alleys and green recesses, "like a green thought in a green shade," where perpetual twilight reigned. There were massed monotones of single colour, and other vistas, bright as the plumage of tropic birds that mingled contrasting hues of a hundred flowers.

118

They passed through gradations of temperature and humidity, the causes of which they did not perceive, but which may have originated in the regulated temperatures of fountain and pool and stream, visible at times, but more often hidden by foliage too luxuriant to expose the sources on which it thrived.

The original surface of these gardens could have been no other than the barren unwatered stone, but millennia of cultivation and irrigation had brought its fertility to the restrained exuberance which, had care relaxed, would have quickly choked the narrow tortuous paths, and closed the cunning prospects by which it was now displayed.

They explored the gardens, as they supposed, to their full extent, but without finding any outlet to the equally subterranean forcing-grounds of utilitarian fruits, grains and vegetables, through a part of which two of them had been led on the night on which they arrived, and which, with the products of the oasis under the open sky, supplied the bulk of the food on which the community must subsist; nor was there any opening through which it became visible, or through which they themselves could have been observed by those who laboured therein. Only, once or twice, they would have a blinking glimpse of bare desert beneath the path of the entering sun.

There were ripe grapes to be plucked at will, hanging in heavy clusters above their heads, but beyond that, the gardens were for secluded beauty, and that alone.

Looking at their established loveliness, which had a quality of freshness which was perpetual in its defiance either of seasons or ancient days, and thinking also of the copper statues who stood, magnificent in reposeful strength, on each side of the gate from which they had come, Leonard found it possible to wonder whether there might not be a stronger case for the methods by which they had been produced (even apart from that which the sterile desert advanced) than the prejudice of his own tradition would willingly grant. And, if that were so, might there not even be some moral argument for rendering the King the service that he required?

And as his reason shook to this unexpected doubt, he was interrupted by Joselyn's voice: "I could almost stay here and forget...," she began, for her breath was shortened, her eyes intoxicated, by the beauty of what she saw.

Helen looked at her, widening puzzled eyes. "I shouldn't have guessed," she said, "it would have hit you as high as that."

"I said almost, not quite."

"And there's a bit of difference—?"

"There's much more than a bit."

The words recalled them to the shadow of the sinister peril in which they stood. They went back silently, giving little heed to the green shadows of a loveliness which could never be home to them.

CHAPTER XXIII.

ENONA sat in her chamber, and her son Ebah also was there. So was Abrah, who had come at Ebah's desire, which might be called a command.

Abrah knew why he had been invited there by those who would have ignored his existence three years before. He had been asked that he might talk of strange things he had seen in another land, which he was not unwilling to do, but he would speak of them with little praise, having peace of mind that he had returned to his own place, and no desire to toil again on a Nile quay at the bidding of lesser men.

Enona was a woman of fifty years who still had beauty of form, though her days of child-bearing were past. She was not slim, but she had avoided the increase of weight which was common to the women of her race after they had passed their fortieth year, and often sooner than that, so that she might have stood beside the Venus de Milo with confidence that sculptors would give her gold-brown body its share of praise.

Abrah was aware that there were some murmurs of discontent, which might have been more easily heard had there been assurance that they could be spoken with safety, but he gave no heeding to them. Had he felt that discretion was needed, he would have ruled a most cautious tongue, for he had no mind to jeopardize the position to which he had been allowed to return; but, feeling as he did, he supposed that he could speak without fear, and especially to these two, for the dread of elimination was not for them, and few could have more reason to be content with the life they knew.

Enona could not only feel security for herself, but for the six children that she had borne, all of whom had assured positions, amid the protection that surrounding inferiorities gave. Indeed, there had been no time of her life when the process by which the population was held in check had had a personal application for her or hers. For herself, she had looked on at a game that she did not play. And it was one that her children had played with ease, and with disaster to those who had been misfortunate to compete with them.

She had not only had the safeguard of her own physical perfection, and the high quality of the children she had produced, she was also the chief garment-maker to the royal household, in which work she had a skill that none of her assistants could reach. The time must come, as she knew, when her body would show signs of weakness, and clearness of sight or cunning of hand would fail. Then she would be put to a test that she could not meet, and the food she took would be required for a better mouth. But that day was far off. For many that were to come, she would have comfort and security from anxiety, privation, or any likely disease, such as those in no other part of the world would be likely to know.

Ebah, twenty years younger, had already attained to one of the two highest positions which a man of the common blood could lawfully win. He was not a cultivator. The toil of the spade, or the skill of the gardener, was not for him. But when the men who handled the spade laid it aside, and lifted their broad-bladed spears, they came under his rule. He was their war-captain, though it might be for a war that would never come. For two thousand years there had been an army without record of war. But it was not therefore an idle command. There was constant competitive practice, by which a high degree of efficiency was maintained, and which was as important to those who engaged in it as though it were a prelude to actual war.

For, every year, there would be young men who had survived the competitions of childhood, applying for places in ranks which did not expand, and they must hold their own lives either by the ordeal of spears, or by an alternative demonstration of proficiency in agricultural pursuits.

The ordeal of spears was a duel in which two warriors would be placed in the arena of the sacred grove, and obliged to hold so far apart that, when they flung a spear, there should be time for an active man to avoid it as it came through the air. Their trouble would be that there were only two spears, so that each must catch up that which had been flung at him for a second throw, and, as he did so, he must give his opponent (unless it were a moment when both spears were on his side) an opportunity more difficult to elude, so that it was a game which, if it were played for a sufficient time, could be relied upon to provide the required number of deaths.

Ebah had played this game at times, but with such skill that it had been small danger to him. It was a sport he enjoyed, and would take in a laughing confident mood. He knew that he was agile, for all his bulk, and that his spears had a deadly second of faster flight than any that would be directed at him. He sat secure in a high place, and if he were loved of few, it might be said that it was a matter which he could be careless to disregard. That he was in a special risk from the King's disfavour was a danger he did not know.

Abrah was questioned of many things, and answered with as much truth as he could, though they were often beyond his range. He could speak of what he had seen of the traffic which goes up and down the Nile, and of the customs of White and Arab in the Sudan; but, beyond that, he could only repeat the talk he had heard from the boatmen and porters with whom he had been obliged to consort. He drew a picture of a vast, disordered, and filthy world, in which were many kingdoms and creeds, of which none was of the power which had once been in the hands of Egypt or Rome, and the strongest were said to be very far. To the southward, Africa was still the wild unsettled land that it had been in the ancient days.

When Enona and Ebah had questioned him long, they let him go, giving no sign of their own thoughts, but when he had left they talked quietly between themselves, and their words were such as Abrah would have been startled to hear.

"The fellow," Ebah said, "has a faint heart. He will lie still, if he can. He would be useless to us."

"I would not say that," Enona replied. "He is wise, and if all were alike to him we could be at ease. But I suppose he would wish to be on the winning side, as we all do."

"That is the whole point. I would keep them still if I could. What is it to us that the King has made the royal apartment bare of all but himself, as you would have me believe? Do we sleep less for that, or does our food have a bitter taste? But if I would hold men back, I am not sure that I can, while if my voice be lifted to stir them up, I have no doubt how it will be. I say Hulah cannot be saved, and I will not take the wrong side, nor let Kobah push himself into the place which of right is mine. Why should I die for Hulah, when I may prove to be a much better king?"

"The wisdom of all the Hulahs is very ancient and very deep. You will do well to be wary in what you do."

Ebah did not deny this, but he put the warning aside in a very confident way. "So I shall. But what can he and the eunuchs do? What is their strength, if the spearmen rebel, which is a most probable thing, and will become sure if they have a leader in me? And are not those of Kobah's who toil underground of the same mind, though in a more morose mood, as is their nature to be? And if the women—of which there is little doubt—will be guided by you?"

"I do not see what he can do. What I say is that there may be things which we do not see. I suppose that you will not try to win over the guards, which I am assured that you could not do. You will say they are only twelve. But you will observe that he has taken the foreign man and his woman into the royal apartment, which was a strange thing for him to do. There must have been a reason for that."

"Well, if there were? Shall we say that Hulah, being weak, looked for any help he could get? Shall we turn aside for one man?"

"He has weapons that reach far, of which men talk with some fear."

"Well, if he have? Has his body a charm which will bring it free, if it be transfixed with a good spear? But I should say he will be of the same will as ourselves. Will not Hulah require that he stay here? And should we not make talk that we would assist him to get away?"

"I have thought of that," Enona replied, "and had thought to make Abrah our mouth to him, had he been of a different mood."

"It would have been a great risk for a small gain. For what is it to him? He will help us, or stand aside, and be grateful if we leave him a whole skin to contain his bones. There is nothing in this which will not be simple to do. But there will be strife at a later day between Kobah and me, which will be harder to win, though I suppose that I may be equal to that."

Ebah went with that word, and while he busied himself about his daily affairs his heart was filled with vague magnificent dreams. He led the whole people over the desert, with little loss beyond that of the children, and the women who were too old to bear, and perhaps of some of the weaker or more turbulent men. These, and the whole of the goats, he would use as water-bearers, slaying them, or leaving them to die when their burdens were emptied. The goats would be food also, with legs to carry itself. He would get most of the people across, including all the young girls, and the fighting men. Indeed, beyond those whom he wished to lose, he might have no losses at all. When he reached the Nile, he would be in a world of contending kings, and there would be no warriors like to his. Surely he would be able to sell his strength on his own terms! There would be competition among the kings. In the end, he would be king himself, as his worth deserved. As to Kobah, he would challenge him at the right time to the ordeal of spears. It would be hopeless for him, of course. He was getting fat. He would be a fool to agree. But Kobah was known to be vain of his own strength, and if he were taunted it would be just what he would be most likely to do.

So he built for the future days, to do which is the greatness and curse of man, as it has been since the tree of knowledge showed fair fruit to a woman's eyes, but if they live long enough they will find that they have come to a place that they did not dream.

CHAPTER XXIV.

BEING left alone while her companions continued the exploration beyond the confines of the King's gates, Helen had leisure to adjust her mind to the facts which she had learnt in the last twenty-four hours. The comfortable idea that she had been kidnapped for a ransom which her father would be able, and even eager, to pay, had not been easy to put aside. But this being finally done, and she having arranged her cushions to the maximum of ease which goats'-hair stuffing supplies, and posed herself with as much care as though an admiring lover were at her knee, she commenced, in a manner equally characteristic, to face the realities of the peril in which she was so strangely and surely trapped.

No one knew where she was. She must face that. No one would be likely to learn. There would be no rescue, no search which would come near by five hundred miles. She must depend on herself, and on these two twelve-hour friends, either for escape, or to make tolerable the prison in which they lay.

If they should elect to remain, rather than face the desperate hazard of flight, or if they should find the subterranean river to be blocked, or guarded in such a way that they could have no hope of gaining it for such a purpose, then it seemed that the fate that offered was that of a union with this English stranger who, she owned in a candid mind, she had already considered for such a position with pleasant thrills before she had known that it might come by other means than the deliberate exercise of her own powers of attraction.

She would naturally have preferred that those attractions should be the unaided lure, but even on that count she was not greatly concerned. "I reckon," she thought, "he fell for me more than a bit before he heard the dirty rotter's ideas"—she would always incline to apply that opprobriously inaccurate description to Hulah's bright yellow skin—"and, anyway, it would be better than if he had tried to get me for Poppa's dough."

No, she told herself, with habitual honesty, she wouldn't be likely to die of grief because she was forced to become Leonard Kinnear's wife, and she had a complaisant confidence that she could reconcile him to such a union without any great difficulty.

Indeed, when she faced the dangers of attempting escape, however vaguely they might be conceived, and the fact—very probable she told herself that it was—that it might result in her watching a duet which she did not share, she was greatly tempted to prefer the evils of remaining to the cost of recovering a civilization which, for itself, she would be very sorry to lose. If her new friends should return to inform her that they could discover no possible avenue of escape, and that they had decided to make the best of the trap in which they were caught, she was not sure that she would be hearing unwelcome words.

But she did not therefore delude herself into the belief that she would hear anything of the kind. She anticipated an opposite attitude; and an instinctive loyalty to the ties of language and blood impelled her to resolve that they should all go by the same road, even before she had realized that her own power of separate decision was not as extensive as she would have liked it to be.

For if they should have decided to stay, could she compel them to a different course? Or could she find means for a single flight which they would not share? Or, if they should be resolved to go, would she be content to be left alone in the King's hands, and for the purpose which she had heard? No, above all, she was sure of that! At the thought her hand went, as Joselyn's had done before, to a secret weapon, smaller, more delicately made than that which was owned by the English girl. Its smallness and polished silver mountings made it look a mere toy in a hand of seeming fragility as delusive as its own, but she knew it for what it was. "It's surprising how it might wake him up!" she said to herself, and the softness left her lips with the thought. And then, much sooner than she had expected to see them, Leonard and Joselyn returned.

"Something spilled on the line?" she asked, observing no satisfaction on either face.

"Just bad luck," Joselyn answered, and proceeded to narrate how caution had overreached itself. For it appeared certain that, had they gone boldly and at once to the discovery of that which they sought to know, they might have found a clear way. But, instead of that, they had loitered as people who looked idly about, with no direction or purpose in what they did. They had done that which, at the likeliest guess, there had been none to observe, so that it became an abortive subtlety, and when they had at last made near approach to the subterranean river, they had chosen about the worst moment they could, for they had been overtaken by a rabble of giant miners, going to a shift of work from the dormitories which Olah had pointed out to Leonard when he had guided him round, and these men had come upon them suddenly while engaged in a loud-voiced disputation among themselves, and had immediately surrounded them in a menacing manner.

Their anger had been inexplicable to Joselyn, who had no clue to its cause, but Leonard had learnt enough of their language to understand that that was just where their fear lay—that he might have understood, and would betray what he had heard.

He had, in fact, understood nothing, or next to that. It had been a babble of angry voices, and little more. But he had seen that his chance of safety lay in convincing them that he knew even less than he did. He answered them quietly, and with such confidence as he could assume, first in English and then in Arabic, but with care neither to speak nor to appear to understand any word of their own language, and what he actually said was addressed to Joselyn, urging her to show no sign of fear or offence, and assuring her that he could shoot before a weapon could be lifted to strike them down.

His attitude had been so far successful that it had produced a fresh dispute among their captors, some arguing that they should be put to death, as the only security against a premature betrayal of the treasonous talk they had overheard, and others replying that they could not betray words which had no meaning for them, while any act of violence would cause inquiry such as would be likely to precipitate the event in the very way which they were concerned to avoid.

In the end the latter argument had prevailed, and they had been allowed, or rather, directed to go, with unmistakable pantomime of what would happen to them if they should be found again in the lower caves.

"They followed us," Joselyn said, "to the very foot of the King's stair, and drew a line round it in the dust, making a pretence with their metal shovels of battering anyone who should cross it. They didn't leave us in any doubt as to what would happen if we should go down that stair again."

"How many were there?"

"Probably not more than a score. There seemed hundreds to me at the time."

"Are they as big as the men that you saw outside?"

"They seemed larger, but I expect they're really the same size. Anyway, they're huge men. They must be nearer eight feet than seven."

"I should say they are scarcely that," Leonard interposed, "but they are different from the over-tall men that we call giants at home, because they are not merely lanky, overgrown weeds, but well-proportioned to their own size." He added: "I didn't think we should get back alive. I suppose they could have killed us and thrown us into the river, and no one could have more than guessed what had happened. If I'd been in their place, I might have thought it the safer way."

"I reckon you could have plugged one or two before they could have done that," Helen replied. She had listened with the pleasant animation of one who hears a good tale, rather than as being personally concerned.

"Probably I could. I had my hand in my pocket, with the pistol pointed at them while I talked, but I didn't think it would have been wise to show it, even if they'd understood what it was. I preferred the attitude of one who was friendly to them, and didn't understand what the trouble was."

"I've heard Poppa say that any fool can let off, but it takes a wise guy to know when to keep his gun where it belongs."

"I dare say it does. Anyway, we had a lucky escape."

So they had, and he might feel some satisfaction in that, and in the trustful admiration expressed in the eyes that were raised to his from where Helen still nestled comfortably among her goats'-hair cushions, but nothing altered the fact that, for the purpose they had in view, the expedition had not been a success.

Judging by the time at which they had seen the miners going to work, it would be the latter part of their own night period before there would be a reasonable prospect of finding the way clear to the subterranean river. They must undertake the attempted flight with no knowledge, or even a reasonable probability, that they would find an accessible raft or boat that they could use for escape by the way that the river took, with no more provision of food than they would be able to accumulate during the day, to face what could not be less than long weeks of river and desert flight—and revealing, if they should be thwarted or discovered in this attempt, by the mere fact of the things they bore, that they were aiming to flee. Probably in the whole history of human flights from confinement or threat of death there may have been nothing wilder than that.

They were discussing this, and Leonard's mind, more than his words, was returning to the possibility of negotiating some more tolerable terms of alliance than had been proposed in the King's name, when Olah entered and said briefly: "The King wishes to see you now."

"But," Leonard protested, "till tomorrow morning. That was agreed."

"He does not ask your decision before that. The King's word does not change. But can he not see you on other matters, if he will? In your land do you question ever the will of kings?"

Leonard saw that it was not a case in which argument would be of any avail, nor was he altogether unwilling to go. If his decision were not prematurely required, he might be more likely to gain than lose by a further conversation with Hulah and the additional knowledge of the position that it would be likely to yield.

He said in English: "I don't suppose I shall be long. You had better wait for me together here."

The two men went away and Joselyn, in response to her companion's acute and eager questions, gave a more detailed account of the observations that they had made before they were overtaken by the crowd of miners.

"I wonder," Helen said, "that you didn't hear them coming soon enough to get out of their way."

"You wouldn't, if you'd seen how it was. And you mayn't have thought that we have to take three strides to their two. Why the steps—I don't mean those that go down from here. They're made the right depth for the King and the others who are more or less of his size. But the further steps down to the mines, as well as those that go lower still, to the level of the river and the great lake, are so wide and steep that it's more like climbing than going upstairs to go up or down."

"Yes, I remember noticing that when they brought me here. I tried counting the steps. I thought it was the right thing for kidnapped people to do. I didn't see much else. It was too dark."

Joselyn was surprised at that. "It was all lit up today. Like it is in the rooms and passages here."

"That sounds as though it must have been specially darkened when I was brought up. Or, more likely, the lights are always put out in what goes for the night here."

"If that's it, we should know when it's safe to go," Joselyn considered, and then had a fresh doubt. She had seen here no form of lantern, nor any kind of portable light. To stumble in the dark down those fenceless steps! To skirt the shore of the lake in a darkness far denser than that of the outer night! To find the river—by sound, or what?—and then grope about for a raft that would not be there! It reduced to the fantastic a plan which had been crazy enough before. But what use was there in saying that? Perhaps Leonard would find a way by which the light could be switched on. The idea did not seem very probable, for she had seen no switches of any kind. It might be that all the light was controlled from the power-house which she had seen where the river entered the lake. Many things might be, on which it would be useless to speculate, and idle cowardice to fear. She was talking to stifle thought when she went on:

"There's no doubt of one thing, and that's the age of the excavations here. The King's steps are worn down till you have to be careful of how you go, and we noticed that the main ones have been cut away, and fresh granite blocks inset, which have become hollow too."

"I shouldn't wonder," Helen replied, "if that's just what's wrong. Everything's gone on here rather too long, and it's time someone made it dance to a new tune.'

CHAPTER XXV.

THE King looked at Leonard in the cold way that he remembered before. It was without hostility, but equally without warmth of human regard. It was as though the whole century of dead Hulahs looked through his eyes, judging the fitness of this man to be the instrument to sustain their age-old experiment in establishing the pedigree of a super-race.

He said: "You may sit." And then to Olah: "You may go. You have that to do which I have told you before. This man can find his own way, when I have finished with him."

Olah went, and Hulah sat looking at Leonard with an intentness hard to sustain, but it was a silence which he had already learnt that it would not be etiquette for him to break, even had he been clear as to what it would be profitable or prudent to say.

After a time, the King spoke. "You have a name?"

"Leonard Kinnear."

"Kinnear will do. Leonard has too high a sound. It is too near to that of a king. You may have it at last, but it must be won."

Leonard did not reply to that. The King could call him what pleased himself. He supposed that there would be more important matters to come.

So there were. The King spoke again. "I have made you an offer, opening a most generous hand."

"It is a generosity I do not deny. But my answer was to be given tomorrow, as I understood."

The King became silent again. He spoke only after a long pause, and these intervals were repeated as the conversation went on, so that there was not very much said, though the interview continued for a long time, and after each answer that Leonard gave, not only the King, but he himself had leisure to reflect upon it.

"So it is. My word stands. Yet it may be well that you do not mistake what you decide."

"I am in a strange place. I am glad to learn what I can."

"You could kill me now."

The words startled Leonard none the less because, in the pause of silence, the thought had entered his mind that he was not more in the King's power than he at that moment in his.

"I have no wish to kill anyone."

"If you did, what would follow?"

"I have not thought about that."

"Think."

Leonard thought several things that it might have been foolish to say. He remained silent until the King spoke again: "Ebah would thank you for that. He thinks himself a king now. So does Kobah, although, being a better man, he is less sure." A faint animation, a flicker of indignation or of contempt, stirred the King's dull brown eyes as he went on: "They would destroy the work of two thousand years! They would end their race. It would be scattered and spoiled. There is no wisdom in what they plan. They have the brains of brigands, not kings."

Leonard listened, but still felt no impulse to speak. What the King said had a sound of truth. The present order of this isolated community might be good or bad; the question of establishing contact with the outside world might be of such a nature that all the arguments would not fall into one scale; but if Ebah thought to pull it up by the roots and march it into the Sudan, it might have any of several ends, but an end of some sort was sure. It might also be true that Ebah's ambitions were for himself rather than for those whom he sought to guide, and so far Hulah might be right when he described him as a potential brigand rather than king. But what was all this to Leonard Kinnear, who had his own troubles, and two women upon his hands? Had the King called for him to tell him this? To make altruistic appeal?

But Hulah was speaking again. "It would be sure ruin for them. What do you think it would be for you? There would be some who would cross the desert alive. And some not. Would they let you live, and another die? Would they count that you would be loyal to them? Would they have you tell their tale in a different way?"

"I have not considered anything of the kind."

"Then you should. You would bear water-bags through the desert heat, and it would not be you who would drain them dry. But when they were, you would either die on a spear's blade, or be left to stumble behind till your strength would end, and the two women, who are now safe, would go to death by the same road."

Leonard still said nothing, realizing that he had been called there to learn rather than to speak, and seeing an unpleasant amount of probability in the prophecy he had heard, though he was disposed to think that he might be of rather more and different uses to the King's enemies than his astuteness thought it well to suggest. He was tempted to disclaim any possibility of joining in rebellion against the King, but how could he tell what, in the end, he might be disposed or driven to do? Why should he forswear himself in advance? He would listen now, and tomorrow, if he were still here, he would answer the King.

The King still did not seem to expect a reply. He spoke again: "You have thought to escape by the way that the woman came."

"With your permission, I should be glad to go by that way."

"You may forget that. It would be your death."

Leonard was silent again, and the King added, after another pause: "You must remain here, but you may live or else die. That is the choice that you have. It is no other than that. It is a matter at which you should look with unblinking eyes."

"What have I done that I should be treated no better than that?"

"You have come here."

"And I am willing to go."

"Which you cannot do. We protect ourselves. But all this has been said before. I may have wit to deal with Ebah without your aid, but with that it is sure."

Leonard was again surprised at a frankness which seemed to give away much more than, in fact, it did. It tempted him to be as sincere in his reply: "If you feel that, you will wish me to be genuinely content."

"Which is to say you are not? I have offered much. Those who ask too much may get less."

"I have said nothing as yet. I am here to learn."

"You have said much."

After this reply, the King became silent for so long a time that Leonard began to wonder whether he had no more to say, and etiquette required his own withdrawal. But when Hulah did speak again, he showed that he had been considering the "much" that Leonard had said, or at least implied, and his own shrewd deductions therefrom: "I must have one, *or else both*. You must bring yourself to see that. And if I die, you will be three who are also dead."

Leonard made no reply, but the King's eyes were on him, and they both knew that the gulf between them was understood.

The King spoke again: "They will break faith, if you bargain with them. You will ask what they will not give. And besides, they think they are enough without you, being foolish men. I also shall break faith if you ask too much. But it is he who strains who must take the blame of a breaking strap."

In the silence that followed, Leonard saw the full dilemma of himself and the two girls who looked to him for protection. It was not so much that the King had urged new arguments or informed him of facts which he had not guessed, as that he had put them with a blunt clarity to which there was no reply.

He saw the essential point to be that he was to resign Joselyn to the King—who, after all, was not his, and which lie might be said to have no power to prevent—and, beyond that, his first service to the King was to shoot down one whom he had never met, and who would have no quarrel with him, on the King's word that he was a disloyal man.

"Speak."

He saw the King's eyes fixed intently upon him, and understood that his mind had been read, at least to the point of perceiving that he had another difficulty which had not been discussed between them. He answered frankly: "I don't like the idea of killing a man with whom I have no quarrel, and who has no chance to defend himself."

The King heard with expressionless eyes, so that Leonard could make no guess of how this further objection was received. But after the usual pause for reflection he answered: "My quarrels would have become yours. If he could slay you, would you be better pleased? Well, there might be no trouble for that."

The King did not smile as he said this. Indeed, it was a great doubt whether a ripple of amusement had ever broken the surface of that tight-skinned face. But there was a tone, very faintly sardonic, which made Leonard aware that his prejudice was ridiculed in the cold logic of the King's mind.

But while he took what satisfaction he could from the fact that the King had shown that the proposals that had been made through Olah's mouth were not beyond modification, Hulah spoke again with a cold finality: "It is enough. Go—and think well."

He went back to where the two girls were still together, waiting for his report. They had tired of discussing a position concerning which, though there was much to dread, there was little useful to say, and had wandered to comparisons of earlier experiences in London and other cities of Western Europe.

Leonard's mind had become clear on one point. After the warning the King had given, and all they knew—and all they did not know, and might guess wrong in a fatal error—it would be madness to attempt to escape during the night.

"There's nothing settled," he said, "and I don't know much more than I did before, except this: the King knows or guesses that we thought of getting away, and he's given me a plain warning that it can't be done, and we shall lose our lives if we try. After that, I don't think it would be a sane thing to attempt, even if it would have been so otherwise. But I'm to see him again in the morning, and I shouldn't worry too much before then. You'll be quite safe for this night at least."

He went rather abruptly, feeling that it was easier to be cheerful in a vague way than if he had been pressed for reassurances of a more definite kind. He wanted time for thought. Surely there must be some better way of escaping death than that which the King designed! Some counter-proposal that the ingenuity of desperation should be sufficient to find.

He left the two girls in better spirits than they were themselves aware, they having taken some confidence from his own tone. And, after all, it is better to go to rest on a goat-skin couch than to spend the night clambering in the black bowels of earth, afraid at every moment to be faced by a sudden light and a circle of lifted spears; or to be launched on a subterranean river, perhaps with no light at all (and how would the place of landing be found under such conditions as that?), and with little food, and dreading that, at any moment, the water might rise, or the cavern roof come down, so that they would bump against it in the dreadful dark, and be scraped off, or choked by the flood as it filled up to the roof above.

Each in her own room, the two girls slept well enough, having youth to aid, and the exhaustion of an eventful day, but Leonard paced the chamber where Peter Brisco may have paced through the night for long hours some hundreds of years before, as he had made resolve to attempt the flight which would be his death. He paced long, seeking for some plan, some expedient that he could not find, and sat down at last on the side of his couch, and as he pondered silently thus he became alert to the fact that his door moved. Slowly, noiselessly, inch by inch, it was being opened by one whom he could not see.

CHAPTER XXVI.

LEONARD remained very still. Who, if his purpose were good, should come with such stealth as this? Had the King decided that he was one whom it would be foolish to trust, and resolved upon his assassination during sleep, when he would be unable to use the fire-arms which might be dreaded the more because they were not entirely understood? It seemed a most probable explanation. But the King would find, for once, that his wisdom had been unequal to foresee the event!

Very quietly he drew his pistol and pointed it at the slowly widening aperture. It was essential that his unseen assailant should not suspect that he sat there. For he supposed that, when he was seen, the next second, if he were not instantly alert, would see him transfixed by a hard-flung spear. But the half-second before that would be his.

In the few moments before the midnight visitor was revealed, his mind went forward to the one resort which would remain. He would rouse the girls. They would shoot their way through the guards. He would find Abrah, and with him as interpreter he would make better terms with the King's foes than that treacherous bloodless monster would ever give. Then the woman who waited upon him appeared through the opening door.

When she saw that he was awake, she showed neither alarm nor surprise. She spoke no word, but turned back to the passage, signalling him to follow.

He hesitated, but rose with the thought that she might be a messenger from one of the girls. Had he not used her himself in the same way? Perhaps they had talked matters over after he left, and decided on flight at whatever cost, which he must not refuse to share. Perhaps they had even succeeded in enlisting the woman's help, and she would show them some secret way.

Cautious, doubtful, but not without some rising hope, he followed her, finding satisfaction in the caution with which she moved, and in the fact that she was leading him away from the King's rooms. But this was also to go away from those where the girls slept.

She led him past the heavy unguarded gates that closed off the royal suite, and on towards the one which he had first entered—the main approach to the whole apartment of the King. He followed her till it became evident that she intended that they should pass the guard, and then paused in a growing doubt. He did not suppose that the guard would obstruct his passage. Olah had told him that he was free to go where he would, and doubtless the woman had right of way. But where, and to what end, was he being led in this furtive manner? Certainly, the girls could not be there. Helen, in particular, would not have been allowed to pass out.

He stood still, and the woman, finding that urgent entreating gestures had no effect, attempted speech.

He could understand little of what she said, but the word "Kobah" was repeated, and that was a name he knew. He made a wise guess when he concluded that he was invited to secret parley with one of the King's principal opponents during the night, but he stood still in a triple doubt.

First, it was a likely thing that his midnight excursion would reach the King's ears, and how he would take it was less than sure. Second, if he should fail to make satisfactory terms with the plotters, was it sure—was it even probable—that he would be allowed to return? And, beyond that, what assurance had he that the invitation was given in good faith at all? He understood Kobah to be the leader of those who worked underground, and he recalled his encounter with the miners a few hours before. Was this a sequel? Had the incident been reported to Kobah, who might have learned from Abrah, or even from this woman, that his ignorance of their language was less absolute than he had professed? It might well be that he was invited to go forth to his own death. He recalled the King's statement that the plotters thought themselves to be strong enough without him. Then was it not likely that they sought to do no more than to eliminate him from the King's side? On the whole, he thought he would remain where he was.

Resolutely ignoring the woman's humble but urgent protests, he went back to his own room.

Arriving there, he closed the door, dragged the heavy metal couch across it, and being thus protected from further surprise, he lay down and slept so well that he was roused only by Olah's voice at the door.

CHAPTER XXVII.

OLAH came in, looking somewhat disturbed, for he had been puzzled by his inability to open the door, and had time to wonder what the obstruction might mean, before Leonard, who had seen no special reason for haste, had dragged it away.

Olah said: "The King waits."

Leonard saw that he must have overslept. But he had waked in a different mood from that of the night before. The hours of thought which had seemed to be inconclusive then had borne fruit while he slept, so that he had become clear as to what he must do. The King needed his help, which he would offer on his own terms, or else none. He would risk all on a firm stand. The King had warned him that, if he were forced to promise too much, it might be a pledge that would not be kept. Well, he must risk that! The King would keep faith as long as his need endured. Crises must be faced as they came. He believed that the King had spoken no more than truth when he had told him that there could be no dependence on those of the other side. For the moment, there was no way of safety for the women whom it was his part to protect but to be very firm with the King.

Olah said again: "The King waits."

Leonard answered. "Well, so he must. When I wake, I eat."

Seeing Olah's distress, he added: "I shall not be long. I was disturbed during the night."

While he ate, he told Olah what had occurred. Olah said: "The plot spreads. You should tell that to the King."

"Why, so I shall. He should know whom he can trust, and how far."

He felt that he had chosen his side, and he would tell Hulah all that he knew. Only, it was an alliance on equal terms that he would offer, which he thought the King could not refuse. And he must be told to leave the women alone!

In this mood, having in fact spent little time on what was no more than a light meal, he went with Olah towards the King's room.

He would have gone to see Joselyn and Helen first, had he waked at a better hour, but he thought now that he would see the King, and when he should come to them he should have more, and perhaps something better to tell.

But they must pass Joselyn's door on the way, and, as they approached, Helen came out. He began at once, before she could speak: "There is no time to talk now. I was disturbed during the night. You may expect that all will be well."

"All be well!" she exclaimed, with a sharpness in her voice which he heard for the first time. "Do you know that Joselyn is gone? Will you tell me where?"

"Gone?" he repeated vaguely. "Gone?" And as he spoke he had a doubt which changed his confident mood to a sudden flame of mingled anger and fear. The King had moved, and had been quicker than he! He had had Joselyn seized in the night! And he had been persuading himself that he could dictate the terms of a game that was already lost, so that only vengeance remained. In a tumult of jealous anger and fear, and self-contempt for the folly which had been outwitted in such a way, he resolved that, if she had suffered violence or wrong during the night, he would shoot the King, let the consequences be what they might.

While these thoughts warred in his mind, he had entered the room, and looked round for signs of a struggle which were not there. The couch had plainly been used, but was not greatly disturbed. Otherwise, all was in order. How had she been lured to leave her room so quietly during the night?

He turned to Olah to ask: "Where is she? You must know this! I must see her first! Till I have seen her, I will not talk to the King."

He spoke to a man who was as bewildered, if not as troubled, as he. "You talk folly," Olah replied. "I know nothing of this. Nor, I suppose, does the King." And as he spoke there came to both of them a better guess, which they read in each other's eyes.

Kobah had failed with him, but had filled his net at a second haul! Whether as hostage, victim, or ally, Joselyn had been lured to place herself in the miners' hands. Thinking this, he had a fresh stirring of self-reproach that, after he had avoided the trap, he had had no thought but for securing himself. He had made his door strong, and had done nothing to warn those whom it should have been his first care to protect. Actually, he had not thought of the possibility of an attempt upon Joselyn similar to that which he had avoided, but there was no comfort in that. *He had not thought!* And he had been confident that he could match his wits against those of the crafty King.

But a later thought brought some modification of these regrets, if no diminution in the sense of his own default. If Joselyn were in the hands either of Kobah or Ebah, for what purpose he could not guess, she was out of those of the King, whose purpose was known, and not lightly to be preferred. Her capture, however hostile in intention, might be an actual advantage, both to her and to himself, in his immediate object of making terms with the King. And yet all this was no more than a second surmise, which might have no better substance than the first—or the first might still be true. But, by any guess, his next move was to see the King. He had no power of himself. Of one side or other he must make allies. He must be instant to see the King.

Briefly, he told Helen his own experiences during the night, and his guess of how Joselyn might have been lured away. He added: "But it is no more than a guess. When I have seen the King, I shall know more. Meanwhile, you should go to my room, for the rifles are there, and I do not want them to fall into other hands. We will not be separated again."

His thought included Joselyn, if she could be recovered from wherever she was. It had been a mistake for them all to have been separated during the nights. Helen did not analyse that, but she liked the way that he spoke.

All the same, as to abandoning her own room, or bearing all her possessions to his, it was a matter to be decided, if at all, in a less casual manner. She said: "I can't do that. I've got too much that I couldn't leave. I'll take the rifles to mine."

He felt a momentary annoyance that she should not be more easy to guide, for he was only beginning to understand that the soft exterior held a tougher core, but he saw that it was not a point to be argued then. He only said: "Then don't overlook the cartridges, if you do that. And don't move for anyone till I come back."

"What a fool," she said to herself, with a dimpling smile, as he turned away—"what a fool he must think I am!" But none the less, as she saw him go, she had a feeling of desolation akin to fear.

CHAPTER XXVIII.

LEONARD walked on with Olah. The remaining distance to the King's audience-chamber was not more than thirty yards, but it was enough for him to observe that his companion was a puzzled and a troubled man, and to obtain a further assurance that Joselyn's disappearance was not to be laid to the King's charge.

When they reached the door, Olah said: "By your leave, I will go in first. I may explain why you are late."

Leonard did not suppose his motive to be no more than that, but it was not a matter opportune to dispute. Olah went in, and the next moment was out again. He said: "There are others in with the King. When they come out, you are to go in at once. There is no occasion for me to stay." He had a look of relief on his face as he said this, making it plain that he was not unwilling to go. Leonard asked: "You will find where she is gone? You will ask the guard who passed in the night?"

"That is what I am meaning to do. I may soon be back."

He hurried away, as one having no time or inclination for further words. Leonard had a shrewd guess that he was concerned for himself, lest the King should blame him for ambiguity of instructions to the guards, which had allowed of Joselyn being cozened through them during the night. Clearly, he was glad to have opportunity for making further inquiry before having to face the King. Leonard waited ten minutes or more, and then four men came out. They were all of the half-bred eunuchs who dwelt in the King's apartment, and were his usual medium for communicating with those who were outside. Being of the royal blood, and a special privileged caste, who might find themselves very awkwardly placed if their present environment should be rooted up, it was a natural supposition that they would be true to the King. He observed that two of them wore armour of an antique kind, and had girded on short broadswords, reminding him of pictures of Roman soldiery that he had seen. These eunuchs were not of particularly poor phy-

142

sique, though some of them, among whom Olah was an exception, had a tendency to superfluous fat. In fact, they varied widely in stature and strength, the characteristics of the royal family predominating in some, and others following more strongly their mothers' race. But Leonard compared them in his mind with the huge bodies of the pure-bred spearmen, whose splendid symmetry made their giant stature seem no more than a natural height—with that of Abrah, with whom he had been closely associated during the weeks of journeying across the desert—and especially with the guards whom he had most recently seen, and who were the elite of their virile race, and the parade of the two eunuch's breastplates and swords seemed an almost comic futility, by which the King would do no more than to expose a consciousness of danger which he had no adequate means to meet.

It gave him an access of confidence in bargaining with one whose military resources were of so puerile a quality, and a doubt of whether he were not being enlisted in a hopeless cause. He had not heard, nor would he have understood, the words in which Hulah had condemned the folly of this display: "Did I tell you that this is a time for swords? You are not my hands: you are eyes and ears. You would be fortunate if they should make you their jest, as they would be likely to do. But they would jest also at me, which I will not have. Take them off before you are seen abroad, as I shall require you to be."

But Leonard had not heard these contemptuous words, and he went into the decisive audience with a confidence which he did not wholly lose, even when confronted by the cold, implacable face of the King.

Hulah asked: "You are now resolved?"

"I have seen that I must take one side or other in a quarrel which is not mine, and which I would avoid if I could; and I am willing to give you my help to control any rebellion which may be made, if we can agree on some conditions, as I hope we may; but there is one matter on which I must first be clear."

The King heard this with a displeasure which was shown by no more than a slight hardening of the yellow thin-lipped mouth. He said only: "Speak."

"It is the question of Miss Wilde's safety, and where she has been taken."

The King gave a time of silence to this reply, as his habit was, but when he spoke it was evident that he had no clue to its meaning. "Your words are not easy to understand. If you still mean that you would choose the woman you brought, it is more than I can allow. The choice must be mine."

"I mean that Miss Wilde disappeared during the night."

This time the King answered without a pause. "Tell me all that you know."

"That was what I was meaning to do." He narrated the events which had occurred since his last interview with the King, including the threatening attitude of the miners towards Joselyn and himself, the attempt to lure him during the night to leave the King's apartment, the discovery that Joselyn had disappeared, and his belief that Olah had gone to investigate what had occurred.

The King's face was not mobile to emotion, but, as the narrative proceeded, Leonard had a conviction that he was profoundly stirred, though whether by anger or apprehension, or outraged pride at the flouting of his own authority, he was unable to guess. It was characteristic that Hulah made no comment on what he heard, but only asked, in his own time: "What is it on which you would first be clear?"

The question momentarily disconcerted Leonard, who had actually put out of his mind the idea that the King might be responsible for Joselyn's disappearance, and was conscious that he might have worded his first statement rather differently. But he knew that he must be firm and fearless in his attitude now, if he were to gain the point that he had in view, and his reply, though courteously expressed, did not recede from the position that he had resolved to maintain.

"It is a point on which I have never had a great doubt, and even that is now less. But I would be assured that it was not by your authority that Miss Wilde has been taken away."

Even Hulah's aloofness of self-control was not sufficient to conceal his anger at this reply, the various implications of which he was not likely to overlook, but he only answered: "You have that. Do you now accept without reserve the offer which I have made?"

"It is a question," Leonard replied firmly, "which I cannot answer in a few words, but I will be as brief as I can. I am in the midst, as I can see, of a dissension which is not mine, but from which I cannot remain apart. You offer to buy my support on terms which you regard as generous, which I do not say they are not, and because you regard them thus, and because you are king here, with a most ancient right, you would have me accept or refuse them without debate. But, if I may say so without a rudeness I do not mean, though you are a king, you are not mine; and if I am to be hired in such a way, you may do better to ask what my price would be than to offer that which, however large, may be without attraction for me.

"So my answer is that, if you cannot alter the offer you have already made, of which it might be said that it has become dubious in itself now that Miss Wilde has gone, then I must decline. But if you require my aid, as I think you do, then it should not be hard for us to come to terms, and that especially if you can aid me to recover Miss Wilde from wherever she may now be."

The King had subdued, by this time, any emotions he may have felt. He listened with an inscrutable face, and answered at his usual contemplative leisure: "It is the women of whom you would have asked the first choice, thinking that it would be yours whom I should prefer, as, in fact, I did. But I am now of a different mind. I will not make a queen of one who has been in Kobah's hands, as I think she is, but will prefer one who, as yet, has been seen of none here. If yours be recovered, at which I suppose we shall not fail, you may have her, as you will. So, if you be content now, we may proceed to plans which are urgent to conclude, for the time of action is very near."

Leonard heard this, and had reason to approve an etiquette of conversation which did not require instant replies.

It was a proposal he had not expected, which, if it were genuinely made, appeared to concede that which, as the King had good reason to think, and as he would himself have admitted to be the case, he had been stubborn to have. It offered protection to the one of the two girls towards whom his first obligation lay. Whether his regard for her were based on personal attraction, the existence of which he had admitted to his own mind even while he had resolved to subdue it in loyalty to his brother, or on a more altruistic impulse to protect that which his brother loved, it was clearly precedent to any obligation he could have towards the American girl. That Joselyn was here at all was owing to her love for his brother, and her mistaken following of himself. Helen's presence was independent of any action of his, and if Joselyn and he should go their own ways tomorrow, she would be no worse off than if they had never come.

Had he been alone, ties of language and race might have seemed to him to impose a quixotic necessity that he should go to the limit of life itself in answering the appeal of the kidnapped girl; but it was a very different proposition that he should jeopardize this opportunity of securing Joselyn's safety and honour in what might prove to be an abortive—and to the King an utterly unreasonable— effort to include Helen in the same immunity.

But the conclusions of logic, and the impulses of inclination, are often so far apart that there is not even a common language for their expression. Leonard was aware, without articulated decision, that he had been offered a bargain that he could never conclude.

He told himself, in support of this instinctive resolve, that he had no reason to suppose that it would be honoured by the King, who might make it a basis for possessing himself of Helen without further delay, and deprive him of Joselyn at a later time, consistently with the plain warning he had received, that he might find himself with nothing, if he should ask for that which the King would not give with a willing hand.

And then—Joselyn was not at present in the King's hands to give, which, for all they knew, she might never be! Was that something which Hulah had good cause to fear? And was this sudden transition of preference due to his appreciation of the value of a bird in the hand? The reason the King had given—that he would not take a bride who had been in Kobah's hands—seemed inadequate in itself, unless a most sinister interpretation were to be placed upon it as to what her experiences under such conditions were likely to be, and that had been contradicted by his own assurance that Leonard should anticipate her safe recovery. An inadequate explanation suggests a *suppressio veri*, if nothing worse.

But he reflected, at this point in his confused thoughts, that Hulah was not of his blood, and that reasons that might weigh heavily with the King might not have equal substance to him, and this reminded him of a kindred argument that he had been intending to use.

"You will think me difficult," he said, "which I do not intend, but you will do me the justice to observe that both I and the women of whom we speak are of blood which is not yours, and our values and ideals may be different in ways which are not easy for you to see.

"I will offer this, as you say that the time is short. We will give aid to your cause in such ways as we may be able to do, without bargain or promise of any kind, beyond this, that neither you nor I will make claim upon either woman until this trouble is done, and the time to talk of rewards will have more fitly come when you have seen what help I may have been able to give."

The King heard this proposal with his usual inscrutability. He pondered it for no more than a short time. He said: "That is well. I must tell you now of the plan I have, and of the part which will be yours, for the time is even shorter than you may think."

After this, the King spoke for some time, explaining the method by which he proposed to confirm his authority, and overawe or destroy the discordant elements which had lately appeared. Leonard learned much as he listened, of which it was not of least interest to himself that his part in the events of the coming hours had been confidently assumed in advance.

He left with an increased respect for the King's wisdom, and an increased doubt of his own.

Had his offer, which Hulah had so readily accepted, been better than a simple folly, by which he had pledged himself to the King's service without assurance of any return? It had that colour, which he could not deny. He told himself that it had postponed a crisis, that it had left him unpledged, that it must now be his part to make himself of such use to the King that the time when he could be discarded would not quickly arrive. His thoughts turned from such considerations to wonder how and where Joselyn might be awaiting a rescue of which she might have no more than a faint hope. Well, the King's plan would resolve that, and much else, with a promptness beyond anything he could have expected or hoped. His step quickened with the thought as he made his way to Helen's room, where the rifles would be.

CHAPTER XXIX.

"You look," Helen said at once, "as though you've had a full house, and picked up the kitty."

"Scarcely that," he replied; "but the King has agreed to leave both you and Joselyn alone until these troubles are at an end, and he has plans by which he appears to expect that we shall have her back almost at once."

"It sounds right while the trouble lasts. Is the plan good?"

"I know it doesn't sound overmuch. But I had to do what I could without leaving either of you out of the bargain. He offered to make do with you instead of Joselyn, if I would deal on that basis and take the chance of getting her back."

Leonard was conscious, as the words left his tongue, that he might have conveyed this information in a more complimentary form, and that he had no reason to be surprised at the manner of its reception. "Why, the dirty rat!" she exclaimed, in wide-eyed indignation. "As though...." And then, as another aspect of the matter entered her mind: "But I will say you're a white man, even if...."

She ended abruptly, her eyes thanking him, and a smile dimpling her cheek, which faded again in a puzzled frown. The auction block may not be a comfortable place for any girl of independence or pride to occupy, and least of all for the half-spoiled daughter of an American millionaire; but still, if you *are* there, it is an additional humiliation to find another girl getting higher bids. What they both saw in Joselyn Wilde! There must be few things more obvious—or more unaccountable—than the folly of men. But the impulse of a generous nature brought her mind back to the question she asked before. "You haven't told me," she said, "what the plan is."

"No. There's a good bit to explain, but we've got time. Probably more than an hour. The King means to bring matters to a crisis at once, and in a manner we couldn't have guessed without knowing more than Olah had told me. He explained some matters very fully, but there were others he didn't touch on at all. I suppose you haven't

thought of whether these people have any religion or religious cere-
monies?"

"I haven't seen any signs. But I don't see how I should, being
shut up here. They may be Particular Baptists for all I know."

"They are not that. But they have some religious traditions—
superstitions might be a better word—as I believe almost all com-
munities have. Unless I'm very much wrong, the King doesn't take
them seriously, except as a means of influencing men to his own
will, and I dare say, among kings, that's common enough too. But
they have a goddess—Artemis of the Greeks she appears to be—of
whom there is a statue in the oasis, where I understand there is also
some kind of amphitheatre in which they hold contests of different
kinds which, under their laws of existence, must often be literal
fights for life, even when there is no actual bloodshed in the arena.

"I remembered, when the King was explaining this, that there
are some notes in my room that Peter Brisco wrote on these matters,
which I didn't understand when I came on them, or I might have
read them more carefully. 'Astarté, Queen of Heaven, with crescent
horns', he quotes, but I didn't see any significance in it, beyond
showing his knowledge of a poem which must have been published
just about when he was leaving England. Anyway, so it is.

"There is an ancient custom, the King tells me, by which he
may order an assembly of the whole people in the amphitheatre, for
what is known as a 'Council of Artemis', and anyone who fails to
attend is unconditionally doomed to death.

"No excuse is allowed, nor exception made. Even a newly-born
child—they don't have any infirm or old people; they would say that
they have abolished such barbarities—must be carried there. And
when the third hour after noon, which is that of assembly, is
reached, two of the King's guards go round to slaughter anyone who
may be found dawdling about. But I don't suppose there's ever been
much bloodshed in that. It's the sort of appointment most people
would remember to keep.

"It appears that this rule applies to the royal household as much
as to others, with the difference that they are not expected to take
their places until after the assembly is otherwise full, and this alone
has been a good reason why the King has not convened such a council, since they succeeded in slaughtering each other, women and
men, except only himself, and he has been trying to keep this position quiet; but he has decided now to put his cards on the table in a
manner they won't expect.

"These Councils have always been popular, as they have been
the sole occasions and method by which the public voice can be

heard with safety to those who speak, and from which any changes have come except those which the Kings have willed. He thinks it certain, from religious and other motives, that the people will obey the call, however surprised they may be. Their leaders will think it to be an act of desperation on his part, and that he is playing into their hands, as he will be providing them with a means of legalizing what they are attempting to do. But he thinks he can both secure himself and turn the tide against those who are conspiring to take the reins out of his hands. He may be right or wrong about that, but it is at least a bold and possible plan.

"Incidentally, it will oblige Kobah to produce Joselyn, as the fact that she is not a worshipper of Artemis would not protect her if she should fail to attend."

"You mean unless he should decide to leave her for the guards to kill?"

"It isn't likely that he would do that!" The idea, which had not entered his mind previously, was disconcerting, even as a possibility of extreme remoteness. But reflection confirmed its first rejection, even before Helen neutralized the effect of her own question by assenting to his exclamation.

"No, I suppose it isn't. They didn't trap her for that, and as to being unwilling to let out where she is—well, they couldn't have thought that there'd be much doubt, when she couldn't be found here." It changed the subject effectually for the moment when she added: "And I suppose I'm in the same boat? What about me? I thought the old rotter didn't want to let out that he'd got me here."

"But that's over now. The King expects you to be there with me. He's going to put all his cards face upwards, as far as I understand, and whatever else there is to be said for or against it, it's certainly a move that his opponents don't expect him to make."

"You think we've got the brains on the right side?"

"I don't know. It's too strange to judge. We've certainly got some. And we need them badly enough. We haven't got much else that I can see, except the twelve guards; unless he thinks that two rifles are going to overawe about five hundred men—I don't know whether the women count."

"Well," Helen concluded cheerfully, "the guards look a hefty lot. But I'm glad something's going to happen. I've got the pip sitting round here."

"Something's certainly likely to happen," Leonard agreed, in a grimmer tone. It was a drama in which the King had cast him for a more active part than Helen was designed to take, and he had some excuse for regarding it in a more serious mood; but he had already learned sufficient of his companion to know that her outward levity was consistent with the functioning of a very cool and resolute mind.

In fact, she showed a practical appreciation of the strategic weakness of the King's position in her next words, when she added: "But isn't it a bit rash for him to take us out there, being as few as you say we are? It sounds rather like a mouse leaving its hole to have a talk with the cat."

"The King hasn't overlooked that. I raised the point with him, and he replied that it was a risk that must be taken, because it is the one method by which he can expect to upset Ebah's plot, and if he can do that the question of retreat will not arise. But he went on to explain that the assembly round the amphitheatre is so arranged that, if it should become necessary, we could retreat towards the Queen's Gate by a shorter way than any by which we could be intercepted. A matter of prudent planning, rather than chance, I suppose, by one of his wily ancestors thousands of years ago."

"Well, it's pleasant to know that there'll be a way back! And you say we shall have to go in the next hour? If that's so, I'd better get myself fit to be seen outside. I suppose we can rely on the sun? It seems to be a fixture round here during the day. I suppose you don't want to make any change yourself?"

"No. I see the rifles are here, and as long as I've got them—"

"Well, I do. No, there's no reason for you to clear out. You can wait here. I'll be ready in ten minutes, or a bit less."

With these words Miss Vincent retired to the partial seclusion of her inner chamber, to prepare herself for the inspection of some hundreds of curious alien eyes beneath the glare of the desert sun; and Leonard settled himself on the couch, with his back to the uncurtained aperture which divided the two rooms.

Waiting thus, his mind turned naturally to thoughts of the girl who had been lured into the hands of the King's enemies, whether as hostage or victim he could not tell; but, as he thought, his fears rose.

The fact that the attempt had been directed to himself as well as to her suggested the probability that it might be connected with their encounter with the miners on the previous day. They would have learnt that he was not as ignorant of their language as he had professed to be. The very fact that he had acted that ignorance would make them the more suspicious that he had overheard the treasons which they had doubtless been disputing among themselves. Had their intention been to put them to a common death, hoping that the King would interpret their disappearance as the folly of desert flight? If so, would they let her live simply because they had failed to secure him also? Even if they should think it wiser to keep her alive, in what fear might she not be? To what violence or indignities might she not have been subjected?

To such thoughts there was no relief beyond the hope that she must be produced in the next two or three hours. But he would be on the King's side, and she would doubtless be far apart, and divided by many spears. In imagination he saw her eyes implore him for aid after the King's subtle arguments and negotiations had been shouted down by a thousand defiant throats. Single, he fought his way to her side—a wild imagination, vivid with the flashing of sunlit spears. To have known his thought at that moment would have changed the smiling dimple of Helen's cheek as she regarded herself in the mirror of polished bronze. That was Olah's step in the passage. A step they knew, though now it moved at an unusual pace. Why had it passed on?

Leonard rose in haste. Olah had gone fast, but he caught him up, even as his hand was on the King's door. He asked: "Is she safe? Why did you not let me know?"

Olah was plainly disturbed, and it was easy to guess that he would have avoided Leonard if he could. But he controlled himself to reply: "Because I was in a great haste. But it was as we thought. Kobah lured her out. But she should be produced at the...." He checked himself, as though fearing that he had said too much. Then he asked: "You will know there is a Council called?"

"Yes, I know that."

"Then you will expect that she will be there. And you will understand I have much to do."

As he said this, he passed into the King's room, leaving Leonard without.

Leonard went back to Helen with more fear in his heart than reason told him there was occasion to have. Olah's words had been good enough. Joselyn was in Kobah's hands. That was what he had expected to hear. He could expect that she would be produced in the next hours. That was what he had hoped.

But why had Olah been in that furtive haste? He had been disturbed—so Leonard thought—by some knowledge or dread that he feared to speak. That might be likely enough, at such a crisis as this, with no relation to Joselyn at all. So reason counselled, and was contemned by a deaf and obstinate fear. "I will not go," he said stubbornly; "I will not go till I am sure."

"And we are to be killed if we stay here?" Helen asked, having a practical mind. But she did not say he was wrong. "If you say that

152

you won't budge till he does, you'll get Olah to spit it out more likely than not."

CHAPTER XXX.

JOSELYN had been wakened by a soft touch on her hand, and had seen the woman who waited upon her kneeling beside the couch.

She slept fully clothed, as it had become prudent to do, but it was no longer with a pistol clutched in a nervous hand. The weapon was now between pillow and wall, where it was hidden and yet easy to reach. The difference showed the measure by which her fear had become less imminent than before.

Seeing that she was awake, the woman rose and moved towards the door, beckoning her to come. There was nothing in her humble, urgent gesture to cause alarm. She was in the King's service, and presumably loyal to him. But she had not refused to act the part of messenger previously. Joselyn's first thought was that Leonard had found some new opportunity of escaping during the night. If that were so, she might ruin everything by refusing or delaying to come.

But she saw, in the next moment, an improbability in that idea. For was it likely that he could have enlisted the woman's service in such a cause? Or would take the needless risk of such a method of communicating with her? Was it not more probable that the woman summoned her to the night-chamber of the King for a purpose which it was too easy to guess?

She hesitated, therefore, from a false doubt; and resolved that she would go only if she were led towards the gates, but if the woman should attempt to draw her towards the King's rooms she would leave her, and seek her friends and any protection that they could give.

She therefore took up the pistol, which to the woman had no meaning at all, gathered together what food there was in the chamber, which might be needed if she were being led to the flight she hoped, and followed her silent guide.

When she found that she was led through the heavy unguarded doors that closed the King's suite, she had a sense of relief, and the hope of escape rose. She was puzzled, but not greatly perturbed, when they went on, not meeting her friends, nor to Leonard's room, but to the gates which led to the caves, for was it not the direction by which they had hoped to make escape?

When the guards let them through without challenge, she felt that one at least of the obstacles to freedom was overcome, and it was not until she found herself surrounded by such a crowd as she had encountered on the previous afternoon that she realized that she had been trapped.

She looked up at the giant forms of men whose elbows were level with her own throat, and she saw that to offer violence would be absurd, especially while none was offered to her. There were a dozen men beside and behind, and though there was some protection in the weapon to which her hand had gone as they closed upon her, it was not much, they being so near and as numerous as they were. How quickly they could strike down a lifted arm with a blow that would break the bone! How easily a hand could reach out from behind and take her neck in a grip which would crush its slender fragility, giving quicker death than would come from the loss of her hindered breath! In front the way was clear, and the woman still beckoned ahead. She went on.

The high vault of the great cave rose above her, and descended, as she came to its limit, without having gone down to the level of river and lake. Beneath was the roar of water-driven machines by which the current of air which now blew to her face was maintained through the lowest cavities of the mines. But she was in no mood to take notice of that which, in fact, they avoided by turning into a long tunnel, through which they came at last to a room where Kobah was stretching his legs and awaiting the fruit of his cunning plan with the satisfaction of one who has trumped the winning trick of the game, and an expectation of private pleasure which was no less because policy recommended what lust desired.

Kobah thought—and may not have been wrong—that he was the most important and also the most capable man in that place, except only the King, concerning whom he was not sure, but it was an issue he was quite willing to test. He thought Ebah to be a muscular fool whom he would supplant at the right time.

For the moment, it was Ebah's strength that he was the head of the spearmen and agriculturists, among whom discontent had been quicker to stir than among the men who worked underground, who, if they should adventure across the desert, might have the more reason to doubt that they would come to a better place for the use of the skills they had. But it was also true that these men, now they were roused, were of a temper more savage, dangerous, and morose, and would be harder to turn aside.

Ebah also, through his mother, had influence among the women which Kobah was too shrewd to despise.

Kobah had plans which differed materially from those of Ebah, with whom he foresaw that a clash would be soon to come. But, in the first place, Ebah was useful—indeed essential—to bell the cat. Kobah's first concern was that he should do that without failure or delay, and to secure this end he was resolved to force a position from which there could be no retreat. Had he known that the King was equally resolved in the same way, he might have seen less reason for what he did, though even then there might have been enough left; but it has been observed already that there were some brains on the King's side.

Kobah's attempt to induce Leonard to parley with him during the night was sincere enough, at least so far that his alliance was something which he would have been glad to have; and, had Leonard gone to him, it is possible that a treaty might have resulted from which the issue, whether better or worse for him and those he sought to protect, would have been very different from that which subsequently occurred. It is equally certain that, had they failed to agree, Leonard would have had a poor chance of recovering even such a slender measure of freedom as that which he enjoyed behind the gates of the King.

Having failed to secure him, Kobah tried again, with better success. He had acted with almost as full a knowledge of what had been going on in the King's apartment as had Hulah himself. Hulah thought that he had concealed the destruction of his own race, the coming of Helen Vincent, and other matters from public knowledge; and so he had, to the extent that rumour, mystery, and surmise had taken the place of simple admitted fact. The mere difference in the provision of food for the royal household, and a score of other unforeseeable or unavoidable details, had gone far to approximate suspicion and fact, but the full truth had not been known until, three days before, the woman who had now decoyed Joselyn to Kobah's power had been drawn into the intrigue of treason against the King, and had naturally told all that humble unregarded observation had learnt, which was about all that there was to know.

It was a defection which even Hulah's wisdom had not considered, though it may be asked what any wisdom could have contrived to avoid the consequences of such an event. It might be his judgment that disloyalty would not spread to those who were of his household, and half of the royal blood (as the woman was), but he might have said that it was a risk which he had no choice but to take, and that if they should fail he played a game that he could not win. But the woman had a mother she loved, and whose special skill, by which she had seemed to be indefinitely secure, was now threatened by failing sight. A bargain that she should betray the King against a promise of her mother's life had proved easy to make.

Kobah had learned not only of Helen's existence, he had been told correctly that the King had shown a decided inclination to prefer the woman who had more recently come. He also learned that while Helen would not be permitted to pass the guards, Joselyn could do so at her own will, and he saw an opportunity, pleasant in itself, of flouting and frustrating the King, and of creating a position in which Ebah must either act, or let the leadership of insurrection pass at once into his own hands, which he did not expect (nor desire) that the rival captain would be of a disposition to do.

As Absalom dealt with his father's concubines on the palace roof, so Kobah thought that it would be both pleasant and wise to deal with the foreign girl whom the King had planned to make the mother of the ninety-third of his royal race. But while there is no record of what the concubines thought of the use to which they were put, or of any violence being required to persuade them to do their allotted part, there could be no doubt that Joselyn's reaction to this programme would not be of a complaisant kind.

Kobah may have recognized such a possibility. To say that he considered it would be to suggest an importance which, to his mind, it was not likely to have. He looked at the woman who followed her female guide, the escort crowding the entrance behind her, and small though she appeared to him, she had a figure and face which he approved. They were attractive in a piquant, unusual way. All things are comparative. Joselyn was a girl of athletic type. By the side of Helen, whose hardness, such as it was, was at the core alone, she was larger, firmer, more muscular, less softly outlined, even more masculine might not be too strong a word for one who looked at her with critical rather than friendly eyes. But when compared with the great bronze women of Kobah's race! Kobah would have agreed with the King, that if you must have a small woman of one of the earth's inferior unselected breeds, Helen by Joselyn's side would not be worthy a second glance.

Joselyn, who had no clue to his thoughts, and supposed herself to have been cajoled there lest she should be in a position to betray those she had overheard, controlled any fear she had, and looked back with brave eyes at the rather burly giant whose regard of her did not appear to be of a particularly unfriendly sort.

Kobah, looking at her, was led to think of the nude statue of Artemis in the grove—she would strip, he thought, to much the same effect, which must be to say that she was one to admire, if you were of a tolerant and religious mind. He said to the woman: "You have done well. Your mother shall be most ancient before she dies, which will spare you grief, though it may be less pleasant for her. Take her to one of the mating-chambers. To number nine, if it be vacant, or else the nearest to that. For, if she cannot talk, I suppose she will go where she is led."

Joselyn thought: "Most likely, it is as a hostage that I am seized. If they meant my death, they would not choose a woman to lead me away. I believe hostages are usually treated well enough, for they are of value to keep."

She went willingly where she was led, even withdrawing her hand from the pistol-butt which had given her some comfort before.

CHAPTER XXXI.

THE social order of this isolated community, by which the very existence of its female members might depend, among other circumstances, upon the quality of their children, required, as an elementary equity, that they should have such measure of freedom in their marital alliances as was consistent with an equal liberty for the fathers of the next generation.

If the basic principle of this social order be accepted as tolerable, then it must be admitted that its application—in theory, if not always in the practice of recent years—had been contrived with a wise and careful justice, elaborated by the experience of many centuries; and this rule of integrity of selection had been enforced by laws which made it a capital offence for any procreative intimacies to take place except in certain specially allocated mating-chambers, which could only be entered voluntarily and with explicit intention.

Kobah, designing that which, although not against one of his own race, was still fundamentally illegal, because explicit intention of any kind was absent from Joselyn's mind, was yet of wit to act, as far as his purpose allowed, in a legal manner.

Joselyn looked round upon a room which, as she supposed, was to be for her use as long as she should be prisoned here, and her brows drew to a puzzled frown. She had, so far, seen nothing of the interior dwelling places of this people. She had seen only some chambers in the King's apartment, which were, in fact, older and smaller than those which had been excavated for the use of the giant population which he controlled.

The different size of the inmates themselves might be considered reason for this, but there was a further explanation in the fact that the royal race had preferred the seclusion of their separate apartment to the superior amenities of the excavations of later centuries. They knew the value of their traditional isolation, and of the mystery which attached to gates through which, for millennia, the feet of those who were not of the royal blood (excepting only the chosen guards), had never ventured to tread. But even there, there were rooms, both private and ceremonial, very different from the single sleeping-chambers which Joselyn had so far seen, and which might have occasioned as much surprise and admiration as the Queen's Gardens, though they might have been differently inspired.

Now she saw a somewhat larger room than those she had entered previously, but that was the least of its bewildering differences. She looked round on walls, three of which were bright with mural paintings, the bizarre quality of which did not obscure the naked frankness of the single subject with which they dealt, and the fourth, from floor to ceiling, was one shining mirror of burnished bronze.

She looked up to a ceiling decorated in the same way as the walls, and lighted more intensely than were the walls or corridors that she had seen previously, so that, at her first entrance, it gave the effect of facing a blaze of light. She saw furnishings which were not numerous, but in which the metal which must have been their foundation was entirely concealed. The goat-skin rug, the woven goats'-hair blanket, had been so freely supplemented with cushions and rugs of vegetable fibre coloured with brilliant dyes that it must all have seemed a luxury of softness and ease to the hard-living giants whose own sleeping-chambers were of a rocky austerity and smaller, in spite of their own bulk, than those in the apartment of the King.

In the centre of the chamber there was a low square, and looking at this, and at the general atmosphere of the room, though she could not understand all that it implied, nor be sure that it was not intended for her solitary occupation, it was easy to have a doubt—which could be no less than a dreadful fear.

Having led her into the room, the woman silently withdrew, and Joselyn had leisure to examine it with greater particularity, which did nothing to allay her first impression. Beneath the bronze wall flowed the usual stream of water from side to side, and beside it was the familiar table laden with pomegranates and grapes and dates. Hanging in the centre of the left-hand wall, for which the mural paintings allowed it an outlined space, so that it was clear that it was part of the original design of the room, was a whip with a metal handle and two leather thongs. It was no more than an ancient ritual symbol of feminine subjection—a sign of subordination when the choice had been made and the room entered. It may not have left its place for once in five hundred years in more than a playful way, but its puzzling significance was another doubt that she did not like.

Her eyes moved from that to examine the wall paintings, which were of an artistic convention different but clearly derived from that of Egyptian art. Under other circumstances, approached in another mood, they might have impressed her in a different way, but she met them now with a coldly hostile virginity both of mind and body. From its first instinct of repulsion, her mind waked to an active fear.

She had become accustomed to unbarred doors in this place, and it was rather through the force of previous habit than in any hope that her eyes turned to that which the woman had gently closed as she withdrew; but hope came to a quick life at the sight of a large horizontal metal bar, which must be very heavy if it were solid, rather highly placed on a door which was designed for the entrance of those who were much taller than she, and having a socket in the solid basalt of the wall. She stepped quickly to it, her plan formed even before it was in her hands.

She could not shut herself in there forever, unless she were willing to die. But there were her friends—there was the King's certain wrath, and his probable power—time might bring rescue before the passing of many hours. And even for days—she had the fruit—she had the running water—and they might not even be able to stay. She would drink deeply at once. It was a long time that she might endure!

It was no use. Maddeningly, the bar was too heavy, too stiff to move. When she had become breathless with a waste of effort which she had not been willing to cease, she considered that, had the bar been lower, she might have been able to bring her strength to bear upon it in a better way. Obviously she must raise herself. She looked round the room and saw nothing of a movable kind on which she could stand. The bed was too massive. The couch at the right-hand side of the room, when its metal foundation was exposed, proved also to be too heavy to be dragged across the floor.

Her only remaining hope was in the rugs and cushions, which she gathered to make a stool for her feet. It was astonishing how many were needed to raise her firmly to the required height. When she had made herself a solid support, she had stripped not only the couch but the bed, revealing that it was not a separate structure at all, but a low platform which had been left when the floor had been quarried out, and had then been hollowed in a shallow, saucer-like shape.

Standing so that she could now put the full strength of her arms upon the end of the bar, she strove again, and thought at first that she was as impotent as before, but as she made what might have been the last effort preceding despair, the bar moved. It was no more than an inch, or perhaps less, but it was enough to show that it could be done.

Straining with a new hope, she had a sudden contrary fear that what was so difficult to drive in might be utterly beyond her strength to draw out again. But she did not slacken effort for that. If she must die in a trap which she had closed with her own hands—well, even that did not seem too high a price for her present peace. And besides, sooner or later, her friends would come—would discover where she had been put. They would find means—they would break it down.

Another inch the bar moved. It had seemed easier that time. Another would close the gap between bar and jamb—a third, and such security would be hers as a bar would give. There was a step on the stone without.

She did not relax her effort for that. It was a step that might pass. Slowly she felt the bar moving again. But the step did not pass. There was a heavy hand on the door. But that the rugs and cushions on which she stood trammelled its movement, catching beneath it, so that it dragged heavily in a way that Kobah did not expect, she might have been thrown to the ground. As it was, she stepped clear.

She retreated to the farther side of the room, so that the wide shallow basin of the stripped bed was between the intruder and her.

Kobah looked, and it was plain what she had been attempting to do. He scowled, and then changed to a laugh which was not pleasant to hear.

He closed the door, shooting the bar with one hand. It was a revelation of how little strength she had beside his, which she did not fail to observe.

He turned to her again. He said: "Put them back," in his own tongue. She did not understand the words, but the gesture with which he pointed to the bed and the rugs which were now scattered over the floor was clear enough, as was the meaning of the tone in which the curt order was given. He had not come to parley, but to command.

As he spoke, he threw off the single garment he wore, revealing the body of one who had once been conspicuous among men who were all splendid statues of living bronze, and was still of magnificent physique, though he had become somewhat obese during recent years.

Joselyn's hand tightened convulsively upon the butt of the pistol which she now held without concealment, but which had no meaning for him, neither had she any words to warn him of what it was. But even it gave her little confidence. He was so huge, so near.

Would he be stopped by one small bullet, or even two? Wounded, even brought to the point of death, would he not reach her at one stride, would he not break her neck with his dying hands? He would not need hands for that. He could squeeze her neck between finger and thumb in a fatal pinch: he could snap her backbone across his knee.

Kobah said again: "Put them back." He spoke in a curter tone than before. He saw that she either did not understand or was not quick to obey, which latter he thought to be the more probable explanation. Well, be that as it might, there was the same thing for him to do. In the one case she must have her wits waked, and in the other she must learn what a woman is.

Had he been able to speak his mind, he would have tried words, and would have expected to find them enough, for he was not a particularly sadistic or brutal man, and it had not occurred to him that this woman, whom he could bring to death with one hand, would be stubborn to foil his will.

But where words fail actions must speak, and if there must be chastisement he would still act in an orderly legal way. It should be by the ancient method the law enjoined for women who entered here, and would not then submit to that which the occasion required.

Therefore he did not move directly towards Joselyn, but to the left-hand wall where the whip hung. Her eyes followed him, watchful as a trapped animal, aware of any inch of distance that shortened between them, alert to every movement he made. She had no doubt that the trigger would soon be pressed, but she had still a disinclination to fire until he should disclose his purpose against herself. It would be like hanging a man for a murder he had not even attempted, because it was judged to be one that he might be disposed to commit.

She saw the whip taken down from the wall, and there could be little doubt that it was intended for her. She said sharply: "Stand back. I shall fire!" She raised the pistol as she spoke, depending upon action and tone in the absence of common speech, as he had done a moment before.

He laughed in answer, a sound of easy contempt, and advanced upon her.

She had a bare second in which to act. She thought: "I must hit his legs. I must bring him down. It is the one way that is sure."

She pointed the pistol downward and fired with no apparent effect, and again. At the second shot he came down. A great leg doubled beneath him. The other stuck out grotesquely across the floor.

As he went down he gave a cry that was half a bellow and half a scream. A hand reached towards her ankle, and was avoided by an inch, but no more.

"Keep back," she said. "I shall fire again." He might know no more of her own tongue, but he knew more of the weapon now. He became still.

After that he gave his wounds an attention that was plainly required. The tiny bullets had made no more than small punctures, but the second had fractured an ankle-bone, where it remained. It was that which had brought him down, but it was the first which had inflicted the more dangerous wound, piercing an artery, from which the blood was pulsing out in a scarlet stream through the tiny hole that had been drilled in the bronze-skinned flesh.

Kobah, muttering wrath and pain, was twisting a tourniquet from one of the bed-coverings which he had contrived to reach, to check that thin fountain of blood that was now making a spreading pool on the floor.

Joselyn's instinct was to go to the aid of a wounded man, but she looked at the scowling face and thought of the strength which had shot the bolt with a single hand, and she had sufficient sense to keep a safe distance away.

CHAPTER XXXII.

HULAH had had one report that was good, though it had been no more than he had expected to hear. The call to the Council of Artemis would be obeyed by Ebah, and by the spearmen and agriculturists whom he controlled. The thought of disobeying it had either not entered his mind, or had been put aside without giving it audible expression. What he was reported to have said was a form of the ancient proverb which has come down to Western Europe by a Latin route, that "whom the gods would destroy, they first make mad."

If Ebah and his followers had no thought but to obey the King's call, then it was likely that Kobah's workers beneath the ground, and the women and children also, who were largely separated from the men, would assemble without demur. If this should occur, it might be said that the King would have won nothing, but that he would have avoided a preliminary defeat.

When Hulah had considered his plan, he had seen this as an initial danger which must be risked. For if his order had been ignored, as a gesture signifying that his power had come to its last hour, and the ritual of the old religion itself contemned, it would have been a position which he would have been impotent to control. For could he have sent two guards (or the whole twelve) to slaughter hundreds for the insult that they had offered to Artemis and to him?

But he had considered that it was fundamentally improbable either that those who plotted treason would regard the call as being any menace to them, or that they would seek to raise a religious issue, to which they could no more than guess, in the short time that was theirs, how their followers would react; and which it was almost certain that many, especially among the women, would be frightened to disobey. The fact that the call must be answered almost as soon as it was received was alone sufficient to render it improbable that a concerted disobedience could be arranged; nor was it likely that individuals would have the separate temerity to risk abstention.

Still, Hulah was aware that he drove with a breaking rein, or at least with one which would snap with too hard a pull, and there must be satisfaction in the fact of a corner turned. It confirmed his judgment. It reassured him that he had gauged the whole position aright, which the inbreeding of two thousand years had rendered one of his race pre-eminently able to do. It might be considered to approximate certainty that, he being what he was, and the tribe being what they also were, he would prove equal to overcoming whatever obstacles discontent might raise, so long as matters pursued a normal logical course; and after long hours of thought he had assured himself that he saw a clear way to a clear end, in which he would be unlikely to fail. His danger lay in the illogical unforeseeable chance, and in the doubt of how far he would be equal to dealing with any emergency for which no precedent could be recalled or tradition applied.

Such a position, it seemed, had arisen now, and it was one that would not wait for the deliberation which cautious wisdom prefers.

Hulah looked at Olah and saw a man who was perturbed and anxious to speak, which etiquette required that he should not be first to do.

"I suppose," the King asked, "that you will tell me that she is in Kobah's hands?"

"That is so," Olah replied. "He sent her to one of the mating-chambers, to which he followed almost at once."

The King frowned at that. It was evil news, both as an open insult to himself, and as giving his alien ally a cause for anger, if nothing more. But Hulah reflected that Leonard could not blame him for what had occurred, and if his indignation were directed upon Kobah, there need be no trouble for that. A bullet in Kobah's brain would be no distress to the King.

Also, though he was annoyed, he was not greatly surprised. It was a possibility he had foreseen when he had so promptly decided that Helen should be the bride for him. He had a fresh occasion to observe how accurately he could forecast what would occur, and there was satisfaction in that.

"Well," he said, "she will have learnt before this whose babe she is like to bear, but there will be no reason to let it live, if it should be one that she does not approve; and as I suppose that Kobah will soon be dead—"

"That," Olah interrupted, as he would not have dared to do had he been less disturbed, or less aware of the urgency of the hour, "is the matter I have to tell. Though that he be dead at this hour is more than I am able to say."

166

The King saw that Olah had more to tell. He said only: "Speak," as his manner was, and became silent and attentive to what he heard.

"Kobah," Olah said, "went in to the girl and did not come out for several hours, so that he was still there when the summons to the Council of Artemis was received. It had not been expected that he would remain with her longer than the occasion required, but he was free to do as he would, and the custom that those who are in the mating chambers shall not be disturbed had caused him to be left alone, as it is scarcely needful to say.

"But after the summons had been announced, and he still did not appear, it was seen that if he were not informed he might ignorantly blaspheme the goddess, he and the woman together, for a default that he had not willed; so that, about an hour ago, there were two who went to the door and informed him of the need that he should appear."

"They had no purpose but that?"

"So," Olah answered cautiously, "it was told to me."

"And were his people already proceeding towards the grove?"

"I believe many of them were preparing to go, or are going now. But there are others who appear to wait for instructions from him, or that he shall lead. They run round in no certain way, as do ants when the anthill is broken through."

The question had been a natural one for the King to ask, for the law was that the people should assemble not less than thirty minutes before the hour at which the royal household should take its place, for which there may have been more reasons than one; but it is evident that a thousand people cannot be seated at once, and that it is unseemly for those of royal rank to sit waiting while the common herd shall range itself on the lower sides.

The King saw that the time had arrived at which Kobah's followers, and the women and children who were also lodged in the subterranean caves, should have been swarming towards the grove, and he sought to learn how far they had obeyed the order as loyal subjects of his, and as the followers of Ebah were proceeding to do.

But he saw also that his question impeded a tale that was not yet done, and the end of which it might be urgent to hear, so he said no more than that it might be well to take record of such as should be last to depart, and became silent until Olah had finished that which he had to tell.

"The two men," Olah went on, "knocked at the door and were answered by Kobah at once. He said that he had a hurt leg, so that he could not rise to open the door, which he ordered should be burst in; and when he heard that the Council had been convened, he called out that a litter should be got ready in haste, so that he should not be left behind for the guards to slay."

Hulah thought that this sounded well enough to make the end of the tale less important than he had supposed it likely to be. Evidently Kobah, like Ebah, had recognized at once that the summons must be obeyed. So that he did that, he might come in a litter, or how he would. Indeed, it might be thought that he could not come in a better way. Evidently the woman had not been docile to do her part. Probably he would have killed her, she having done such damage to him. That was the worst that there could still be to hear, and the King felt that he could endure it with ease, but he did not interrupt again.

"The time being as short as it was, they did not attempt to cut through the door at a place where the bar could have been forced back, but brought sledge-hammers to burst the hinge. But at the first blow there was the sound of the woman's voice in an unknown tongue, which had not been heard before, and after that Kobah called upon them to desist in an urgent voice, saying that the woman would kill him before they could burst it through.

"After that he asked that one should be fetched who could interpret between him and her, and they would have constrained me to do that part, but I thought that I should first make report and have instructions of what you would have me do; and I replied that I had no skill in talking with her (of which I have a real doubt), and that I must fetch the man of her own race, which they released me to do."

"And meanwhile do the people stand?"

"Kobah has called that none shall move till he be free, and some obey and some not."

"Have you told this to the man?"

"I avoided speech with him to come here."

"You have done well."

Hulah had a problem to solve at a short count. He might take the simple, obvious course of informing Leonard, and requesting him to go to the scene of dilemma and interpret between Joselyn and the man who was in her power. It would be risking that he would be detained by those who had tried to entice him during the night, and it might appear that it would be difficult for Kobah to give satisfactory guarantees that any terms that might be made would be honoured when the door had been broken in. But Hulah had the less doubt of this because he guessed the argument that Kobah would use. He would explain the common necessity they were under of vacating the caves and appearing in the sacred grove, and assert both the impossibility of detaining her longer under such circumstances, and that she would be in the same peril as himself if they should remain there.

Yet if Leonard should place himself in the miners' hands, through anxiety to rescue Joselyn therefrom, it was easy to see several possible developments which might be bad for him, and unsatisfactory for Hulah himself, with which point he was most concerned.

Against that, it was an obviously dangerous complication to allow the matter to take its course, with the probability that Kobah's detention might continue, and that he might prevail upon a considerable number of his supporters to remain, which he would be certain to command or implore.

Hulah had some excuse for feeling that Fate had hit him below the belt, and at a time when he was breathless enough from more legitimate blows. If it were imperative to send someone, and inexpedient to ask Leonard to go, who else remained with knowledge of tongues sufficient to bridge the dividing gap? He considered Helen, and dismissed her as one whom it would be even more foolish to place within Kobah's power, and also as being too ill-equipped with his speech, in which, as we know, she had professed an even denser ignorance than she had. Only Abrah remained, and in him, it seemed, the solution lay. But time was short, and Abrah might not be easy to find. He might be already seeking his place in the amphitheatre, or he might not turn in that direction until the last moment that punctuality required, by which time Kobah, who had farther to go, should already be on the way. And after Abrah should be fetched, and conducted beneath the ground, there would be parley to hold, a door to be broken down, and Kobah to be carried along narrow passages, and by steps and causeways of stone, and then a mile, if not two, under open sky.

Hulah might have sent for Abrah in a dozen directions at once, but he did not wish to scatter his eunuchs about, who were the only reliable messengers that he had. They were to be dressed in a ceremonial garb, and marshalled beneath the royal seats, which would themselves be bare except for himself and the white strangers whom he would introduce to his lofty place.

And—final doubt—suppose Abrah should make excuse which, as the time shortened, he would have increased reason to do?

Hulah saw all these things, but he saw also a position which would not improve. It was evidence both of his wit and his fitness to lead, as it should be fairly judged without reference to later event, that he said in a brief style: "It is Abrah must do this. I will keep the white man at my side. Seek Abrah without delay and charge him from me that he be instant to Kobah's aid. I will reward him largely, and with the exemptions he will desire, if he bring this to a good end."

Olah asked, "Have I time for this?" He had a thought for his own garments, which he should change, and of the pace of the flying hour, but at the look in the King's eyes he became silent and hurried away.

CHAPTER XXXIII.

HULAH was alone when he had sent Olah away. Eunuchs and guards were preparing themselves for the occasion, as he had ordered them to do, and he should have been occupied in the same way with the help of Olah, and of a woman who was not likely to come. But for this exasperating, last-minute event, his dispositions would have been complete, and he would have attended the Council, as a King should, without haste of body or mind. He cursed Kobah in his heart, both for the woman he stole, and that he had been too clumsy a fool to deal with her as a man should.

But his curses took little time. He saw that there was something else still to be done, which should have been Olah's part had it not been necessary to send him away. He must be his own messenger now! It was such a thing as no Hulah may have done in two thousand years, but it is to his credit again that he did not pause, nor look round for someone who was not there to perform his will. He first completed his own dress, putting on the robes and rubies of state which he would wear when he appeared in the light of the open day, and started to find Leonard as though he had the legs and mode of a common man.

And because he had been thorough in his knowledge and comprehension of what had occurred beyond the sight of his own eyes, he found him at once. For he chose the way that led by Helen's room, and the voices he heard therein told him that he would have no farther to go.

His entrance surprised Leonard, who rose up from the couch where he had been sitting, feeling it to be a mark of respect due even to a yellow king and one whom he had no great reason to like.

Helen, whose toilet was now complete, standing at the back of the room, a ripe fig in her hand, surveyed the intruder with wide-open eyes that were blankly blue. He would always be a dirty rotter to her. It was a fresh offence that he commenced to speak to Leonard in tongue that she had neglected at school, considering that her

own attractions, and her father's wealth, should be sufficient to secure the prizes of life that a woman seeks without the assistance of
Latin verbs; though, had he preferred the use of his own tongue, it is
improbable that she would have been much better informed.

The King said, "You will understand that, in the emergency of
the hour, I put formality by. Having sent Olah on an errand that
could not wait, I had no other who could speak to you so that he
would surely be understood. So I have come myself to say that you
should be prepared to join me at the Queen's Gate, where we shall
assemble and go forth at a time which is now near."

He looked at Helen, who had dressed herself in a manner which
she had not thought previously necessary, or perhaps expedient,
from the resources of the baggage which had been brought away
with her from the Cairo train, with more satisfaction than she had
aroused before in his dull-brown eyes, as he added: "Which I observe that your companion has already been prompt to do."

Leonard heard this without a direct answer. He said: "I saw
Olah when he was coming to you. He knew something he would not
tell."

"He was in haste."

"It concerned Miss Wilde," Leonard replied, making assertion
of what was no more than a likely guess. "It is what I should be
grateful to hear." He spoke without heat, recognizing that his com-
plaint against Olah, if such he had, could not be laid as yet at the
King's door.

Courtesy had its reward. The King considered that tomorrow
must bear the weight of today's lie. He must not refuse truth, in
ways which a few hours would expose, without more evident cause
than he now had. "Olah," he answered, "is a timid and foolish man,
and his haste was without pretence. The news he had you should call
good. Kobah, whom we will find occasion for you to slay, had
tricked the woman into his power, as we already supposed. He
would have raped her some hours ago, meaning despite therein to
me rather than you, but she found means to do him so great a hurt
that he will be unable to reach the Council except he be carried by
other legs."

"She being still safe and unharmed?"

"So there is some reason to think. But we shall know more
when the Council meets."

"There is, I think, more you could tell me now."

Hulah, so directly challenged, and at the disadvantage of one
who had come to wait on another rather than being attended by him,
which may have had more effect on the processes of the ancestral

mind than would have been the case with a king of more casual blood, did not deny that there was. He had outlined a picture which he could not now refuse to fill in with the details that were required. In the next minutes Leonard had the tale, somewhat glossed and not entirely simple for him to understand, but substantially as Olah had related it to the King.

After that, Hulah must wait, as a king has little practice to do, while Leonard told Helen what he had learned, and they discussed it in words that had no meaning for him.

When she knew the position, Leonard found that she echoed the decision of his own mind. "You can't leave her there," she said.

"You can't tell that they'll find Abrah at all, or that she'll be willing to listen to him; and, if she does, they'll double-cross her more likely than not. It's a case, if you ask me, for calling up the marines. Tell him, if he wants any help from you, he's got a dozen guards who can come along and give us a leg up before his own funeral begins."

Leonard saw the advantages of a proposal the audacity of which was beyond his own intention. It was not a position in which he could either delay or scruple in what he asked. He turned at once to the King to say: "We cannot risk leaving her there. With your guards to aid, I will bring her out, and the people will see that they cannot do as they will, even before the Council begins."

The King stared. He exclaimed, "You would have my guards!" Beyond that he was dumb. Astonishment and anger were controlled by his habitual reserve, but at that moment, Helen thought: "He almost looks like a live man."

Leonard added: "I cannot come till she be free. I will go alone to fetch her, if you prefer. But it may be better to give me the guard, if you would have me live to be useful to you."

The King was still silent, and Leonard was aware that his anger burned, but not sure that he would refuse, being in the dilemma he was. He spoke again, thinking of all he could that might tip the scale: "You say that many of Kobah's men will have gone already towards the grove. The rest will be in confusion. Will Kobah order them to oppose your guards, he being placed as he is? If it be done in a bold way, there will be no danger of complication at all."

Hulah saw that he was right, and though he was wroth, he would not therefore put his judgment aside. He thought Leonard's demeanour to be as insolent as the proposal he made, for both of which he resolved that he should be chastised on a better day. "There would be two kings," he thought, "or perhaps he would make me the lackey to do his will!" He resolved also that he would not be

173

left with only the eunuchs to be his guard, and that if the plan should succeed, as he thought it would, it should not be to Leonard's credit, but to his own.

"So it shall be," he said. "Wait for me here. We will all go."

He went even more quickly than he had come. He gave command for the eunuchs to proceed to the grove, and, at the due time, if he were not there, to take their appointed seats, and to let it be known that he would appear as soon as the assembly was full; and (if there should be occasion for further words) that he had gone to the release of Kobah, he being hurt in the mines, and it being the royal will that no man should fall to the goddess' wrath for a contempt that he did not mean.

He then went to where the guards were already arrayed and waiting, and it was but a few minutes before he was at Helen's chamber again.

"I suppose," Helen said, "he will let me come?"

"It may not be safe. We shall be soon back."

"Oh, but I—I should be afraid to be alone—to be left here!"

Leonard hesitated. To keep together in such a place—there was much to be said for that. He looked at the King, who made no sign, and may not have guessed what the question was. Or he may have avoided attempt to exercise authority which might not be obeyed. He merely watched what they would do.

Six of the guard moved ahead. Then came the King. Leonard followed and Helen kept at his side. The remaining guards fell in behind.

As they moved along the rock-passages, ceiling-lit, they could see nothing but the heads and shoulders of the guards towering above them both before and behind. Their bronze bodies were now clothed in armour of copper and bronze, over which they had cast gay scarves and drawn surcoats of yellow and red. The King wore a scarlet robe, and round his neck a circle of rubies shone. Rubies were the only stones that he wore. They gleamed along the white edge of the scarlet cloth. The whole effect was a barbaric splendour, all yellows and reds, that toned with the yellow skin of the King and the guards' muscular bronze. The King looked small, insignificant now, as he walked with shorter, quicker steps behind the giant strides of the guards, but he would appear formidable enough when he would be in his high seat, with his thin, hawk-like face looking down on the crowded amphitheatre beneath and around.

"It was a good thing," Helen said, "that I decided to come. I don't see how you'd have carried both." She had the lighter rifle under her arm.

"I don't suppose we shall need either. We'll hope not, anyhow. But if we do, be ready to hand it to me when I've emptied mine. You'd better not try to use it yourself."

She was submissive to that, with a reservation in her own mind which he need not know. He thought she showed more timidity even than the occasion required. They seemed safe enough between the huge forms and gleaming spears of the guards, but in fact she had a fear which was not of her own kind. It was that of the great cavern through which they passed, and the wide black waters of the lake that stretched away into a far darkness below. It was a recollection of the terror she had endured as she had travelled the dayless, endless tunnel that had no sound but that of the flowing water that never ceased. It was the other way she had thought they were near to go— to the sight of the long-lost day. But she was no less resolved that Joselyn's rescue should be accompanied by someone with more sense than any man was likely to have.

CHAPTER XXXIV.

KOBAH'S naked bulk sprawled over the bed, to soften which he had drawn such rugs as were within his reach, and some others that Joselyn had thrown his way, hate and fear not having entirely overcome her inclination to give such help as she could to a wounded man.

But she looked for no gratitude in return. A sure instinct told her that Kobah had become one whom she could never trust: one who would take his first opportunity of revenge in dreadful, re-morseless ways. She would have seen him bleed to death before she would have come within reach of those restless hands.

But the question did not arise. He had stanched the wound, though not before he had seen more of his own blood than he had been willing to lose, and he was aware that a careless movement would be likely to start it again.

Yet there had been a time when he had tried to rise: when he had made cautious, awkward attempts to see what could be done with his arms and a single leg. But he had become still at the sound of a sharp word and the pointing of a weapon which he was begin-ning to understand. Joselyn watched him with the strained, pitiless eyes of an animal that has been cornered by too-numerous foes, who may still be held off so long as vigilance does not relax—but to what end?

She had the one hope that her friends might come; that they might have the support of the King. Without them, even if she could have spoken in Kobah's tongue, she saw no possible way by which she could make a bargain that he would be likely to keep. In the end, she supposed, she would become too drowsy to hold her watch, and must kill him lest he should crawl upon her while she would be un-aware. And after that? Well, she must stand siege while she could.

When she heard a clamour of voices around the door, she stirred to a little hope, which became less as she observed that Kobah shouted orders to those without. But when the sledge-hammer commenced to beat on the door, she was instant in her menace of tongue and weapon. Sulkily he ordered the smiths to cease, and then held further conversation that Joselyn could only wish she could understand. But she would not interfere with that which might have a good sequel for her.

She judged correctly that if she could keep Kobah at that side of the barred door he would try to get someone called who could interpret between them, so that he might make terms for his release; but as she understood nothing that had been said, the urgency arising from the King's summons was hidden from her. She could only observe a continual clamour about the door, in reply to which Kobah had much to say, sometimes in pleading or imperative tones. But she would offer no interference while the door was allowed to stand, and the time came when her patience had its reward.

It was after a time during which the noise and movement in the corridor had much diminished, and she had caught a tone of bitter, alarmed remonstrance in Kobah's voice as it had pursued the retreating steps, that there came a new volume of sound, a prelude of excited chatter and confused feet on the stones, and then the heavy, regular tread of a column of marching men.

Her lips tightened at the sound, and her finger itched on the trigger. Had they some fresh device by which they would burst through the door so that it would be down before she would be aware? Well, they would find that she could be quicker than that! Kobah, till his last minute should come, would never be nearer death than he was then.

Helen's voice sounded outside the door. "Joselyn, are you there? What do you want us to do?"

"Who've you got with you?" she queried in reply. "Shall you be able to get me away?"

Leonard answered: "You needn't worry about that. The King's here, with the whole twelve of his guards, and most of Kobah's men have gone off, or are going now. The question is, can you let yourself out? There's no time to lose."

"If it's like that, I don't see what the hurry is. But it sounded as though they'd got a sledge-hammer outside. A few good blows at the hinge—"

"There may have been a hammer here once, but there isn't now." With brief sufficiency he told her of the Council the King had called, and of the consequent reason for releasing her without delay. "If you're sure you can't open from inside," he said, "I'll tell the King, and I expect he'll soon find means of battering it down."

"Wait a minute," she answered. "We may be able to do better than that. I've got a great brute here that I shot in the leg. I don't see why he shouldn't do it, if it's to save his own skin. Can you talk in a way that he'll understand? Well then, tell him I shall shoot to kill if the door isn't open in twenty seconds, or a bit less."

Kobah, who had suffered Joselyn's previous experience of listening to conversation of vital interest to herself which she had been unable to understand, now heard himself addressed in his own tongue, and with greater fluency than Leonard would have been able to use, for Abrah had been found, and arrived in time for a part which, under the King's eye, he was quite willing to undertake.

Kobah, menaced by the pistol-barrel, with the messages of which he had already made closer acquaintance than he desired, crawled over the floor, and dragged himself up with a hand on the door's hinge till he could reach the bar, which he pulled out, sinking to the ground again at the side of the opened door.

"You are unhurt?" Leonard asked, as Joselyn came forward.

"Yes," she said. "No thanks to him." She looked down at the groaning, somewhat corpulent figure of naked bronze, and there was a common hate in their meeting eyes which would not cease while their lives remained. Kobah, seeing the King, and that his guards filled the corridor, had a doubt whether he might not have been safer behind the bar of the door. He knew that he had done that which the King would be unlikely to misunderstand or forgive, and he had intended that when next they met, it should be under different circumstances than these. But Hulah said no more to him than: "I see that you have a litter awaiting. You will tell the bearers to hasten the most they can. And your wounds must wait to be dressed at a freer time."

Helen was saying: "You cannot go like that. If you could see how you look! I suppose we shall pass my room, if not yours. We are to go out by the Queen's Gate. Leonard, you must tell the King that he will have to delay for five minutes, or perhaps more, if he wishes to have Joselyn there."

And when they came to Helen's door, Hulah found that he must agree, even to that. But he was not ill-content. He saw that the first skirmish was his, though it had not been one that he had sought or foreseen, and might have brought his plans to a quick wreck.

CHAPTER XXXV.

EBAH considered a tale which he had not expected to hear, and which might have ended either in a better way or a worse, but, as it was, he concluded that it was good enough.

The King, as he saw the position, had given to him and to others who were of the same mind an opportunity of talking treason in a constitutional manner to which no immediate penalty could be attached; and though it gave Hulah an equal occasion of public oratory, it was a form of conflict in which—or so it seemed to him—the issues must be fairly and logically faced, which he supposed to be favourable to his own plans.

He knew nothing of what capacity for public speaking the King might have, while he was confident of his own, which had been practised before. And if argument should not prevail, the appeal to force would remain, and should be as potent tomorrow as today.

That was how he had regarded the position when the summons had first come to his ears. Nor did he observe occasion to change his mind when he heard that Kobah had committed an outrage upon the authority and prestige of the King, and a violation of his private apartment, such as must in itself be productive of immediate crisis, but which had brought its own retribution upon him in advance of the dash which it would be natural for it to cause.

Kobah on his back was a poor leader for the miners to have, either for speech or strife. Ebah, a short-seeing man, smiled at that in a satisfied way. He ordered that all men should be punctual to obey the word of the King. He did not doubt that they would have done so had he said nothing at all, but they must be practised in obedience of orders that came from him.

So they had thronged into the amphitheatre, women, children, and men, in the punctual, orderly manner that the occasion required, and, in a somewhat more laggard and straggling throng, came those who were under Kobah's control. The amphitheatre was a place to which they resorted often enough, and around which everyone, from the day of being loosed from a nurse's arms, had an allotted place. But the games and contests which they watched, or in which they engaged in many perilous ways, were not of the solemnity of this occasion, nor were they commonly attended by those of the royal household, except at the Annual Games, which were now nearly due, and which were the principal occasion of resolving the eliminations that the maximum of population required. And even the Annual Games were not of the portentous nature of one of these Councils of Artemis, which could be summoned by the reigning Hulah alone.

There had been times when more than one of such Councils had been held in a single year, and others when a whole century had seen none, so that they had assumed an almost mythical character in the tales the Recorders told, and in the Legal Creed which all must learn to repeat, without error or halt, by the end of their seventh year.

The present King had not sat on the high throne, having attended, in the ten months of his reign, no public ceremony, for such must have exposed the fact that the royal race now consisted of none but he; but he had sat near to his grandfather's throne on such occasions often enough, and he had twice watched the ritual at which he would now preside, besides having been well instructed thereupon during earlier youth, before discord came.

The fact that he was, by two generations, another king from him who had last been seen in this public view was not a matter to cause concern to himself, or one of which Ebah could make a song. The line of Hulahs was one. A king's death might be rumoured or even known in the general talk, but it was not an official event outside the privacy of the royal house. The dead body would go in darkness the river's way. It made no change, for a Hulah ruled, and the line of Hulah's was one.

Nonetheless, there was a lively wonder to see how far rumour and guess would be confirmed by that which the royal seats would show, which, till the hour was close, and even, it was murmured, for a full minute beyond the hour, was just nothing at all. Or, at least, no more than the entrance of the eunuchs, who were more or less known by number and sight and name, and but little esteemed; and even they did not all enter at once, as it would have been seemlier for them to do.

The amphitheatre was sunk below the level of the surrounding rocks. Its centre was an oval of level sand. Its tiers of a thousand seats were hewn from the black rock, and polished so that it shone in the sun like a giant's ring, with a centre of tawny stone.

But the sun was descending now, and the larger half of the amphitheatre was already shadowed by the thick palms that were an outer girdle of green and, being on the ground level, were high above the hollowed saucer of stone. Most densely shadowed of all were the royal seats, though they were placed high, for immediately above them was the statue of Artemis, and behind it the sacred grove, the trees of which were higher and of nobler girth than were those that stretched right and left to curve round the narrower ends of the oval and meet on the farther side.

It was through the sacred grove that the pathway ran which was the private approach from the Queen's Gardens for the use of those of the royal blood.

The shade that the grove supplied was welcome to those who came by that way, for though the caverns from which they would not often emerge were well lighted enough, their eyes might have been shy of the glare of the desert sun. There might be others who worked much in the caves who would have blinked at too strong a light, which was cause enough for the amphitheatre to be sunk as it was, and belted with shade, and for the Council to be called when the sun was three hours from its height of noon.

Hulah came to his high seat, and the guards, splendid in yellow and red and the shining bronze, ranged themselves, being no more than ten and then twelve, but with the aspect of mighty men, in a line beneath him, but above the tier where the eunuchs sat. The guards stood, where all men were seated but they, which gave them the better show.

Leonard and the two girls came in with the King, and were given seats beside him, Leonard at his right, and Helen and Joselyn on his left hand. It was a strange sight for the people to see these strangers, one of whom had been undiscovered till then, seated in the places which were the rights of the Queen and the closest kin of the King. But there was no time for wonder to reach the lips of the circling crowd, for the King's entrance was the signal for them to rise, and to unite in an anthem of praise to the goddess of ancient days.

The chant was one that Ebah had learnt in youth, as all men did, and which he must sing now, but as he did so he had his first doubt that the King might have been wiser than he. For he must praise Artemis of the moon-shaped horns for the old laws and customs and kings with which she had blessed his race, and that she had held them so securely apart in a changing world, and given them, by the austere wisdom of the rule through which they improved their race, an excellence of vigour and form which was unmatched among heathen men.

And after that there was a ritual of questions which must be asked by the King, and to which the people must make response. Hulah's voice, as he spoke these questions, had a cold, inhuman austerity, a kingly remoteness, which was surely not that of a fearful man. Rather there was menace in it, showing him to be so exactly adapted for, and so equal to, what he did.

With these responses, the ritual closed. The first Hulahs, while observing the cohesive advantages that a form of religion gives, had seen no reason to perpetuate a priesthood which must always threaten to rival the authority of the secular power. With its abolition, the demand for sacrifices, the tyranny of dogmas had, in natural consequence, disappeared. Only the grove remained, the statue stood, and the mystery of the moon-goddess was for each to dream in the imaginations of torrid nights.

This preliminary ritual, which could have little meaning for those to whom its language was strange, gave Hulah's three white supporters (as his diplomacy had caused them to appear to be) leisure to look round upon an assembly the most of whom gave as much attention to them.

They observed that the women and children were ranged separately from each other, and from the men. The children, numbering over two hundred, were seated, girls above boys, around the two lowest tiers of seats, in the order of their births, each having the next eldest on the right, and the one whose birth followed his or her own on the left hand. It was a method of marshalling the youth of the tribe which emphasized any disparity of strength or growth by which the individual exceeded or fell behind the average of their splendid race, in a merciless but equitable comparison.

Above them were three tiers of women and five of men, which did not indicate their comparative numbers unless allowance were made for the larger seats, and this was discounted by the fact that the higher, being the outer tiers, formed larger circles than those below.

The whole assembly was dressed in white, as their custom was, but they had a kind of turban upon the head, the colours and shapes of which differentiated between them.

Ebah's followers, highest of all, wore turbans of yellow and red, their colours being those of the King's guards, which may have been an honour to them. They were unarmed, but their spears were stacked uprightly under the palms, and it would be seconds rather than minutes which would be required for them to be in their hands again.

Kobah's men sat below them, turbaned in yellow and black. The women wore blue-indigo for the mothers and cobalt for barren or unwedded girls. The white of the children was unrelieved, indicating that their classification was still to come.

There may have been other distinctions, finer than these, but if so, they were too obscure to be observed by a stranger's eyes.

In appearance, there was a curious uniformity of form and features among them, and Leonard, regarding them in bulk, could not deny to himself that the experiment of pitiless selection, continued for so long a period, had been justified in its physical results. Contrasted with the method of his own civilization, which gave its first care to the survival of the unfit, it was difficult to condemn.

But he was also aware that he looked on those whom he might admire, but could never like. "Splendid brutes" was the designation which came to his mind. Even the women, magnificently formed as they were, and with beautifully regular though rather heavy features, did not rouse more than a frigid admiration. They were fine animals, but hard. Not easy to consider as lovers, and less as friends.

What they thought of him and his companions may have held more contempt than his opinion of them. In contrast to the guards who were ranged below them, they must have appeared poor specimens of their kind. But beside Hulah, they made a different comparison. Indeed, had not his seat been raised, he would have appeared smaller than they. But size is not all, and Hulah was one who might rouse aversion or fear, but contempt would be less easy to feel.

Now Hulah stood up to speak. His words were deliberate and slow. Leonard could only partly follow their sense, but he could perceive that the King was depending upon argument rather than passionate appeal, and the cold authority in his voice could not be easy for these people, bred and educated as they were, to disregard.

What he was saying was this: "I have called you to meet here, in the presence of the goddess who guards our race, because a time of unrest has come. Ten months ago it disturbed the minds of my royal house. The goddess spoke, and I only am left, who observe her will.

"I asked her then: what can I do for a wife, seeing that I cannot wed in the ancient way? Artemis answered, and there are two here for my choice, being two of the best that the world contains.

"This is a new thing, for a new time. The old order must change. Are there foolish men who suppose I am blind to that? But it must not cease: it must wed the new that it may endure, as my example will be.

183

"We cannot remain apart and unknown. That time is ended by the new birds of the sky. But there may be some here who think that we should endure if we were cut off from our ancient root. Let Ebah speak if he will."

Ebah was not quick of wit, and he was confused by the King's words, which were different from anything which he had been expecting to hear. He had supposed that the King would have denounced him, and those who were of his mind, and he had prepared himself for a defiant reply. Now he could not tell what the King meant, beyond that he was called upon to blow a bladder which Hulah said in advance that he would be able to prick with a better plan.

But he was a vain and arrogant man, and aware that he was the centre of attention of all the world that he knew. His rival, Kobah, was on his back. Surely the moment was his! He rose boldly, a splendid, confident figure of virile power.

"Oh, King Hulah," he said, "is it I alone? You have said that there is discontent which has even stirred in your own house to the degree that you only are left alive. Among us it moves like a colic pain in the hidden bowels of all but few, and it is too violent to be controlled. It must vomit forth. It is not solely of me, but I will speak that which is in the minds of all here, both women and men, except that there may be those who are faint of heart, and not fit to endure.

"Our fathers and we, for more than two thousand years, have felt the yoke of a hard law, but it is one that hath made us strong. Now we must be the best men in a world of those who are puny or even rotted with disease which they permit to endure.

"Is it forever that we shall slay those of our own blood in a narrow place? That we shall walk on the edge of death, as we all do, while there are wide realms that are filled by the fecund breeding of meaner men?"

Ebah's pause at this point was rhetorical only; in two seconds he would have started again. But Hulah, without rising, or haste of speech, showed that the slowness which he preferred did not come from a lagging wit. His interjection was instant, and charged with a full measure of cold contempt: "Do not ask questions of me. I am here to learn. Tell me what you propose to do."

"We will leave this barren place, where there is no more than a measured portion of food. We will swell our strength in the fertile lands. We will cross the desert, for which we have a sound plan, and which we shall be well able to do. Did not Abrah do that on his two legs, with no more of water or food than his back could bear?"

Here he paused again, and looked round for the support which he expected to have. But he found little either of that, or of sign that he was not approved, for the people were disposed, by their manner of life and death, to conceal thought which it would be peril to show, and now they looked on as those who regard a play which they do not share. It did not follow from that that they would not be on his side if they should be forced to the point of choice, but they would not show their thoughts in a random way; and, in some degree, the most of them were overawed by the King.

CHAPTER XXXVI.

HULAH saw that it was the moment for him to rise, which he did quickly, though without aspect of haste. He said, with the same contempt as before: "Now you have told us what you would do, you can sit down, for I have something to say." He addressed these words to Ebah, but after that he turned his eyes and words to the general throng as having finished with him till a further time.

"You have heard," he said, "what Ebah would do, and you may think him to be more wise than your ancient kings. If you will be guided by him, so you may, for you will go where I would not lead, and I will be gentle beyond your worth when I tell you why.

"Ebah says that you could cross the desert and live, and so some of you would, but there would be many deaths, and you can each guess who would live and who not. That might be well, if the need were great, and the end good. It is our law that the weak must die, that the strong may have better life. But I tell you that you would go to an evil end. You would be slaves if you did not die.

"Abrah found his way to the fertile lands. Was he greatly esteemed for the strength he had, or did he toil in a servile way? Was he glad to return, even to the danger to which he came? Do you think that there will be better welcome to you, if you make a show of five hundred spears? Will you conquer a million men, even though they be puny and foul with sores? Will they give you their fertile land, that they may starve while they watch you feed?

"I tell you that if you leave this place which is yours, being as few as you know you are, you will be slaves, or else dead."

Here he paused a moment, but as Ebah would have risen to make reply he checked him with a gesture that even he did not venture to disregard.

"Not yet," he said. "I have not done. We have come to a hard time, when wisdom is needed to lead us through. The great birds that have been built and are ridden by little men will search us out, and the days of isolation are nearly done. But we must remain in our own place. We must meet them here. They must come to our door. You would lose all when you snatch at that which will come to your hand in a better way, though even then you may find that it comes too soon."

His eyes settled upon Ebah again. He went on: "You would like to say that you are wiser than I. So you may be. I will ask you this: there is one man of the puny folk who has wandered here. Will you meet him in single strife for the prize of the place you hold? Or will you say that you are fit to lead our people against his race, though you be too weak for a single man?"

For the first time a murmur of interest, a rustle of anticipation, stirred the assembly, as a sudden breeze may ripple the summer wheat. It might not mean that the people took the part of the King. They might not care though Ebah should give a quick death to the stranger who came unasked. But they were offered the sport they loved. It should be a strife that would be pleasant to see. And Ebah was too arrogant to be a popular man.

Kobah's litter had been laid in a gangway that gave approach to the seats, and he had raised himself, with the help of friends, to a sitting position. The method by which his followers were seated in a wide circle around the amphitheatre was not favourable to consultation or concerted action, but he had made excuse of his wound to keep around him two or three of those on whom he most surely relied. Now he spoke a quick word to one of these, who rose up to say: "It is but fair that it should be thus. For it were unjust to depose Ebah from the position he fills so well, and to place a stranger therein, unless he have first shown us that he is the better man."

This was twisting it into more than the King had said, but its purpose was to make the challenge one that Ebah could not decline.

Ebah, arrogant and vain though he might be, saw himself on the edge of a pit which he had the wisdom to dread. Yet it was a pit which he would find it hard to avoid without a shame that, by the laws he knew, would be a death as sure as that he could meet from the strange weapon the white man bore. He was silent for more time than he should have been, or Kobah could not have interposed, but when he spoke it was with a bold front: "I will meet him, or a dozen such, if he be ready for death, having spears of an equal length, as our custom is, and no weapon but only that."

The King asked coldly: "And if you lead your folk to the stranger's land, will you make bargain for the weapons with which they fight?"

Leonard had watched the event to this point with an attention the closer, because it was not possible for him to follow more than half of what was said. He thought, perhaps beyond the fact, that the King prevailed, and that the opposition had little heart to oppose his will. If he should meet and kill Ebah, as the King desired, would not Hulah rest on an easy seat, and his use be done? It was a prospect he liked no better because he had come to see that, however the social order of this strange people might be appraised, the position of the King was worthy of more respect than was due to that of those who plotted to end his power.

The King might be right or wrong, but he considered the good of those he ruled as, perhaps, with the ancestry that he had, he had no choice but to do, and there was also wisdom in what he said. As to those who opposed his will, Leonard remembered his remark that they had the minds of brigands, not kings, and did not think it was widely wrong.

But all the same, it was an issue in which he had no concern; a quarrel which was not his. The King's idea that they might each wed one of the two girls might be sound—and indeed attractive—enough if either (but which would he have wished?) had been willing to become Hulah's wife. But it appeared that to both it would be a repellent fate, such as they would not lightly endure, and while that were so every instinct and tradition he owned called upon him to protect them from such a dread.

To do that he would go far, even to killing Ebah, if he could, with a light heart; but what if that were to be the end of his influence on the King?

Or would Kobah's followers be a further problem with which to deal?

That he could kill Ebah, if he had the use of firearms, he had not doubted—he did not doubt. But as he looked at the narrow confines of that oval arena, a doubt came of another kind. He could kill Ebah—but was it not equally true that Ebah could kill him?

Even if they should be separated to the extreme limits of the arena, he was not sure that a spear could not reach him, being cast by Ebah's practised and muscular arm. A bullet would be faster than any spear? Yes. That would be bad for Ebah, but would it be equally good for him? Not unless the bullet should reach before the spear could be launched on its deadly flight.

It seemed a likely chance that they would both die. There would be no gain in that, either for the women or him. Was it that which the King designed in a subtle mind? No, he did not think that. But it might happen, no less. What was the King saying now?

It appeared that Ebah was arguing his position with some front of legality, which the King could not easily override, and which gained a murmur of support. He claimed that the choice of weapons was his, by some established custom, perhaps that he was the challenged man, but Leonard could not clearly understand what it was. He only saw that the King paused to reply, as being confronted by that which was not simple to overcome.

The two rifles, like the spears, had been left a few feet behind the King's seat, under the trees of the sacred grove, there being an ancient law that arms should not be brought into the amphitheatre, except such as the combatants in the arena might require. Leonard had accepted Hulah's assurance that they would be untouched there, the more readily for the confidence he felt in the smaller weapon he carried, of which the King was not aware.

Now he thought that he might be able to offer a compromise which would end the difficulty, perhaps with no actual disadvantage to himself, and relieve a fear that he might be required to accept the duel with spears alone, which would be no better than certain death. He said to the King, producing the automatic his pocket held: "I have this, which is no more than the child of the long weapons which Ebah has learned to fear. It can neither kill so far away, nor is it so certain in what it does. I will meet him with this alone, if it will give him courage to test his skill."

He could not clearly follow the interpretation which Hulah gave to this offer, but it appeared to draw Ebah over the edge of that doubt to the argument of another point—that of what his status and immunity would be when he had conquered this foreign man.

As to that, Hulah gave him all the assurance he would. He said, in a faintly derisive tone, as dealing with that which certainly would not occur: "If you win, you win all. The ancient wisdom of Hulah would have declined, without which power is a fruitless and withered stem. If you can do that, you may lead your brothers to death in your own way."

Hulah may have seen that, if he should lose on this throw, he was lost indeed; or he may have spoken thus to encourage Ebah to what he anticipated to be his fall. Such, at least, was its effect. He became his usual truculent, boastful self as he replied: "Well, let it be done now. It is but one to add to the fourteen I have killed before." He left his place and retired by the back of the amphitheatre to the southern entrance of the arena, which was under the tiers of seats.

Leonard rose also, seeing that the fateful moment had come. He had been informed by Hulah of the procedure at these combats at the last conference at which he had confided his plans. Now the King called to Olah to guide him to the arena, at the reverse end from that to which Ebah had gone.

The rule was that each combatant should remain for ten minutes in a chamber of absolute darkness, so that when they should be let out to the arena at the same moment, they could do no better than blink at a strong light. They would each be provided with two spears, which they could cast at their own time, with the knowledge that if they should delay they would aim with a better sight, but with the risk that they might feel a blade between their own ribs before that moment should come, and having the further danger to bear in mind that an ill-flung spear would soon become a weapon in an enemy's hand. Such duels differed only from the more frequent, and equally deadly, contests of skill, in that the combatants were not held the full length of the arena apart, but might close upon each other the most they could.

So for the next ten minutes the arena was empty, and a murmur of voices rose as the spectators speculated upon the result and consequences of the duel they were to see.

Kobah spoke at this time to the man whom he most trusted, and whom he had prompted before. "Ebah," he said, "is a dead man; and the King had meant to feed me with the same fare, so that I may have the less cause to fret for the hurt I have, which may have spilt a part of his plan. But I can see that we must win now, or we never shall, it having gone too far for compromise or accord. So when the combat is such that all men's eyes will be there, you will send two on the errand of which I told you before, and after that the King will be no more than ourselves, and that, I suppose, for a time which will not be long."

For those who waited above in the cheerful light for what would be no more to them than a pleasant show, the minutes were quickly done; but for those who waited in darkness for what must be the death of one or else two, the time may have seemed more, and yet less.

To Ebah there came a thought that he did not like. He had asked, and received assurance, that if his opponent preferred to fight with his own weapon he should not also be provided with spears, which had been allowed as no more than just, but now he observed a consequence which might be evil for him. For if he should throw two spears which the white man would be active to dodge, and none should be thrown at him in return, he would be left weaponless, and could be speared even by one who was much weaker than he, and who would have had no practice in such a game. He remembered scenes he had enjoyed watching, in which all the spears had passed

190

into the possession of one, and how he would chase his victim about, wounding him in fantastic ways, and taunting him with his coming death. That was why two spears were allowed to each, and why a prudent man would not cast the second for a long throw until one had been cast at him.

But his fear of this was not much, for he reminded himself of his own skill, which had saved his head so often before. Besides that, he had questioned Abrah shrewdly concerning the weapons of the white man, and had a more accurate idea of what they were, and their limitations, than even Hulah had been able to gain.

He knew that, though they can be deadly and swift, they will often send their bullets wide of the mark, and particularly if they are held in a flurried hand. But he had no wish to be shot down by a man who had been in no danger from him, and his last resolve, as the door slid open and he must step out to the blinding light, was that he would cast a spear the first moment he could focus his foe, such as, if it did not make a quick end, would be likely to spoil his aim, and the next, if it should be needed at all, in a more deliberate manner. But he had found in the past that one was most often enough.

Leonard had thought much on the same lines, except that he could calculate on six shots, which would be the most he could hope to use, for it was not probable that he could reload while avoiding the spears. He also had observed that when Ebah had cast two spears at him he would be unarmed, but he might have found more comfort in that had he felt confidence in himself that he could avoid even one as it would come flying from Ebah's hand.

The light fell between them, for which the arena was equitably designed. The whole amphitheatre was now sheltered from the direct rays of the sun, except the highest tiers opposite to the King's seat and the sacred grove. Yet those who came from the black interior darkness could be aware at first of mere dazzle and glare. But there was advantage to Leonard here in the fact that his opponent was so much larger and more gaily arrayed. A blurred vision will be conscious of colour before shape can be clearly seen. Ebah's turban, flaming yellow and red, moved confusingly, low and fast; for Ebah, a skilful man at a game he knew, was running forward at a slant, and crouching low as he ran. Leonard was confused, but he had resolved to aim low, among other reasons because he did not wish an errant bullet to do mischief among those who looked on. Ebah's belly was aware of a stinging pain, even before he heard the sound of the shot.

Instantly he straightened himself, and threw. The spear, from which Leonard shrank aside a full second too late, so that it would have been his death had it been better aimed, passed within a foot of his side. It had been thrown so truly and hard that it pierced the stout metal door through which he had come, and remained unbroken there with a quivering shaft.

The spectators, seeing so much better than those more nearly concerned, were divided between laughter at the poor aim, and admiration at the virility of the throw. The next moment the strife was done.

Maddeningly conscious of his wound, and now seeing with clearer eyes, Ebah drew himself to his full height, and lifted the second spear. His adversary, unaware that he had already inflicted a severe though not a disabling wound, felt no confidence that he could fire in time to stay the spear on its deadly way. It would be no satisfaction to him to kill at the cost of his own life. His first care was to sink to earth at the moment the cast was made, when it would be too late to deflect the aim. Doing this, the broad blade, intended to transfix his body, whistled between shoulder and ear, leaving torn cloth and a bleeding lobe to witness how near it came. And as it passed, the five bullets that the pistol could still discharge poured out in a stream of death. The massive muscular body received them as though stricken with an upright paralysis, then swayed, bent, and fell forward upon its knees in a blind way. Ebah put his hands to the ground and remained thus with a hanging head.

Leonard looked down at the spears. It had been so instant a strife that, now that it was done, he was conscious only of wonder and great relief. He saw two men come out of the door through which Ebah had entered. One of them carried a heavy metal club with which he struck the wounded man on the back of the drooping head, a skull-shattering blow. The other bore ropes and hooks, with which they grappled the body of the man, dead or alive, and dragged him away. It must have been such a sight as that arena had often seen.

Overhead, the King's voice, slow and clear, spoke in the Latin tongue, accenting it in the way that Leonard, but perhaps not even those eunuchs who were instructed in tongues, would be able to understand.

CHAPTER XXXVII.

"You have done well," the King said; "but come quickly, for Kobah plots."

Reloading the pistol as he went, Leonard hurried back to the King's seat, Olah guiding him as before. He looked round on a scene of confusion. The King had said in a sudden way: "There is an end now. You will meet here tomorrow at the same hour, when there will be more to be told." And he had called his guards to withdraw. To the eunuchs, he gave the brief order: "Scatter and learn," not using the common tongue.

The decision, the abrupt closing of a Council of this description, was a violation at once of political and of religious ceremonial law, the effect of which, being with out precedent as it was, and at such a time, it could not be easy to guess. The King took no heed of the confusion his words had caused. As Leonard came back, the guards were already moving towards the grove; the eunuchs, hurrying on their shorter legs, were scattering about.

The two girls came to his side. Joselyn was pale, but with a look of excited pleasure in her eyes which Leonard might attribute to joy at his own safety without violation of probability—though he would have been wrong. Helen showed no evidence of emotion of any kind—unless it were in a slightly heightened colour, a slight rise above the usual pitch of her voice as she said, in explanation of the sudden movement: "Just as you shot that great brute two of Kobah's men went off at a run. I should say no one saw them except the King, but the next moment he made us jump."

"No one but the King—except you?"

"Oh, I was born with my eyes wide. And there was something more you may not have seen, having enough on your hands."

Joselyn took up the explanation, this being of more concern to her, with the guess she had, than whether Kobah's men had found occasion to run. "It was an aeroplane. It was coming from the east when we saw it first. It went away to the west."

"You mean it came overhead?"

"Not exactly."

"But you think they saw what was happening here?"

"Yes, of course."

Helen was less sure. "It's what we want to believe," she said. "But it may just have happened to cross the desert. The pilot mayn't even have been looking down."

"It isn't very likely it would have come from the west. It must have seen us, and turned," Joselyn persisted.

"So it may, but it's no more than a guess. We didn't see it soon enough to be sure," Helen replied, holding, as she considered, to saner judgment.

"Anyway," Leonard said, "it's quite certain it didn't stay."

"It was Denis, of course," Joselyn answered, with a note of obstinacy in her voice. "I've always known he would come."

This had been a vague possibility at the back of Leonard's mind also, but he had felt it to be too faint to be entertained. Now, so confidently affirmed, it had a different sound. After all, Denis would be sure to hear, sooner or later, that he had disappeared in the Libyan desert. He would be likely to learn that Joselyn had vanished in the same direction. He would have a double motive for making search. If he could get leave, it was what he would be very likely to try. But to search may not be to find, and, realizing that, Leonard had put the idea from his mind, being in a position in which action was required rather than reliance on doubtful dreams.

But it was an idea that recurred at a moment which appeared to have its own urgency. The King clearly feared, if he did not correctly guess, what Kobah's men had been sent to do. He pushed on, regardless of dignity, at the pace that the guards made, hurrying in single file along the narrow paths of the royal gardens, and coming at last to the place from which Leonard had looked back the morning before, to see the two guards at the open gates, waiting for his return.

The gates were open now, solitary and quiet. A slight expression of relief came to the immobile countenance of the King. But next moment it had occasion to change. Kobah's men appeared from the inside, and were seen to be closing the gates. Hulah looked back for Leonard. "Can you kill those men at the distance they are?"

He might have done that, had there not been a five seconds' delay in reaching the King's side and then the need to call to the guards ahead to draw their huge bulks aside to give him a clear shot; and, meanwhile, the short chance had passed and the gates were shut.

CHAPTER XXXVIII.

IT may be said that Hulah made a mistake. It was a fact that he had failed to arrive in time, and to fail must always be a mistake of the worst kind. Yet he had been almost there, and the minute more would have foiled Kobah's design, and justified the swiftness of that retreat.

Hulah had, at least, been alert to see that which Kobah had thought to do unobserved, and quick and accurate in judgment of what it was most likely to be.

Kobah had sent two men to shut him out from the royal apartment, where the race of Hulahs had dwelt for two thousand years in a mysterious isolation, from which their authority may have largely derived.

It might seem a small thing, though it was one which would have brought swift punishment upon any who had made incredible attempt at another time; but at this moment, when his power shook, it must have the effect of stripping the King of the dignity, the prestige, on which his authority so largely relied, and which was now more vital to him than the security which he could gain from its heavy gates.

Now these gates were shut in his face, and he had no force that could break them in. They were not built so that they could easily be forced from the outside, and so that which should have been his strength had become his foe.

He saw that he had broken up the Council in a disastrous manner, with no resulting gain to himself. It is to his credit again that he was instant to see how he now stood, and where his danger was most.

Had he kept the Council together, he might have won Kobah's followers to himself, and his wiser plans, or he might have overawed them by asserting his influence over those others who had seen their own leader fall. Coming away, almost in flight, as he had, it was to be supposed that treason would lift a bolder head, which would not sink at the news that he had been ignominiously shut out from his royal rooms. Had he been first at the gates, he could at least have secured himself from immediate attack—which would have been an improbable development—and there would have been time to foster dissensions between the two sections of his opponents, on which his foresight had astutely relied.

Now he judged correctly that Kobah would lose no instant in making attack with such of his followers, many or few, as could be stirred to active rebellion by hopes of favour from him, or warning that they had already gone so far as to leave forgiveness behind. The part the leaderless spearmen would take might be less sure, but it was a poor chance that they would be as prompt and resolute for the royal cause as Kobah would be to destroy a king who would leave no heir, which had the look of a clear field for himself, now that Ebah was dead.

The first and vital necessity, as the King saw, was to get clear of the close entanglement of the garden growths; for to be attacked, even by a mere fraction of Kobah's men, amidst the bushes and vines, the narrow paths and grottos, might bring a swift and fatal end to the millenniums of his race's reign. But if he could get clear to the light and the open ground, his little force, small though it was numerically, would not be overcome at a low cost. The twelve guards were not only very powerful resolute men, chosen for skill in arms as much as for fidelity of character and muscular strength, they had protective armour of proof, in which their opponents were not arrayed, for this (perhaps by the prudence of former kings) had not been allowed to be forged for the general use. With Leonard's rifles to help, Hulah might well think that if he could get clear space he would have a strength that would grieve his foes.

"Back!" he ordered the guards. "Back with haste!" For perhaps the first time in his life, as it might be the last, the King ran.

When Kobah saw that Hulah broke up the Council abruptly, having evidently guessed his design, he saw also that it would be a close race, which either might lose or win. His men had the longer route, but the King, for all his promptness of action, could not prevent that they would have a good start, being unable to move until Leonard had come back to his side.

But whether the King should be shut out, to be ignominiously exposed, like a snail that has lost its shell, or should be swift enough to regain his lair, Kobah knew that his own actions of the last twenty-four hours had brought matters to an issue of open war. If he would live himself, and still more if he would seize the leadership, the way to which had been made clearer by Ebah's death, he must act at once, before Hulah could draw together such men as might be loyal to him, or merely anxious to be on the stronger side, which they might still think his to be.

Kobah saw also, as clearly as did the King, that Leonard's weapons and the metalled strength of the guards would be more formidable on open ground, and as the people swarmed from the amphitheatre, debating in excited groups, he said to those who were nearest to him: "If the King be shut from his lair, as I have a good hope, he must not be let to come out of the gardens again, either to make head of strife or to use his tongue on the crowd. He must be slaughtered among the leaves. But as for the guards, and the foreign women and man, let them live or die at their own choice. If they yield, they may be put to uses of diverse kinds, and there is one with whom I would deal myself when my wounds are well.

"Omrah, and you, Terah, must raise a cry that the King flies, and get together such of our men as are of stubborn and merciless mood, and tell them to arm themselves as they can in a hasty way, in particular seizing the stacks of spears which are kept in the vestibules of the arena, and follow the King boldly where he may be safely approached through the hanging boughs. Be he dead, it is all done; and those who are with him now must teach their knees to be humble to us, for what else will there be left for them to do? But be swift, for the scale tips, and this moment is surely ours."

When most men doubt and debate, much can be done by a few who have a clear aim and a settled will. There were two score or more of the miners who were soon drawn to a head, and armed either with spears or with tools and bars that could be used to a deadly end. Terah, who had the name of the tallest of Kobah's men, and who excelled all in the throwing of ball or bar, led them without scruple through the sacred grove, and by the path which till that hour, for two thousand years, had been reserved for those of the royal blood, and so came at a run to the edge of the Queen's Gardens.

At this time the King's party had returned far enough to look ahead on the sunlit sand, beyond the shadow of vine-clad roof by which the gardens were overhung, and Terah's men were plainly visible to them, though they were themselves unseen in the half-darkness of the narrow green-roofed path which, at this place, was closely walled with the trailing of trellised vines.

If Hulah had a doubt of what he should do when he saw Terah's approach, it was too short to be apparent to those he led. He saw that his guards might charge out, and perhaps break through the advancing mob, they being better armed, and likely to move in a more dis-

197

ciplined way. But they would have to emerge from the narrow path singly, or two abreast at the most, against opponents who would be already there, and who might break into the garden also to right and left (though that could not have been quickly done), to attack them on either side while they would be drawn out in a narrow string. He may have thought of spears being blindly thrust through that wall of green to vex those who would be unable to make effectual reply. He may have seen that, behind the black-and-yellow turbans of Kobah's men, there was a larger body who came in his own colours of yellow and red, and with the flashing of many spears in the low rays of a setting sun. (Enona, bitter now for her son's death, had some part in persuading these who, without her words, might have been less sure of what they would choose to do.) He may have thought that he himself had no armour against the casting of many spears, and that he might die before the guards could make formation to close him in, as he had meant them to do. He had the advantage of knowing these shadowy gardens, in which he had wandered from childhood, as none else, even the eunuch-gardeners, would be likely to do. Abruptly, he changed his plan.

He turned to the left-hand side of the path, where the trellis-work was a heavy metal barrier, not easily to be broken through. He said to the guards: "You must make a way."

Leonard, watching and following where his opinion was not required, thought that Hulah, with a failing nerve, had paused where he should have gone boldly out. It was not sure that all those who ran would have proved his foes, had he appeared more equal to the event. But bolting back, as it seemed his purpose to do, must increase and hearten those who would seek his end. But Leonard saw no less that the course of events had allied his fortunes inextricably with those of the King, even though they might show a draggled front.

Yet, for the moment, there would be an end to any talk of the taking of wives, either by bargain or force. That was well, if it were a position that could endure, which did not appear. Would it be better if Hulah were dead? That was not easy to think. Probably a compromise, a limited victory, such as would leave the King largely dependent upon himself, would be the best hope for him, and more particularly for the two girls whom it was his first duty to guard. But that position would not be reached by bolting into the garden growth like rabbits when the dogs are prowling about.

The King asked him: "Could you hold them back here for a short time, shooting who may be first to approach?"

The guards, using all their strength, had torn the metal trellis away, making a gap large enough for their own passage, and were going through, one by one. The tangle of down-torn vines, suspended by other tendrils towards the roof and the trellis-work where it still stood, would form a screen behind which he could kneel and fire along the narrow way of approach; but what use would there be in that?

The King explained in his next words. "If we have but a short delay, we can make a retreat strong. They cannot come behind you quickly to left or right, for the trellis stretches both ways, and there is impediment on the outer front. How many deaths does your weapon bear?"

Leonard showed him a handful of cartridges from a jacket-pocket. "I have twice these," he said. "And some for the pistol beside. But if I use them without care, they will soon be done. There are many more in my own room."

"You will not see your room till the occasion is past. I will send one to be your guide at the first moment I may."

Leonard observed that the King spoke with decision and without haste, as one having gained control of himself, making it the more likely that he would control the position in which he stood. He saw also that he could take a bold risk at sufficient need, for such it certainly was to station him there. For he did not suppose that Hulah would lightly lose the support which his firearms gave.

Seeing this, he had the better heart for that which he was asked, or commanded, to do. But he looked doubtfully at the two girls, with whom he was neither willing to part, nor that they should be exposed to the risk he took.

Hulah looked at them also, in what may have been the same doubt, but he did not speak, and Joselyn, who had understood more than Helen of what was said, answered with decision for both: "If you stay here, we shall do the same."

Leonard accepted this, as what might be the better of alternatives that he did not like, and Hulah, keeping his mind on essential things, went through the gap without further words, for he must lead the guards on a way that they did not know.

CHAPTER XXXIX.

HULAH had scarcely gone before the entrance to the path was darkened by the coming of Terah's men, who, being too many and too grim of mood to be daunted by any fear of the guards, and now being joined by a larger number of the leaderless spearmen, were resolved to search the gardens, and make a quick end of a king who, as it was now plain, could not assert his power at a less cost than that of their own deaths.

Leonard saw that the time for scruple had gone, and that for parley had not yet come, if it ever would. After the insolence of those closing gates, there could be no doubt of what was meant for the King, and for any who were faithful to him. Taking careful aim, he fired. The shot rang out deafeningly in the low cavernous vault, and echoed along the roof. The entrance to the path became quickly clear, except for one sprawling giant, who half rose, and also crawled out of sight.

After that there was silence, broken by real or imagined sounds, as of those who cut through bushes and vines, avoiding the open paths. It was a tense waiting more hard to endure than would have been the approach of any visible foe.

Seeing that there was no probability that the path would be used again, the three watchers withdrew through the gap, thinking that they were occupying a position of greater safety, or at least that they reduced the directions from which death, sharp and sudden, might thrust at them from under tendril and bough.

Joselyn, nervous but quietly intent, held the shotgun in ready hands, though she had seldom, if ever, handled such a weapon before. Helen, her face curiously changed and strained, but in a childish way, as though her spirit had reverted to earlier, more primitive days, whispered: "Say, can you shoot straight?"

"If they're near enough, I expect I can."

"Then if that's all, you'd better pass it to me."

Leonard asked, in some surprise: "Are you used to guns?"

"I used to shoot off rattlers' heads when I was ten."

"Rattlesnakes?"

"Yes, of course."

Joselyn passed her the gun.

So they waited, tensely alert, while nothing happened beyond the doubtful sounds that might mean nothing, or the approach of deadly peril that still delayed, until, in what was probably less than half an hour, though it had seemed longer to them, a strange voice shouted a queerly accented Latin phrase which the King had surely told it to call lest a bullet should be too hastily fired, and one of the guards appeared to guide them to whatever safety might lie in the King's retreat.

After a short scramble through broken bushes, made easy by the bulk of those who had passed before, and with the guard now leading the way, they waded a shallow stream, crossed a little ridge of rock-garden, and descended through trampled flowers to a clear path.

As they came here, they saw men at no great distance away, who withdrew into the bushes too suddenly for them to judge whether they were many or few, but the guard led in the opposite direction, striding on with an indifference which might well give courage to those who followed his armoured form. Threading a succession of twisting paths, they came to a hollow grotto, the sides of which were raised to within four or five feet of the roof, which came low, particularly on one side.

The centre of this grotto was filled by a pool of three or four feet depth, which had been fed by an entering stream, and drained off by another on the opposite side. The entering stream had now been damned and diverted, this being the work for which Hulah had wished to have unmolested time, of which he would have felt less sure had his enemies not been discouraged from following in the direct way that he had broken through to the place he sought.

This diversion did no more than to reduce the depth of the pool by six inches or eight, but Hulah's object went farther than that. As it was, those who took refuge there must stand middle-deep or more in the lukewarm water, or cling to the shelving side of the grotto, in positions which would be irksome to maintain as the hours passed. There being no light in the roof above, and only on one side where the path adjoined, the grotto was dimly lighted above, and dimly shadowed within, the water being felt rather than seen, even by those whose eyes had become used to so poor a light.

The grotto was large enough to accommodate twice the number of those who had taken refuge within it, if they were indifferent to the depth of water in which they stood. But whatever might be thought of its defensive qualities, it seemed a poor place of refuge to choose, and one the discomforts of which would make it impossible for more than a short time even though it were not strongly attacked.

Hulah's voice, cold as ever, but yet with a more human quality than he had heard in it before, greeted Leonard's approach: "You have done well; and it seems that more terror is bred by one bullet's flight than by the flinging of twenty spears. There was more reason for coming here than you will understand till you see what I am preparing to do. For the time, I must ask you and the women to watch, and to keep away those who would attack us, for this pool must be baled dry."

Leonard heard an allocation of parts which he disliked less for himself than for those whom, he thought, should have been last asked to take the danger of looking out over the grotto's rim, but it had reason which he could not deny.

It did not require knowledge of the King's ultimate purpose to recognize the advantage of baling the water out, and it was work which the guards were best fitted to undertake. They stood middle-deep where Helen's mouth would have been hardly sure of its breath. They had longer reach to cast the water into the channel by which the overflow had been drained off.

The worst feature of the position was that the men had nothing better than leaves, hollow and broad, of a tropic plant which they had gathered on Hulah's instructions as they came, with which to bale the water away, and how long it would take might be hard to guess, but it was clear that it would not be quickly done.

Leonard translated to his companions: "It seems that we must watch, and keep Kobah's men back, if we can, till the pool is dry. If you keep well covered, it may be as safe, and will surely be a dryer task than the balers have, for if a spear be flung over the top it may fall in the midst of the pool. But shoot at once if you see any movement without, for though you miss it may be enough to scare them away, and you should not be targets for Kobah's spears."

So they agreed on stations which gave Joselyn, who had no more than her revolver to use, the side on which the roof came low, and which attack was least likely to choose, and settled down to a further period of watchfulness, with hazard of death as the stake if it should relax or they should be outwitted by the stealth of those who might be round them on every side.

CHAPTER XL.

NIGHT fell on the desert. The hard hot light of the sun was changed for the softer brilliance of a full tropic moon. At such an hour, if the winds were still, there would, for these hours, be utter silence and peace, and no movement except the creeping change of the long black tufted shadows of the oasis palms.

But now the whole space around the mushroom rock was alive as with the stirring of bees from an outraged hive. The light of the cloudless moon was enough for those who sought the life of the King, as though, like Joshua, they had been blessed with a lasting day. It was, indeed, brighter than that which shone in the dimly lighted gardens, which had now been desecrated and trampled through by hundreds who regarded its long-secret beauties only as they would give cover to an attack which had been converging upon the King's grotto during three cautious hours. They had been punctuated by no more than three shots, one of which must have gone wide, one had shattered the elbow of a man who had obtruded it as he pulled himself forward from rock to rock, and the third, at a shorter range, had given a wide wound of a different kind, from which one of Ebah's spearmen must bleed to death, for he had crawled too near for the shotgun's charge to scatter widely before it struck.

But to these shots there had been no reply. Kobah, ordering all from a couch which had been spread for him upon the sand, had forbidden that in emphatic words. Till the attackers had surrounded the grotto closely on every side, they were to do nothing to rouse a desultory abortive flinging of spears, at which he thought that those who were first within the short range that such a cast will require might be disheartened and driven back.

He delayed that he might overwhelm at a single rush. And meanwhile, those who watched from the grotto's ridge reserved their limited ammunition for a clearer aim and a more imminent need. And the guards, even if they had not been fully occupied in the baling that showed so slow a change in the level of the water in which they stood, would have been unwilling to throw their spears until they could be sure of the use of others which would be directed upon themselves.

The attackers were greatly helped in their approach by the fact that the gardens had not been equally lighted. The roof-lights followed the twisting occasional paths, and the spaces between, of whatever width, had been left unlit, unless for the short morning and evening hours of the entering sun.

Amid the dense exuberant growths of that heated and humid air, Kobah's men, in spite of their giant size, had wormed themselves forward until three score were within a short distance of the dark circle of grotto walls. Each was armed with a throwing-spear, which was to be cast when a goat's horn would sound, and with either a second spear or some other weapon or tool which could be used as such in a strong hand, for the rush with which they were to follow the flying spears.

Farther back, a more numerous body of men, who were of a more prudent courage, or else less sure of what they expected or hoped the end would be, were to close in when the fight was joined, and make sure of that which should, indeed, require little help from them.

Such Kobah's orders had been, and so Omrah reported to him that it now stood. Kobah might chafe that he lay as he did, but he was of a shrewdness to see that he was saved thereby from peril of death, or of a worse wound than he yet had, for he would have been expected to be in the foremost rank had he been able to stand; and it is always better to live than die, especially when a man is near to his greatest dream. Besides that, he had in Terah, and in Omrah also—a man as valiant, and more astute, though he was scarcely equal to Terah in strength and stride—two who would be most active to do his will.

Terah was now among those who had the grotto no more than a long spear-cast away. Omrah stood at Kobah's side, making report to him. "They are now," he said, "as near as they are likely to get, unless they are to be seen. Shall the horn sound?"

"Yes," Kobah replied, "so it may, when you are returned to your place, which must be that of a safe rear, from which you must urge, or if need be lead, the supporting charge. It is an attack that must not falter nor cease till you have the King's body to make a show, for there are more than enough who would be inclined to his side, if they should see that we have the worse of this bout."

"That," Omrah said, "is what you have no good reason to fear. There are too many who close him in." Omrah went, and Kobah listened for the sound of the horn, which was soon to come. After that, there was a sudden uproar of distant sound, with more noise of the white man's weapons than Kobah liked, or had expected, to hear. The sound rolled out, a volume of tortured air, from under the low roof of the mushroom rock. It continued until Kobah's face took an expression of more content, as the moonlight showed. "It is a stout fight," he said, "at the least. They are not thrust back. But the white man must be hard to kill."

Then the noise fell, and broke out afresh. He said: "There is the second wave. It should overwhelm." And then silence came, and remained, and he must wait till there should be word from a runner's mouth.

CHAPTER XLI.

THE King had made no show of arms until now, but it appeared that he wore a knife, long and broad, like a dagger-sword, under his robes. He used this to dislodge some stones, by which he made for himself a sheltered niche under the grotto wall, where it would be an ill chance indeed if a spear should come.

He had no shame in this, having no armour of proof such as his guards wore, and his first care being for his own life, without which he could do nothing to foil his foes. But he was alert to watch and direct, seeing the water decline, inch by inch, and wondering somewhat the while why the attack was so long delayed.

He asked Leonard from time to time what assurance he felt that Kobah's men were not close enough for a sudden rush, and the time came when he had reply: "They are closing on this side, and to right and left. There is one I could kill now, and perhaps more; but if I fire it may be signal for them to rise. Are you ready for that to be?"

Hulah was reluctant for the men to stop that which they had so nearly done, but he said: "There shall be six behind you with spears (which should be enough), and you shall kill the man that you see. It may not cause them to charge. It may send them back."

Leonard delayed only to call Joselyn from where she was on the farther side, towards which there had been no sign of assault, but he thought that, if there should be throwing of spears, she might be in most danger there, having her back so high and exposed to those which would come over the top on his side; but while he delayed for this, and the six guards stood to his support on a floor that was nearly dry, there was the sound of a horn that blew, very near and shrill, and the shot he took was not at a crouching man, but at one who rose with a flourished spear.

It was no shame that the next moment he shrank, withdrawing even his eyes from above the edge, for there came a flight of three score of spears that made a rushing, whistling wind overhead, such as no man could meet and live. It was well for Joselyn that she had moved, for the place where she had stood would have been that of her death; but when the flight was done, it had worked no ill, for, the roof being so low, the spears could not be cast so that they would fall into the pit. They must come over the edge in a level flight that passed clear away, or struck the inside of the farther wall, where there was no one to be hurt. And so the spears ceased, and the rush came.

Leonard stood back from that, as had been agreed, and it was met by the armoured guards, who were six at first, and the next moment were twelve. With the girls at his side, he watched where a shot could be sent to a deathful end, or for the relief of one who would have been pressed too hard.

The guards, being skilful and strong, and having the good armour they had against men who had no equal defence, would not have been easy to overcome had they had no support, but with the help of a shot here and there at the right time, they made a slaughter which would have daunted less stubborn men than the miners were. As it was, their numbers prolonged the strife, and those who still stood had scarcely withdrawn, as at length they did, from the grotto's edge (which was now near to level with the bodies of those who fell), when Omrah came up at a run, with more men than the first had been.

He saw Terah lying dead enough, with a cleft head, and might have run on to the same end had he not caught his foot in a vine, and come to earth in a better way.

This last charge was the worst of all, they who came being so many and fresh against those who were weary and blown with the bout before; and for a moment the line of the guards, who were no more than eleven now, was burst through, and men fought in a struggling heap.

When it was done, Hulah had had time to forget that he was King of a Sacred Line. His yellow lip had been drawn back as a beast will snarl, and his knife was red.

Leonard, his cartridges done, had fought with a rifle-butt to keep clear a space for those whom it was his first duty to guard, till a back-thrust spear-shaft, whether handled by friend or foe, had caught his knee at the side with a bruise, so that he came down, and looked up to see Helen's face over his own, and the flash-flash of her pistol that spit death enough to give him leisure to rise.

Joselyn, at his side, asked: "Are you much hurt?" Her pistol had been emptied before, and she had a black bruise crossing her face which she could never guess how she had got.

The King said: "They have had enough. We shall do well to be gone."

He spoke to the guards, who were now but nine, and they bleeding and bruised. He pointed to the floor, on which the water—if so the red puddle could still be called—was no more than three or four inches deep. A guard groped, pulling aside one who was or would soon be dead, and finding a metal ring.

There was a trap-door, which would not lift, being fixed by age, till there had been straining by several men, but at last it did.

Hulah said: "We must go in haste, for if they should find we are gone this way, they may turn the stream on us before we shall be through."

There might be need for haste, but there was no pleasure in hearing that, when they must drop in the utter dark to a floor that was ten feet below, which might have been dry enough but for the curdling filth which had drained into it as the trap was raised.

Holding hands, and he who led feeling a wall of stone that was hard and dry, they hurried the long half-mile that the tunnel stretched, and came at last to a metal door that was much trouble to force, being banked with earth on its outer side, and closed for centuries that even Hulah could only guess.

But at the last they came out to the tropic night, which was a dazzling brightness to them as they stepped from the utter dark, and looked up to the statue of Artemis of the moon-shaped horns, and the silent mystery of the grove.

CHAPTER XLII.

IT is likely that many things, including Kobah himself, might have come to a different end had he been of a less frugal mind, but when it was asked at an early hour: "Shall the eunuchs die? They run round. They are the ears of the King," he had replied: "No, for it would be waste at this time. They shall bear weights in the desert heat, and be useful to us." So it came to be that when the news spread that the King was gone down into a black pit, into which water was being pumped, so that he would have a poor time if he were staying there, it came to Olah's ears, and he was the one man who was so far in the confidence of the King, and aware of the ancient tales, that he knew where the tunnel would be likely to end, though he could not have said where it began.

It was not long before he came to the King, and after that he whispered to trusty men, and succour was brought, and a watch set around those who were soon taking the sleep of which they had need enough.

Kobah did not overlook that the King might appear in another place, but his thoughts went to the royal rooms, and other points in the caves, where he wasted men, setting strong watches for those who would not be there. And meanwhile Olah had told the eunuchs to talk in a confident tone, saying that the Council would meet again at the hour that the King had set, when he would surely be there, and after that he would be equal to scourge his foes.

There was talk also of how many had gone to death under the strong arms of the guards, and most of all from the deadly weapons the strangers bore, so that there were some who lost heart for the cause of a wounded man who had himself been taught what those bullets were.

It followed that when the great battle-plane appeared like a vulture from the bare height of the sky, and with the English symbol beneath its wings, it settled down to a place where there was bicker of words, but the clamour of strife was still, though it had become known that the King was alive in the sacred grove, having Artemis for his friend, as she was likely to be.

Hiram Vincent stepped from the plane, and should have been enough for his daughter's eyes; but she was able to see that Denis Kinnear also was there, and that Joselyn's arms were around his neck, as though there were none to observe her joy. Helen looked more pleased at that than that her father had come. "One from three," she said to herself, "will leave two"—which was arithmetic to her of a good kind, to which she thought that Leonard would not be slow to agree.

Wing-Commander Truscott inquired: "Miss Wilde, do you complain of your treatment here, or shall I make a report that these natives had been friendly to you?"

He looked at the twin machine-guns that projected from the forward gun-ring, as though he would be pleased to open fire on the doubtful crowd at a word from her.

"No," she answered; "the King has done us no wrong. There is one—" Her eyes hardened with a hate that she could not lose. "But I should say that he will not live if we leave him here."

ABOUT THE AUTHOR

SYDNEY FOWLER WRIGHT (1874-1965) penned over seventy volumes of science fiction, fantasy, classic mysteries, historical novels, poetry, and non-fiction, many of them being published by the Borgo Press Imprint of Wildside Press.